JACK'S BACK

CYNARRA TREGARTH

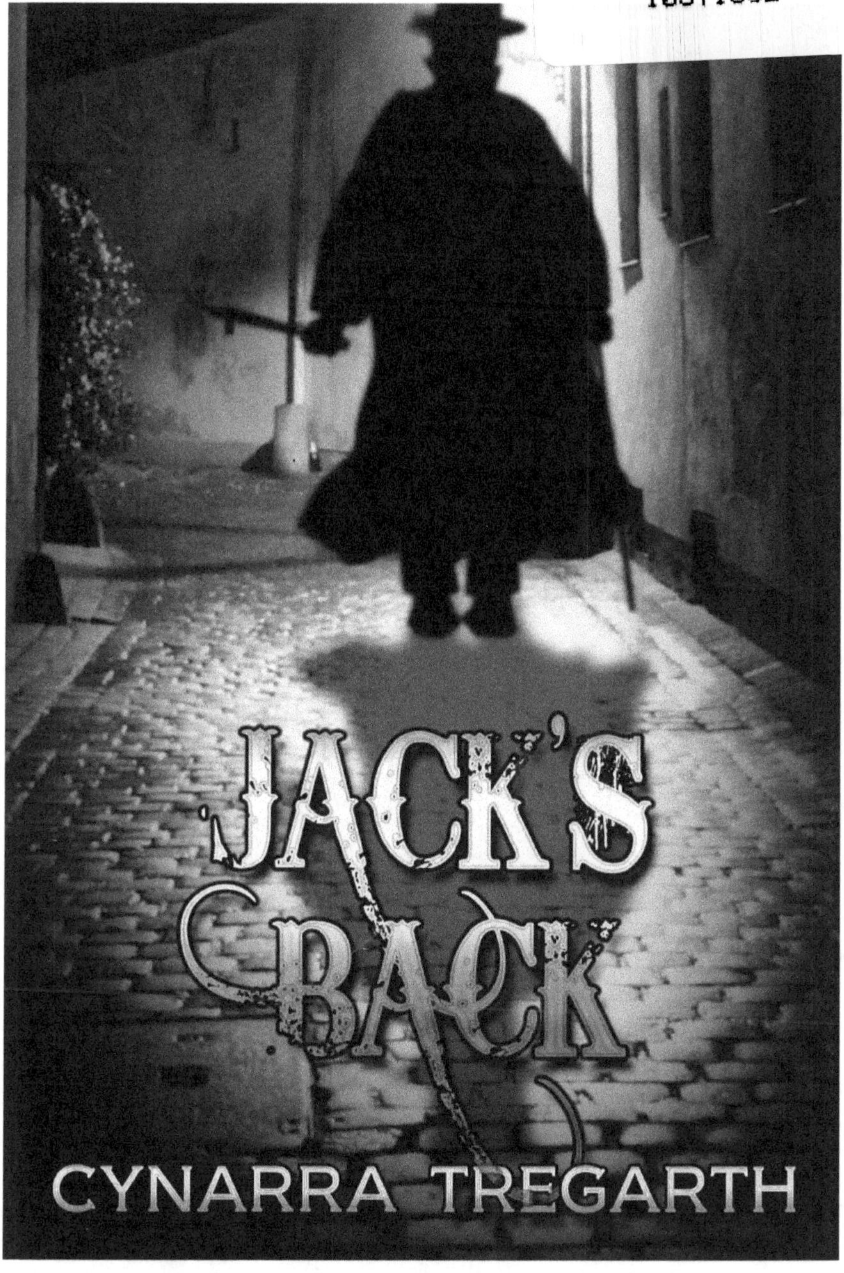

JACK'S BACK

Cynnara Tregarth

Warning

This e-book contains adult scenes and language. This story is meant for adults only as defined by the laws of the country in which you made your purchase. Store your e-books carefully where they cannot be accessed by younger readers.

This e-book is a work of fiction. While references may be made to actual places or events, the Names, characters, incidents, and locations within are from the author's imagination and are not a resemblance to actual living or dead persons, businesses, or events. Any similarity is coincidental.

This book is licensed to the original purchase only. Duplication or distribution via any means is illegal and a violation of International Copyright Law, subject to criminal prosecution and upon conviction, fines and/or imprisonment. The e-book cannot be legally loaned or given to others. No part of this e-book can be shared or reproduced without the express permission of the publisher.

Copyright © February 2015 by Cynnara Tregarth

Dedication

To my Mom – This book is for you and all the times you fed my passion for reading.

To my special people in my life – Thank you for being there when I needed you most.

Prologue

Tiana looked at her friend Kyrie with concern. "Are you sure you want to do this spell?" She was concerned that releasing this magical binding might cause more trouble, especially since they didn't know who had placed it upon Kyrie. Tiana fingered her pewter pendant, the warmth reassuring her of protection.

"I'm sure. What do I have to lose? Would you put up with someone binding you, preventing you from doing something because it's against what they want, regardless of what you want?"

"Well, we don't know who did the spell. It might've been something done to you as a child in order to protect you."

Kyrie's features scrunched up. Tiana resisted the urge to laugh at her raven-haired friend. "I don't care. It's not fair to place a binding on me and not tell me why."

Jules nodded. "I agree with Kyrie, Ti. I think we should do the unbinding ceremony, and then, once the person figures out it's undone, they can explain the reason behind its existence."

"Okay, Jules. Since you're just as fanatic about this as Kyrie, we'll do it," Tiana acceded as she stood in the northern part of the room. The two women stood in the middle, where a small table acted as an altar. On the table were the implements they'd use to break the binding surrounding their friend, including candles, a bowl of water, and other items that might be necessary for the ritual.

Once the circle of protection was invoked and they had thanked the elements and gods for their presence, protection, and blessing, Tiana lit a deep-amethyst candle.

"This is Kyrie, the one bound by forces unknown. Hear our plea to break the binding." Kyrie spoke the words she'd been told to say. "I beg the elements to release me from the binding. Just as this cord has knots that I undo, let me be unbound."

Tiana watched as Kyrie undid each of the nine knots. When Kyrie got to the last one, Tiana nodded to Jules as Kyrie handed the undone cord to Tiana.

"Let the last knot be undone, let the binding be let loose. Thus we three ask and demand acquiescence," intoned Jules.

Tiana's hand slipped to her pendant, feeling strong warmth pulsating within it. Feeling nervous, but also reassured, she spoke the final words as she placed the cord in the bowl and lit the cord fire. "Let the elements release the binding that exists in this circle. Let it hold no more."

As the cord burned to ash, Tiana sensed something happening. Looking at both Jules and Kyrie, Tiana saw that they seemed at peace with the ritual so far. She seemed to be the only one who felt a cool rush of air swirling around them. Suddenly, a huge cloud seemed to float up from in front of her, swirling around, then disappearing out the window. Neither of her friends seemed to see what she did. A chill crept down her back, and she noticed that her pendant was cold to the touch. Then it warmed again, slightly. *What just happened, and why do I feel it's not good?*

"Well, that's done," Jules said with a slight smile. "Now we can enjoy the rest of the weekend."

Kyrie nodded. "Thanks, you two. I know it's not one of your things, Jules, but I feel much better now. How about you, Ti?"

Tiana nodded her head and pasted a smile on her face as she began the cleansing ceremony to help speed out whatever negative energy might remain. "I'm okay. Let me close this circle, then we can go lie about and watch movies."

Silently, she used a sage and sweetgrass braid to smudge the air and cleanse it. Once she was done with the ritual and had released the circle, she joined her friends. "There, all done. Let's put this stuff away, and we can bury the ashes in the morning to make sure the binding is released."

As they left the basement of Kyrie's house, Tiana looked back and wondered what it was she felt.

* * * * *

Free. I'm finally free of that damned witch! Once again, I am free to continue what I want to do. With that thought, the spirit released went searching for a way to cause fear and havoc. Having been bound for such a long time, he felt the need to feed once again upon the blood he would spill and the people who deserved to be terrorized. Searching for a way to slake his thirst, the spirit roamed the night, searching for someone to inhabit. For him it would be an indirect kill, as the person's spirit would crumble before the sauciest killer known to London.

Chapter One

Tiana Wells walked toward her office with a spring in her step, and peeked in on the guys in the computer forensics lab. "Hi, guys, I'm home," she called to the three men in the room. They looked toward the doorway and responded in kind.

"Hullo, Tiana."

"Hello, boss lady."

"Welcome home, Tiana. How was your holiday with Jules and Kyrie?"

"It was great, as always. Thanks for asking, Damian. How were things while I was gone?" Entering the room, she slid the one free chair toward the guys and sat down.

"I finished up a couple of variables in the program you asked me to review. I think you're right; it does produce a smoother composite."

She lightly punched her colleague, Dr. Damian Collins, on the arm. His brown eyes smiled at her playfulness. "Told ya it would. Next time, believe in this half-Yank."

Her eyes professionally scanned over the skull showing on Damian's computer screen. "Looks like someone with Asian features; notice the cheekbone area and the forehead spacing. Missing person?"

Damian and Dr. Kyle Mortimer nodded simultaneously. Kyle added, "Her remains were found near York. Cause of death is thought to be blunt trauma to the back of the head, and strangulation."

Tiana controlled her reaction. "Well, at least it's not a knife victim or one who was chopped up, which would make it harder."

Damian, Kyle, and their graduate student, Lawrence Tanner, shared a look with each other, then looked at Tiana. They all seemed a bit discomfited.

"Actually, Ti, her remains were discovered having been hacked apart," Damian said softly. "They found her remains in four separate pits near each other."

Tiana turned from the screen, and three pairs of eyes watched as she tried to catch her breath.

She knew the looks they were giving her. They all knew about her issue with edged weapons since she'd been attacked over five years before. The ongoing joke dealt with the fact that she had a slight obsession with Jack the Ripper, a man known to love blades. Though her friends didn't understand her behaviour, they kept their teasing to a minimum when it came to professional cases.

Lawrence softly mumbled, "Good thing she was found after the soft tissue rotted away. It must have been gruesome enough for discoverers, without having to deal with cut-up body parts."

"Might have been able to get more clues from the crime scene, if they had," chimed in Kyle. "In fact, they would've had more to work with, even if it was in separate pieces."

He was the one that Tiana thought really could get into being a killer, if it weren't for his squeamishness about blood. She recalled one night a couple years back when he had happily dissected two corpses and reveled in how they were killed. She'd thought he was unhinged, and he'd done nothing since then to change her mind on that fundamental issue.

Tiana looked at the three men, giving Kyle and Lawrence a disdainful glance. "Horrid. I swear, at times you do this specifically to make me shudder."

Kyle smirked as Lawrence shook his head. "Lawrence wouldn't do that; he's not got his doctoral thesis done yet."

Tiana smacked Kyle on his back. "Behave. He's been with us in this program long enough to know my idiosyncrasies. Just ease off a bit, all right?"

Damian put his arm around her shoulders in a friendly hug. "This isn't the Tiana we know and love to tease. What's the deal?"

She rubbed her arms and looked at her friend. "To be honest, I'm not sure. I've been feeling a bit on edge since vacation. Did a ritual for Kyrie to help her feel better, but I got weird vibes."

Kyle lifted a brow. "A magic ritual? You?"

Tiana rolled her eyes. "Yes, me. You know I'm a Druid by beliefs. She asked me to do the ritual to help her feel freer. I didn't see anything happen, but as long as she feels better, that's what counts, right?" She knew she was lying, but there were some things that couldn't be shared, even with these men she trusted. Though she couldn't put her finger on what had happened that night, she couldn't shake her unease. Even her dreams were uneasy and unmerciful.

"Somehow, I've got trouble picturing you, Kyrie, and Jules doing magic," Damian stated, having met Tiana's best friends in the past. "Jules doesn't seem the type for anything magic-oriented."

A smile crept onto Tiana's face. "No, Jules isn't one for anything that smacks of ghosts, goblins, and other weird, unexplainable things. But she figured it was best to humor Kyrie. I have to admit, it was great to get away with them. Thanks for covering for me so I could go for a holiday."

"Ah, that explains much," Kyle snorted. "Somehow your friends like getting you into things you're never completely comfortable with doing."

Tiana pushed herself back from the workstation. She really didn't want to get more into what happened over the weekend. It was one thing to get into it with people who could understand, but these guys didn't comprehend the subtleties that went into working magick.

"Well, if you boys don't have anything you need me for, I'm going to my office to catch up on paperwork. Don't forget that I'll be in London the latter part of the week, giving a talk and dealing with consultancy stuff before the school year starts."

She moved gracefully off the chair and out the door with a wave to her colleagues. Her purposeful walk brought her to her office, further down the hall. Though most professors had their private offices in another building, Tiana had hers near where she worked, because the Sheffield forensic reconstruction lab was often called upon by various government agencies. Tiana unlocked and opened her office door, then flipped on the light switch.

The office was furnished with her own personal furniture: a modern-looking desk, a computer system hooked into the university network, a swivel chair, and tons of bookcases. The nearest small bookcase held the only evidence that Tiana was more than just a forensic anthropologist. Fingering a couple of the well-used books, especially those dealing with Jack the Ripper, she realized that Jack was, in some way, her own private obsession. The books were only the tip of the iceberg for her -- on her computer rested about fifteen articles she'd written dealing with various aspects of the murders attributed to Jack. Shaking her head, she sat down behind her desk, booting up her computer system while dialing the number for her phone messages on the nearby phone.

Quickly and efficiently, she retrieved her messages and noted down numbers she would need to return calls, including to a fellow Ripperologist, someone who specialized in the Jack the Ripper murders. She and Hamish McGowan were working on a joint paper dealing with the autopsies of all the canonical and noncanonical victims, showing similarities that might prove that Jack the Ripper had hunted after his last known victim. Just as she was hanging up the phone, her other line lit up.

"Hello. Dr. Tiana Wells. Can I help you?"

"Dr. Wells? This is Inspector Frederick Saducci from Scotland Yard."

Tiana leaned back in her chair, recalling the tall, barrel-like man. "What can I do for you, Inspector?"

"I'm calling to thank you for your help in the McDonald case. We've received a conviction, and the perpetrator received a life sentence. Your help was invaluable."

Resisting the urge to whoop, Tiana contented herself with a Cheshire-cat grin and pumping her fist in the air. "I'm glad that Sheffield University could help, Inspector Saducci. I accept your thanks, on behalf of my team."

"You might be hearing from one of my superiors. We're interested in having you come up for a talk regarding forensic anthropology, as well as how we can help preserve a scene for you and your people."

Tiana jotted down his comment and circled it. "Well, I do consultancy work, as well. Let them know I've no problems giving a talk to your crew. They were a tremendous help in preserving ancillary evidence that helped in verifying our finds. Have them call me, and I'll make sure that Scotland Yard is put on the priority list."

"Dr. Wells?" His tone turned inquiring and a bit soft.

"Yes, Inspector?"

"Some of us have heard you're a Ripperologist. Is this true?"

Tiana shook her head, chuckling softly. "Yes, it's true. Do I dare ask how that came out?"

"Dr. Gerald, in our forensic department, mentioned it."

Tiana recalled the older man, who specialized in trace evidence, particularly fiber analysis. "Ah, yes, I remember now. He's a fellow enthusiast; he helped me to receive copies of some of the autopsy reports I'd been searching for." She brushed back her hair, feeling that something more was coming. Sometimes it didn't pay to have not-so-latent psi talents.

"Have you ever considered doing a reconstruction project to see what Jack's victims looked like before they were slashed in the face?"

Tiana was shocked into stillness. "I couldn't be completely objective, as I've seen the autopsy photographs, Inspector; but, yes, I've wondered what Catherine Eddowes and Mary Kelly looked like prior to death." The quietness on the other end spoke volumes to Tiana. "Inspector, are you also a Ripperologist?"

There was a soft sigh. "Not in the traditional sense, as you and Dr. Gerald are, but it's a case that many of us feel was handled incorrectly. Though in those days, it was handled the best way possible."

"I agree there were some errors made, but the Metropolitan Police tried their best."

"One of the things that has always bothered us was the fact that the last two known victims were slashed beyond easy identification. The only pictures you ever see are the horrific ones of the autopsy. Or, in the case of Mary Kelly, those taken at the crime scene." The Inspector paused, as if weighing his words. "Would it be possible to reconstruct their faces using your forensic computer program, to show what they looked like before?"

"Yes, it's possible, but there are certain things we'd need in order to do such a project; and I'm not sure we'd get the approval for it. First, I'd need detailed reference points of the skulls, many x-rays, or the skull itself. Otherwise, it would not be as accurate as it should be." Tiana's brain began focusing on the intriguing idea. They'd done reconstruction of ancient skulls before, so she knew it was possible to do the re-creation work. Working with two of Jack's victims was something she'd want to be a part of.

The inspector cleared his throat. "If the proper clearances were given, would you be interested in the project, Dr. Wells?"

"If it was properly cleared, with no major upheaval, publicly or otherwise, yes, I'd jump at the chance to reconstruct their faces." Her voice betrayed her interest and eagerness. "Inspector Saducci, if you manage to pull that off, I'd be first in line to offer my services of not just the computer reconstruction, but also a clay reconstruction of both women." Tiana swiveled in her chair, pulling up her email as she tried to quell her excitement. She had to get herself under control before she sounded like a prepubescent horror fan.

"Then I'll place you at the top of the list, though I never considered anyone else for the idea. I'm not sure when it will be taking place or if clearance can be gotten, but knowing that we have someone who would be willing to work on the project is a great help. Thank you, Dr. Wells."

"Call me Tiana. If this pans out, Inspector Saducci, you'll probably see a lot more of me than you plan on. Thank you for thinking of me for the project, even if it doesn't work out."

"Thank you for all of your help, Tiana. Please call me Frederick or Fred. The Yard has enjoyed a great association with your group over the past few years, and there is no one better qualified or who'd do this with dignity. I'll keep you informed as things get underway. If you ever need anything, even access to some police records from that time that might not be readily available, please feel free to call or email me."

"Great, I appreciate it. I've got your card on my file system, so I might take you up on your generous offer. Thank you for your call."

They both hung up, Tiana twirling happily in her chair. What an opportunity it'd be if she could work on that project. Not just on a personal level, but also professionally. "Wow," she whispered aloud, packing that single word with all the happiness, excitement, and more that she felt.

With a renewed enthusiasm, she went back to work. The phone call made work a joy instead of something tolerated. The day seemed to pass by quickly as she got back into her working routine.

* * * * *

Later that night, a man stood in the city of London, grinning. There was no time to waste, now that he had the opportunity to indulge in the secret fantasies that had kept him going for so many years. Many a night, he had dreamt about something totally evil, and now it was here. It roared up within him and took over in the clear, chilly night ...

Freedom. I am finally ready to begin again.
Too long he had been bound in that eternal emptiness. His only hope was that whoever had released him wouldn't realize what they'd done. He didn't want to go back to the emptiness that was neither Heaven nor Hell. Perhaps it was the Purgatory that the Catholics spoke of. All he knew was that he was never going back, if he had anything to say about it. *God forefend if I ever go back. I shall not be put back there! Not now that I'm free to reign supreme!*

Having spent part of the afternoon finding out more about this day and age, he'd discovered he was one of history's unsolved mysteries and the epitome of what was known as a "serial killer." It had been somewhat of a shock to see the many books speculating on what he was really like. Perhaps he'd let them all know just exactly what his thoughts were while he killed those whores. Even now, there were women who used men, who deserved to die. The voice of the man he'd taken over protested at his choice, but the man's voice grew more silent as time passed.

Do you want the taste of power, or are you a coward? You will not speak in this woman's defense. There is no defense for a woman out this late, strutting her wares for men to look at!

Grinning, he watched as a young lady walked purposefully past his concealed presence. *You shouldn't be out this late, unless you're trolling for company, luv. Now you've got company.* Taking the opportunity, he grabbed her, pressing his hands around her neck until she lost consciousness. The memories of his avatar, the medical training in this body, helped him disable his victims more effectively.

Knife glinting in the moonlight, Jack re-created his very first murder. "I'm free," he muttered gleefully as he began carving up the woman. As he ran the risk of being caught being outside like this, Jack quickly, but methodically, took care of his first victim.

"Never again shall I be caged. Never again," he growled as he was drawn into the throes of his work.

Chapter Two

Detective Ian Spencer looked at the crime scene and controlled his shudder of revulsion. The sight before him was something he'd never wish on a new detective, not for *any* money. This had been brutally executed; deep inside, he knew this case would haunt him. The young woman's body lay before him, the crime scene carefully tagged. She'd been brutally stabbed in the throat, breasts, and abdomen. There were other cuts, but it would be up to the coroner to give them more information. Ian suppressed a shiver as he looked down at the young woman, rounded in features, perhaps in her mid-twenties. They had found her purse beneath her, identification and money intact.

"Well, guv, we've got the photographs taken. The forensic team wants to take her out and then reinvestigate the site itself," said the gangly, blond detective next to Ian. They had been partners for a long time now, enough time for Ian to take the teasing nickname of "governor."

"Thanks, John," he murmured. "Tell me something, does this remind you of anything else?" Somehow, this scene on Gunthorpe Street made him uneasy. There was something significant about it and he wasn't quite sure what. He had learned to listen to his instincts, but first he had to figure out why this place got to him. Why did this murder scene seem so familiar?

Ian had been with the Metropolitan Police for a few years. He'd recently turned down a chance to work for Scotland Yard, on the grounds that he hadn't learned enough to be part of that prestigious law enforcement arm. *Which is true. I've got much more to learn before I could consider being part of that elite team.* Running a hand through his short black hair, he wondered if he should notify them, just in case the murder matched up on their violent-offender listings. He'd do it later when there was more time.

"Did anyone hear any cries for help?"

John piped up. "Notta one, guv. Which seems odd."

Ian turned and looked at his partner. "What do you mean?"

"That's the thing, Ian. You'd think where she was found, someone would've heard a struggle or something; but no one heard anything. There were a couple higher up in the flats who claimed to hear the cry 'Murder!' but those closest to the crime scene heard nothing."

Ian considered his partner's words. You'd think the woman would've yelled for help. He stood up and stepped back, motioning to the forensic technicians to do their part in securing all evidence at the crime scene. Pulling his arms over his head, Ian stretched out the back and shoulder muscles that had tensed as he leaned over the woman. What was her name? Martha Cathridge.

His eyes raked the scene once more, wishing for some clue about the person responsible for this brutal killing. There seemed to be nothing. *How could a man kill a woman with a knife and leave nothing behind, not even bloodied footprints? Does he know how to kill without getting himself splattered? Is he from this area? What the hell are we dealing with here?*

Ian called to a couple of uniformed officers and directed them to start a door-to-door campaign, asking people if they'd seen anything or anyone who might be a possible suspect. "John, I'm heading back to the station. I want to run this through to see if there've been any similar murders reported in the last couple of years."

"This one spooks you, too, guv?"

Ian turned his eyes on his partner. "I hate to admit it, but yes."

* * * * *

Four hours later found Ian at the pathology lab, waiting to see if he'd be allowed to watch the autopsy. An older man opened the door and looked at him. "Detective Spencer."

"Yes."

"Come with me if you want to watch. You know the rules?"

"Dr. Campion, you know I do."

The older man grinned as he ushered in the detective. "Yes, but it's regulation to ask."

Ian shook his head. "How are you doing, Al?"

The doctor chuckled as both he and Ian began washing up before going in to the actual autopsy area. "Not bad, Ian. How's your father doing?"

Ian took off his coat, rolled up his sleeves, and scrubbed his hands and arms with the disinfectant. "He and Mum are well. They're going to Cornwall for holiday soon. He's asked me to make sure that you're coming to the Thursday bridge game with Ginny."

Dr. Alexander Campion was one of Metropolitan's foremost medical examiners. He'd helped refine, from other fields, some of the techniques used here. It was an honor to work with him. Al was close to retirement; Ian hoped that didn't mean that he couldn't be dragged out on the harder cases when they popped up.

"Yes, you can tell my bridge partner I'll be there, along with our mortal enemy, Ginny."

Ian chuckled as he gloved up and watched Al don his protective gown. "You call your wife the 'mortal enemy'?"

Al's twinkling gray eyes caught Ian's sapphire ones. "You bet your arse I do. She's managed to wipe your father and me out, three weeks running. If I didn't know better, I'd say she was cheating."

Al nodded at Ian, who opened the doorway to the autopsy room. In the center of the sterile room was a stainless steel table, its almost trough-like design meant to channel bodily fluids and drain at the end. There were also microscopes, materials to make slides, and numerous other instruments. This was one of the best-equipped forensic rooms that Ian was aware of outside of New Scotland Yard.

"The trace team has already vacuumed her and her clothes, so we're free to take a look at her wounds and figure out what the cause of death was," Al said, his voice taking on a more official tone. His right hand reached up and touched the recorder as his left pulled back the sheet, exposing a naked Martha to him and Ian. "Before me is a young woman named Martha Cathridge. Age at death is twenty-five. Height is five-foot-four. Her weight is one hundred fifty pounds."

21

While Al went through dissecting and weighing various things, taking notes on a pad as well as reciting them, Ian tried to put together who could've killed such an apparently innocuous young woman. The autopsy process was a long one, usually an hour or so. Several times, Ian went to look at various organs Al pointed to wordlessly for his examination. Al eventually finished the main parts and started on his review.

"This is a review of the body wounds. There are at least twenty-two stab wounds to the trunk; seventeen in the breast, including five stabs wounds to the left lung, two stabs to the right lung. The heart was stabbed once, which caused some bleeding in the pericardial sac. Liver stabbed five times, the spleen cut twice. The lower half of the body has one major cut, while the stomach also had one slash in it. There is a lot of blood between her legs. Nine stab wounds to the throat, though there is no evidence that the carotid arteries were severed. The breasts, stomach, abdomen, and vagina seemed to have been the main areas. Death is due to hemorrhage and loss of blood. No evidence of a struggle, except for the wound on the chest bone. Almost all injuries seem to have been inflicted by a right-handed person using a short, non-serrated knife, though one of the wounds looks to have been done left-handed," Al stated. "I'd like a second opinion by another expert to confirm the findings regarding handedness. Recommendations -- any New Scotland forensic examiner or Dr. Tiana Wells, forensic anthropologist and part-time examiner."

Switching off the recorder, Al began restoring the young woman to a semblance of order again. Ian stepped back to give him room; Al motioned him forward. "Ian, you see this stab wound, yes?"

Ian looked to where Al pointed, the one stab wound that seemed a bit out of place, the stab to the heart. Hearing the soft, emotionless review had caused a shiver to crawl up Ian's spine. It sounded like a review he had heard somewhere before, though he couldn't place it. But now wasn't the time to think on it. He had a murder to solve. "What about it?"

The older man shook his head. "Something about that doesn't sit with all the other wounds. It's like he deliberately tried to cause problems. The wound doesn't look or seem like the others; it's as though he used another instrument to cause confusion for the coroners. Look at the edges of the wound. I'd like another expert to consult on this. I've taken snapshots and recorded this fully, but still. Do you think we can get a rush on a second opinion?"

Ian thought on it. "If it's you asking, I don't see why not. Who would you prefer?" Al's smirk was his answer. "Wait, let me guess: Dr. Wells." At Al's assent, Ian continued. "I take it she's competent and pretty."

"She also specializes in knife wounds. Though she doesn't like being called in for examiner work— prefers doing those skull restorations— Tiana would help tremendously on this. She works at Sheffield University. I'm going to place the call once I get this done."

Ian nodded. "Let me know when she comes, so I can sit in on the procedure. I'd love to get her ideas on this." Taking off his gloves, Ian tossed them into the trash on his way to the clean room again. Picking up his coat, he pressed the intercom button.

"Al?"

"Yes?"

"Does this murder remind you of any past crimes?"

Al hesitated, then answered. "It does, but I can't quite put my finger on it."

"Me, too. Thanks, old man. I'll tell Mum and Dad you'll be over on Thursday."

"Thanks, tyke. Now go find this killer before he strikes again."

Ian left, confident Al would do what was necessary to get Dr. Wells to be part of this investigative team.

* * * * *

"You want what?" Tiana asked, wishing she had learned to drink tea, as the caffeine from her cappuccino flooded her system. She refused to look at Damian. There was no way he was asking her to do what had come out of his mouth. She'd come to work a bit late, plagued by nightmares she hadn't had in ages. Now, a real-life nightmare seemed to be starting. "Who asked for this?"

"Dr. Alexander Campion from London Metro called and specifically asked for your help."

Rubbing her hands up and down her face, she let out a sigh, then turned toward her colleague and friend. "He wants me to do what?"

"He's asked you to come down and examine some knife wounds on a victim from the Metro area. It's not like you haven't done an autopsy before. I do believe you've done it a handful of times."

Tiana glared at the dark-haired man. "You know, if I didn't know better, I'd say you were all for this."

"Ti, it was years ago. You need to move forward now. This is a new case, and someone needs your expertise. Will you do it or not?"

Hands behind her head, squeezing it with her arms, she nodded. "Call Dr. Campion and tell him I'll head down as soon as I'm able." She paused and swallowed. "Damian, I'm scared."

He clasped her shoulder as she brought down her arms. "I know, but it's time to turn that fear into strength, Ti. You survived, and became knowledgeable in that specialty. Don't let him keep winning because of fear." He left her in her office.

Tiana bit her lower lip. *Is he right? Am I letting that bastard win, because of my fear?* Letting out an anguished sigh, she closed her eyes and relived the moment when she'd faced death and known it wasn't soft or gentle as her Grandmum had promised.

"You're beautiful, squirming like that. Will you beg for mercy as I cut you?" The voice was roughened and American.

Tiana twisted, trying to get out of the ropes around her wrists as she heard the sharpening of a knife in the background. "Why are you doing this? Let me go. I'm no danger to you." Her throat was raw from screaming through the earlier blows to her body. How many hours ago had that been? "What do you want from me?"

"Simple, lady. I want your body mutilated as a testimony to my power. Nothing more or less." The huge shadow moved forward. She almost screamed as the face she had thought was a nightmare became real once more. "I see you remember me now. You cringe pretty when trying not to get hit. What a shame you've got nothing more of value that I want."

Tiana closed her eyes for a brief moment, trying to remember the self-defense lessons she had taken.

*How did you protect yourself from a man with a
Bowie knife?*

*The first slash against her naked abdomen
burned, but wouldn't give her abductor the
satisfaction of screaming in pain again. She
concentrated on keeping her heart rate even as the
second, third, fourth slashes slid across her belly.
Runnels of blood coated the sweat-slicked skin as she
bit back her cries.*

*Dark, wild eyes glimmered before hers, a hot
tongue trailing the sweat that rolled down her cheek.
She tried to control her revulsion as the fetid breath
rushed at her face. At that moment, she saw
something move out of the corner of her eye.
Something white and flowing, perhaps a cat, though
she didn't remember seeing one in the two days she'd
been locked in this basement. Her dangling body
shuddered as her blood dripped down.*

"Let me go."

*"The only way you're getting free is if you kill
me." The predator grabbed her shoulder-length hair
and yanked her head back. "You talk too much."*

*The glint of the knife filled her mind. She felt the
bite of the blade on her throat as she kicked at him.
She gasped for air as the blood seemed to pour from
her throat ...*

Tiana gasped, grabbing at her throat as her body heaved forward. She placed her head between her knees and sucked in air greedily. *Dear gods, the memories!* This was why she didn't deal with knives or edged weapons anymore. Remembering her two days of hell on earth, she shuddered as she tried to gain control. Damian was right. She had let that bastard keep his reign of terror over her; it wasn't easy to let go of that fear. She was afraid she'd never be able to.

Shakily, she grabbed the phone and punched in Damian's extension. "Call Dr. Campion. Tell him I'll be there in three hours." Pausing, she considered her next words. "Damian, he hurt me more than I can ever tell you. But you're right, I need to move forward."

Hanging up the phone, Tiana took a tissue from her desk and wiped her face. This was going to be tough. Five years ago, the victim on the table could have been her. Closing her eyes, Tiana tried to get her balance back before she made the journey to London. She picked up the personal reference book she had put together and dropped it into her attaché.

Edged weapons were a subspecialty of hers. When she'd decided to become a doctor, both medical and anthropological, her love of edged weapons had been a bonus in helping her determine cause of death for crime victims. Little did she realize that her knowledge would put her up there among the top of those who specialized in particular wound types. When she wrote her first article on edged weapons and how to identify certain features in regards to depth, cuts, and blade edges, her writing style captured the interest of many scholars, who helped her with further research just prior to her kidnapping.

Now she tried not to think about knives. Even her personal collection of edged weapons, including her favorite sword and dagger, were locked up and out of sight. At one time, Tiana had loved working out with her katana and her daggers. The sight of them now made her shiver in horror. She remembered her first autopsy dealing with knife wounds after her rescue. Blackness had rushed in when she realized she was looking at cuts from a knife similar to the one that had caused her so many stitches and had almost ruined her voice.

Rubbing her arms, Tiana steadied herself. Dr. Campion was counting on her to help him out. She had to do this. Sighing, she rose from her chair, making sure everything was in place for when she got back.

"Here I go. I can do this. I can face my fear and overcome it." *I hope.*

Chapter Three

The phone beside Ian rang. "Detective Spencer."

"Ian, this is Al. Dr. Wells will be here by five."

Ian looked upward and quietly thanked whomever it was that had blessed Al's ability to get help. "I'll be there."

The older man cleared his throat. "Before you do, you need to do something for me."

Ian looked at the phone receiver in disbelief. "You want a favor?"

"Yes. This won't cost you anything more than pulling up an old file. I want you to know more about Dr. Wells. Your forthright manner might overwhelm our lady doctor."

"Then she needs to get over it."

"No, Ian Andrew Spencer. You need to be more circumspect." There was a hardness in Al's voice that was rarely heard, except when he dressed down new hires in the forensic department.

"Why?"

"Pull up the file dealing with Messy Mike and the Sheffield Killings."

Ian's brow lifted. He remembered the case -- vaguely, as it was in the early days of his time as an officer. "As you wish. You want a hard copy?"

"No, I want you to pay attention to the names of the victims and how he was stopped. I'll see you in an hour."

Al hung up his end and Ian followed suit. Turning in his chair, he turned on his computer. He pulled up online records regarding the case Al had mentioned. As he began reading the case notes, the hairs on the back of his neck stood up. Getting a flash, Ian scrolled down to the last page of notes. As he read the findings, his stomach dropped. The last victim, the only one left alive, was one Tiana Wells, graduate student. Damn.

As he read further, Ian was horrified by what Dr. Wells had lived through. He was beginning to understand what Al had meant. Tiana Wells had lived through what most people wouldn't. He catalogued her injuries, amazed she'd managed to disarm and escape her captor, then notify police. The fact that she'd gone back to finish her studies was simply amazing.

31

Her picture haunted him. She possessed simple beauty, made ethereal because of her experience. Her auburn hair framed her face; her eyes were shuttered, holding the pain of many people, so many people who had died before her. Ian felt something touch his soul as he memorized her features. She had come out of hell looking like a fey lost in the world of men, but with an inner strength that would turn a killer back on his heels.

Ian leaned back in his chair and sighed. "Unbelievable. This woman lived through hell, and now she regularly gives of herself to help the police."

His partner leaned over and glanced at the information on the screen. "Who?"

"The forensic anthropologist who specializes in knife wounds."

John read some of the report. "Dr. Tiana Wells. She's one of the group up in Sheffield, isn't she?"

"Yeah. Al asked her to come help us with this case of ours." Ian's eyes glanced again at the five-year-old picture of the young, battered woman. Something in him clenched and held tight. Her eyes were that of a warrior, and he knew all about being strong in the face of the enemy.

"She looks like she's seen hell and isn't sure she's alive."

"Yeah. Let's hope she's recovered enough to be of help to us." Ian continued reading the case reports, his admiration for this woman growing with each passing moment.

* * * * *

Tiana rolled her head around, loosening up tense muscles as she pulled into the division's parking lot. She was vaguely familiar with the terrain, since she was a freelance consultant as well as an expert on knife wounds. After parking the car, Tiana grabbed her medical bag and her ID badge and alighted from the car, making sure the door closed and locked securely. With a confident stride, she made her way up the steps toward the entrance.

The gray building was old-looking— well, old-looking to her. Like many government buildings, the bland exterior was created to conceal that important happenings occurred inside. Tiana never understood why they didn't draw attention, as the other buildings in the area were more decorative, almost forcing you to consider the slightly shabby structure. Just as churches were huge so as to be seen as sanctuaries against crime and spiritual wrongs, Tiana thought the police force should stand out to be a safety for those who might need them.

"Oh. Excuse me," she said as she bumped into the tall man in front of her. He turned around, and her first thought was that she'd never seen the likes of those eyes anywhere on this earth. They were blue, almost too blue for his dark hair. A wave of instant lust hit her hard. It had been a long time since she'd been with anyone, and this male was just her type, had she been dating. *Gods above, he's beyond gorgeous. Save me before I do something stupid, like follow him around.*

"It's alright, miss." He paused and tilted his head as if to take in her every feature. "Tiana Wells? Dr. Wells?"

Tiana stepped back, feeling as if she was being dissected. "Um, yes. I'm Dr. Tiana Wells."

The tall, broad-shouldered man put out his hand. "Welcome. I'm Detective Ian Spencer. Al asked you here because of my case."

"Oh. Nice to meet you, Detective Spencer. Do you know where Dr. Campion is?" She shook his hand and was aware of the sparks that flared between them. *Ack! No, no, no! I did not feel that. I didn't. Okay, I did, but now is not the time to feel lust. I'm on a job, for Arawn's sake! Okay, no taking the Celtic god of the dead in vain, Ti; he might just kick your arse for doing so. Then again, he might just laugh at you and make the dead walk.*

Ian gestured behind him. "More than likely, he's in the autopsy area, waiting for us." He shot her a lopsided grin. "Follow me and I'll take you to him."

"Thanks, I appreciate that. Do I need to check in with anyone?" She fell into step next to the man, letting her instincts as well as her gaze register him into her consciousness. Tiana had been with men before, but none had affected her like this. Again she reminded herself that now was not the time or place for such lust. "Last time, I had to go through a whole process to get inside."

Ian waved his hand as they walked past one of the desks. "No, we've been expecting you; plus, we already have you on file from last time. You've got your badge on, so you remembered the routine."

Tiana grinned, despite trying to maintain her calm. "Something like that. I'm used to wearing a badge, so it's second nature to me."

She followed him down the small flight of stairs to where the forensics department was relegated. Tiana watched as Ian took the stairs two at a time, his muscles bunching and releasing as he moved. Yeah, there was something about men in uniform, even if the uniform was a nice suit. Damn her hormones. It had to be a side-effect from the vacation with her friends. Doomed. She had been doomed without knowing it.

Shaking her head, she negotiated the stairs easily. Tiana shivered slightly. The hallway always seemed darker, scarier to her, regardless that the fluorescent lighting illuminated the area completely. "Is it just me, or does this place make you feel like you're walking into a horror film setting?"

"You're not alone." Ian smiled as he waited for her. "I keep waiting for the morgue doors to open and the zombies to walk out."

Tiana chuckled. "*Night of the Living Dead.* Yeah, that could be a bit tough."

Ian pretended to shudder as she walked past him. She saw the older man waiting for her.

"Tiana, my dear. You look wonderful. It's good to see you again, even though it's business."

"Thanks, Dr. Campion," she said. Tiana put down her briefcase and hugged the doctor. Noting his look, she chuckled. "Okay— Al. What's this I hear about you wanting another opinion on some knife wounds?"

"I wanted a second opinion. You're the top of the field."

Tiana's brow rose. "Since when does my teacher need help?" Her voice lowered to keep with the teasing between former mentor and student.

He squeezed her shoulder lightly, a slight grin on his face. "Because the student has outdone the teacher."

Tiana blushed and looked away. "Not by choice, Al," she responded ruefully. "Let's glove up and get this over with." Looking back at Ian, she shot her former mentor a questioning gaze.

"Detective Spencer will stay and ask questions, as this is his case. Ian's got a vested interest."

"I see. Makes sense, in a police way. They're always hovering around when you want room and space to work," Tiana teased. Grabbing a set of scrub clothes that were laid out in the guest cubby area, Tiana stripped off her shirt and pants after she kicked off her gym shoes. Once she was down to her underwear and bra, Tiana grabbed the pea-green top and pulled it over her head. Then she slid the pants on, tying them at her waist. Sliding her feet back into her shoes, she sat on the bench, lacing them.

Tiana looked up, noting that both men watched her. She chuckled. "Not had female docs in here lately, have you?" Reaching over, she pulled a hair scrunchie from her bag and put her hair back in a ponytail. She gave Dr. Campion a playful glance. "Do I need to tell the missus on you, Al?"

Giving her a look of mock horror, Al answered. "Oh, no! She'll punish me by beating me again at bridge— or worse, she'll make me give up my comfortable chair!"

"It'd serve you right, you bridge cheater you." Turning her gaze to Ian, she took in the younger man's dark blue gaze. Involuntarily, she stepped back from the heat of his gaze. "And will your wife mind that you were ogling a female doctor?"

Ian's head tilted back and out came a low, rumbling laugh. "If I had a wife, my dad and Al would be celebrating, or at least convincing me to learn how to play bridge. No, I'm not captured and browbeaten as of yet."

Tiana chuckled. "Me, neither. In addition, I play bridge badly. More of a pinochle player, myself." She walked to the sinks and began scrubbing up. "Anything I need to know going in?"

The room seemed to sober with her question. Both men rolled up their sleeves and began scrubbing up alongside her. Al spoke first. "She's young, Tiana. About your age, perhaps a bit younger."

Tiana nodded, encouraging him to continue as she dried off her hands and arms. She needed to prep herself mentally for this, and she knew that Al knew it. It had been a while since she was in the position of actually dealing with a recently deceased body, not just bones. This was going to be very difficult for her. Very difficult indeed.

His voice broke her reverie. "Multiple stab wounds. Some look like they were done with a penknife or some thin, small-sized blade. Then there's another wound that is a bit different ..."

Inclining her head, Tiana looked at her mentor. "Understood." They both knew that she didn't need details. It would be her job to do this without anything that could cloud her judgment. She sucked in a deep breath and slowly released it. "Let's get this done and over with."

Al opened the door between the changing room and the autopsy room. It was the same pale colors as most of the autopsy rooms she'd been in. Not like the green rooms in America, but pale, blah beige. She wasn't sure which she hated more. How she missed her computer room and studio. Stepping forward, Tiana didn't quite catch the shared look between the two men.

She made her way quickly to the shroud-covered gurney. She felt a shiver pass through her entire body. Swallowing the dryness in her throat, Tiana clutched the pewter pendant that dangled between her breasts. Reassuring warmth stole over her and she released the antique locket, thanking her family for being with her, even if it was only through the family heirloom.

The men stood opposite her, waiting for her signal. From the clipboard lying next to the gurney, she read the victim's basic information, including name, age, and weight at death. Inclining her head, she took a breath as Al pulled the covering from the young woman's body. At the first glimpse of the dead woman, Tiana's stomach rolled and pitched as she willed herself to stay strong. Letting out her breath and then inhaling deeply, she picked up the first set of instruments as she spoke into the recorder.

"This is Dr. Tiana Wells, doing a secondary inspection of the wounds sustained by Martha Cathridge." She glanced at her mentor. "Was there a tremendous blood loss where she was found?"

Ian answered. "The recovery scene is almost guaranteed to be the crime scene as well. There was a pool of blood under her. We kept the clothing for evidence in case there's any trace of our killer on her."

"Hmm, that explains some of the discoloration." Leaning forward, she touched the skin with one metal probe. With a mental kick, she forced herself to the first set of wounds in the left breast area. "These look brutal. Yet, they do seem to differ in depth."

Taking a thin, clear ruler, Tiana measured the length, depth, and angle of each wound in the area. She called out her measurements to be recorded. When she got to the last set, she began comparing a couple of them. A few times, she switched instruments and remeasured them for accuracy.

"What would cause the variation of depth?" Ian queried.

"Honestly? Too many things, actually." Tiana paused, biting her lip while she lifted the woman's breast, checking underneath for exit wounds and other marks. "She doesn't seem to have any defensive injuries. That means she was alive but unconscious when he started his vicious assault. However, she'd twitch, perhaps even start to awaken, unless he had given one of the killing blows early on."

Tiana continued to methodically measure each cut, bruise, and mark upon the young woman's body. She paused only to give the measurements for each wound as she poked and prodded them to give up the answers that might help them find out more about the killer. When she got to the longest cut, the one on the abdomen, she measured it as she had the others. Curious. Calling out the numbers quickly, Tiana measured the depth, the angle, and brought out a special magnifier to check the wound even more closely. Unconsciously, she started clucking her tongue against the roof of her mouth.

"What's going on, Al?" Ian whispered to his friend.

Al answered softly. "It means that it's possible there wasn't another blade used on Martha. That it might've been the same blade."

"Oh."

Tiana looked up at Ian's response. A chestnut brow lifted in slight amusement, distracted from the corpse for a moment. "From the measurements, including the width of the cut, the knife was pulled a bit before it was removed."

"Can we tell if he was right- or left-handed?"

Tiana smiled a bit at Ian. "Good question. But the answer isn't quite that simple."

Ian looked at Al. "I thought you said --"

"What I postulated was the killer being left-handed. I wanted Tiana's opinion to verify."

Tiana continued making her final measurements before answering. Rubbing her face with her forearm, she motioned Ian closer to the body. When he stood next to her, Tiana brought the magnifier closer to Ian's level.

"There are various factors, including edge placement. But at the same time, that also makes it tough." She paused as she moved the magnifier over a cut.

"What do you mean?"

Tiana took a probe and pointed toward the one larger cut. "See how it's thicker in the cut on this side?" Seeing his nod, she continued. "That means he used a single-edged blade. That is where the blunt portion entered her body." She moved the probe toward herself. "See how the cut seems to thin?"

"So he moved it towards him."

"Possibly. We don't know how he held the knife. Though from studying angles and depths, I'd say the wounds on the upper chest were done overhand." Tiana gestured to the longest cut. "He held it underhand here. The angle of the cut suggests that he held her as he cut her, probably to send her system into shock."

"Show me," Ian interjected.

Tiana blinked in surprise, her eyes meeting Ian's. She picked up a scalpel in her left hand, fisting it, with the blade coming out near her pinkie. As she raised her hand to shoulder level, her eyes went to her hand. "Overhand causes deeper wounds. There's more force behind the puncture."

Without missing a beat, she switched her hold on the scalpel. Now the blade was out near her the index finger. "This is sneakier. However, it has less thrust than overhand."

She went on to show him how certain wounds could look similar, again demonstrating the angle of the cut in relation to the various poses. Without knowing the killer's preference, it was hard to say whether he was left- or right-handed. She did admit, though, that it looked like the killer had right-handed tendencies, due to the angle of the wounds and the pulling of the blade. More than likely, the initial wounds were done from behind. But she wouldn't commit to it completely. As she told him, it could be either way, depending on the risks the murderer was willing to take.

When she stopped, Ian spoke. "I want to thank you for this, Dr. Wells. You'd make a deadly enemy with your knowledge." He admired Tiana's professionalism and form. She had come through her own tragedy to be strong for others. It amazed him.

Tiana blinked at him and dropped the scalpel onto the table. "Excuse me?"

"Your skill and movement look lethal. They also show me how a killer might've done it. You've come a long way to help us, and I appreciate it greatly."

She looked slightly mollified by his words. He hadn't meant to refer to her past, but he could see that her knowledge of edged weapons was intimate. Having watched her move and act with the scalpel had shown him exactly how proficient she was with edged weapons and their uses. It was a bond that many people never had with any kind of weapon. "I have a question, though. Do you think the assailant has the same skill or knowledge?"

Tiana bit her lip as she thought upon how to answer the question. "I'm not sure. For some reason, these wound patterns look somewhat familiar to me. It could be how they're clustered that reminds me of an old case, or it could be something as simple as the hatred involved."

"You mean perhaps an unsolved murder of some kind?"

Tiana shook her head. "I'm not sure. That's what makes this difficult. It looks familiar, but I can't remember where I've seen something similar to this. I'll look at my reference books and such when I get a chance to see where I've seen this pattern before."

Al spoke up. "Are you driving home tonight, Tiana?"

Tiana looked up at the clock. It was now seven at night. They'd been at this for a couple of hours, and she was in no shape to drive home. "No, I'm going to check into the hotel I normally stay at when I come up here for my consulting work."

"Ah, the Brighton Square. At least you can get a hot meal and relax before heading back home to Snaith, then."

"Definitely." She pulled off the latex gloves and tossed them into the trash bin. Then she went to the sink and washed her hands again. "This is an unusual case, Detective. I wouldn't be surprised if your assailant strikes again."

Ian's eyes met hers in the mirror above the sink. "How so, Doctor?"

Her face was grim and there was no hint of mischief in her eyes. "Easy. Those are wounds from a very vindictive person, with murder on his mind. He won't wait long before claiming another victim."

Chapter Four

After her pronouncement, Tiana changed clothes, finished her report, and made her way to Brighton Square. It was a modest hotel, but one that was comfortable for her. Checking in was simple, and she couldn't wait to throw herself on the bed and shiver herself to sleep. Amazingly, she'd struggled through the postmortem without freaking out and fainting, which surprised her. Definitely something to celebrate. Nevertheless, she needed food to ground her before she could spend time looking at her reactions to the time in the basement.

Then there was the mysterious Detective Ian Spencer. What was it about him that made her tremble in lust? "Stop being silly, Ti. You're gonna make yourself look foolish if you think of him as anything other than a detective."

After spending some time meditating and doing some stretching exercises to help relax her, she realized it was getting late. She'd better go to the restaurant down the street and grab some food before going to bed. In the morning, she'd look through the reference books she always brought with her. Maybe she could figure out what about the victim's wounds seemed so damn familiar. She felt like she should recognize the significance of the wound pattern. Grabbing her wallet, she made her way downstairs.

As she walked toward the front door, Tiana heard her name called, but couldn't see who was calling to her. Someone tapped her shoulder. Turning to her left, there stood Detective Spencer. "Dr. Wells, I'm sorry to have scared you like that. I wanted to thank you again for today. Would you allow me to take you out for dinner?"

Tiana's brows lifted high under her bangs in shock. Normally, she was the "untouchable" Dr. Wells. People didn't like the bone doc around unless there was a victim to be brought to life. "Why?"

The detective stepped back. Tiana realized probably not many people, especially women, ever questioned his motives. However, she knew to be cautious; sometimes the ones trusted turn out to be dangerous. She'd found that out when a guy she'd dated at university had been related to that ... creature. She swallowed back the bile that rose in her throat. No more thinking on how sometimes the supposed good guys are bad guys in disguise.

The detective's head tilted a bit as if to really look at her. It seemed to be one of his habits and endeared him to her easily. "Have I really stymied you that much, Detective Spencer?"

"Ian, please. Actually, I think so. I figured you'd have guessed I wanted to take you to dinner as a 'thank you' for coming up on such short notice."

Now it was Tiana's turn to be stunned. No one had offered to take her to dinner before. Well, unless it was her mother, sister, or aunt. *Amazing.* "I'd be honored. I was only going to walk down the street to a fish-and-chips stand or to the family-owned Italian restaurant."

"Ah, Arrabiata's. That's a great place, I'll be your escort." Without waiting for her reply, Ian gathered her hand in his, pulling her toward the entrance. She walked along with him.

"You know about Arrabiata's? I thought it was one of those places not many people knew about." As they walked down the street, their strides slowly matched together, despite Ian's longer legs.

"I'm not many people. I love Italian food and make it a point to find the best Italian restaurants when I need to rejuvenate myself or when I need comfort." His voice possessed a smiling tone that relaxed her.

"It's a wonderful restaurant. I discovered it about eight years ago, and I've been a fairly regular patron since. Only my work at Sheffield University keeps me from coming around more often." Tiana chuckled. "If I could get them to agree to overnight me food three times a week, I'd be in heaven."

"Wouldn't we all?" Ian joined in. "Pierre has considered expanding the business, but he's not quite ready yet."

"Oh, you know Pierre and Isabella, then?" Tiana tried not to seem surprised by this information. "They're a wonderful couple. I'm glad they sent their son to business school and Felicia to culinary school. They will carry on their family's quality over the next twenty years, if they choose to keep up the family business."

"Yes, Paolo and I are friends. His sister is a beauty."

"Definitely. But she cooks even more divinely than she looks," Tiana countered.

Ian sighed happily. "Yes, she does."

They stood before the elegant, yet not ostentatious doors of Arrabiata's. Ian pulled open the door and held it for Tiana. As she entered, the smell of fresh-baked yeast rolls and various Italian spices wafted to her nostrils, causing her stomach to growl. "Mmm."

"Indeed." Ian walked her to where Isabella stood as the hostess for the evening. "*Buone notte,* Isabella."

"Good evening to you as well, Ian." Isabella smiled at Tiana. "Tiana, my dear, it's good to see you again." The older woman hugged her as she whispered words in Tiana's ear.

"I'm fine, Madre. Honestly, I am. Yes, I'm here on business, but Ian is taking me out to dinner so he can question me further on a case that he's working on."

Isabella looked back at her adopted son and clucked her tongue. "Ian, tell me this is not true? Instead of wining and dining this beautiful woman, you'd make her work while eating one of our dinners?"

Tiana hid her smile behind her hand as Ian shuffled his feet and his eyes refused to meet Isabella's gaze. "Madre, that's not entirely true --"

"It had better not be if you expect your usual table, young man. I will not have my daughter upset while she dines tonight."

"Daughter?" Ian looked from Isabella to Tiana in slight confusion; then it clicked. "You mean like how I'm your son."

"Sí, and I won't tolerate you harassing her. She and Felicia are close friends, and there will not be any—I repeat, *any*—work talk until after dessert, understood?" The older woman crossed her arms and glared at Ian.

"Sí, Madre. I understand." Ian shot a glance at Tiana, who tried desperately not to laugh.

Isabella had adopted her when Tiana first found the restaurant after meeting Felicia at boarding school her final year. However, she wasn't telling this devastatingly handsome man anything about that. It was bad enough that Paolo teased her at times over what happened during those years. There was no need to allow another male to tease her while Paolo cheered him on.

Isabella escorted them both toward a table in a corner area near the kitchen. Kissing her adopted mother's cheek, Tiana thanked her quietly. Isabella had come to the hospital during her recovery and understood Tiana needed to feel secure in any setting. Handing them both menus, she told them one of the waiters would come by in a few moments.

Tiana glanced over at Ian, who kissed Isabella's hand. As the older woman left them alone, Tiana couldn't resist teasing. "Seems to me that Madre has you under control."

Ian turned towards her, glaring, though she could tell by the smile in his eyes that he was teasing her. "You got me in trouble."

Nodding unrepentantly, Tiana responded, "Sure did. I make no excuses. No work talk during dinner. This way, it's set in stone. Madre won't hear of it, and she'll check on us to make sure you follow her law."

He shook his head, a grin playing on his lips. "I can't believe you did that. Granted, I did want to talk business, but I would not have done it until after we ate. It's a bit crass talking about murder when people are eating."

"True, but there are many people who would do so. I forestalled that by getting Isabella involved." Tiana chuckled again as Isabella looked over and glared at Ian, who, in turn, smiled and waved to her. This was one way to help tone down the attraction she had for this dark-haired, blue-eyed, sexy devil. Madre would watch over them and make sure that things stayed low key.

"Brat."

"Yes."

"She protects you like you're one of hers."

Tiana smiled softly, a glow appearing in her eyes. "Yes, she does. And I adore her for that. She was one of the few who didn't walk away from me when I needed someone."

Ian nodded. "After the attack, you mean."

Tiana gaped at him. "Yes, how did—?"

Ian clasped one of her hands in his. "I'm a detective, remember? Plus, Al gave me a heads-up and told me to look at a file before meeting you. For some reason, he thinks I need to work on my manners."

They both chuckled, knowing Al thought everyone needed lessons in manners, including his dearest wife. Talk shifted toward the forensic doctor and how they both knew him. Subconsciously, they both decided to not speak of Tiana's trauma.

"He and my father have been best chums since their early years at Eton. Trust me, I've heard *all* of their stories. Nothing like a member of the landed gentry being with a guy who knew everything but unknighted."

Tiana grinned. "I got to him when he agreed to teach a couple of forensic courses for my residency. He was reluctant at first, but then warmed up to me when he realized I was also majoring in forensic anthropology. At that point, he brought me home to meet Ginny. After that, whenever I needed someone to help me with my studies, he was there."

Ian stuck out his tongue at Tiana. She snorted with laughter. "I've known them both my entire life. They're my godparents as well as my parents' best friends," he said. "I don't remember a time when Al wasn't regaling me with tales of grisly murders and autopsies. My father blames him for my becoming a detective."

"Surely not! Being an upholder of the law is quite important work."

"But not as important as being heir."

"Ah," Tiana responded, feeling a bit sorry for Ian. In some ways, she forgot about those who were considered royalty or upper peerage, their duties often precluding having a choice in their destiny.

"Don't pity me. My father got over it quick enough when he realized that it meant his son would be able to protect the inheritance, as well as run it with my business degree."

Tiana clapped her hands as she chuckled. "Sounds like my mother. She wasn't too thrilled when she found out her daughter wanted to play with bones; but then she realized how close to many men I'd be, and, suddenly, I could do almost no wrong."

Their waiter came at that moment. He announced that Signorina Felicia was preparing something special for them both, but he'd be honored to take their drink and appetizer orders. They ordered a carafe of zinfandel and the house minestrone soup. As they regaled each other with the various times they'd been fed the soup when they were sick and ailing, the two began to bond in friendship. For a moment, the spark of lust was tempered with the overtures of something deeper.

* * * * *

"I can't eat another bite. I love Madre and Felicia, but I swear they try to stuff me to the gills when I come." Tiana moaned as she tasted one last bite of chocolate mocha tiramisu. "This is too sinful for words. How is your dessert, Ian?"

They had dropped formality within the first course and discovered they had much in common, including their love of various music and movies. Tiana fully relaxed after the second glass of wine, as Ian made her laugh over some of his stupider stunts in his early years on the police force.

"Divine. I hadn't realized how good Italian gelato truly was. Thank you for recommending it." Ian paused. "Do you think I could convince Felicia to sell me a pint or two to bring home?"

"Hmm, good question. If she gives you one, I want one for when I go home. I'll pack it in ice so it'll last the trip home to Snaith."

Ian summoned the waiter and asked him to ask Felicia to come to their table so they could thank her for such a wonderful meal. They had feasted on roasted capon *arrabiata*, a new dish on the menu. They'd both agreed after the first few bites that heaven had to be in any Italian food created. As they waited for Felicia's appearance, Ian turned to Tiana.

"I wanted to thank you again for everything. I know it was difficult to deal with our mess."

Tiana inclined her head. "I'm glad I could help, though I figure I've frustrated you as well."

"Nothing insurmountable. I realize you need more than one body as evidence."

Tiana sighed. "Yes, but I hope the killer is stopped before he kills again."

"I agree."

Ian stretched his arms overhead, releasing the day's tension, then laid his hands on the table. "Tell me something, Tiana. What made you continue your studies after what happened?"

Tiana bit her lip and looked away. She knew this would come up, but in a way, she still wasn't prepared. Somehow, she wasn't certain she really knew the reason why. "I'm not sure. Part of me refuses to give up, I suppose."

"You have my deepest respect for that and more. You're a brave woman, Tiana Wells." Ian's hand squeezed hers.

"No, I'm not. I've not been active in any edged-weapons training or anything that requires any edged instrument beyond a scalpel since that awful time." Tiana's voice cracked slightly. She hoped he hadn't noticed. "There are moments, when I see certain blades, when I feel like I'm reliving my worst fear. Yet, for the longest time, I loved all kinds of edged weapons -- the feel of them, their honed blades, their balance. It hurts that I'm too scared to pick one up and start training with it again."

He drew her against him and hugged her compassionately. "That takes time to put away. The fact that you've kept up with the latest information, and more, is a credit to you. Most people would've completely changed their goals to avoid their nightmares."

"Thanks. It's nice to hear that I'm strong somewhere in this aftermath." Tiana quietly voiced her fear. "I worry that, one day, they might let him loose, you know."

Ian squeezed her so hard that she gasped for breath. Releasing her, he tilted up her chin. "They'd never let him out after what he did. He's in a high-security facility and slated for death."

Tiana closed her eyes for a short moment, opening them to find Ian's blue ones staring at her. "I want him dead. When I hear people speak on human rights and how even criminals deserve them, I have to bite my tongue not to make comments back to the idiots who would have freed madmen by thinking that they're human."

Ian nodded and said nothing. He agreed with her completely. After all she'd gone through, her voice was the one that should be listened to and heeded, as should all victims that survived inhumanity on any scale. He caressed her cheek and leaned his forehead against hers. This was ballsier than anything he'd done before, but there was something about this woman that called to him. Just this one moment, he would give her comfort and part of himself he rarely showed most people, much less people in his field of expertise. She was so strong, yet so delicate. Something inside him clenched at the idea of her attacker going free, and he vowed to keep track of the case to make sure it would never happen.

"Agreed. Perhaps you should speak out against some of these people who seem to lump-sum all criminals as needing human rights. Not everyone sees that it's those who are repressed who are denied human rights, not criminals."

Tiana smiled at him. "I think you hit the nail on the head, Ian. To me, that's what's happening. People are beginning to confuse the fact that there are innocents whose rights have been ripped from them, and that the call for human rights should be to restore those rights. Yet, time and again, I've seen petitions by these people who claim that these terrorists and killers deserve to have rights." She sat up, her eyes flashing as she thought back to one of those gatherings when she'd wanted to backhand them all and show them the scars made by someone who'd been given his human rights and then killed again. "They forget that when those people make the choice to commit acts of violence upon other humans, they forgo their rights. They've chosen to live outside the law and the decency of humanity. They don't deserve any rights, because often, when given a second chance at having rights, those same killers and terrorists pick up where they've left off. In those cases, I blame those who scream 'human rights' for the deaths of those people, as well as the actual perpetrator of the crime."

Ian was about to concur when a slim young woman with waist-length black hair approached their table. "Evening, Tiana and Ian. You called?"

Tiana slid from the table and hugged Felicia close. "Good to see you, *sorella*, sister. The meal was lovely."

Felicia's smile was bright. "You enjoyed the new *arrabiata*?"

"Definitely," Ian answered. "But we were both wondering about that delicious lime gelato."

Felicia's laughter tinkled like a bright bell. "Let me guess— you both want some."

"Are we that obvious?" Tiana queried. "Sister, it was divine. I snuck a taste of it from Ian's dish."

"Yes, you are. But I figured as much. Just call here anytime, and we'll ice-pack you a pint or two to bring home. If you're very good, I might include a new flavor."

Both sets of eyes landed on the young Italian woman. "New flavor?"

A huge, white grin greeted them both. "Oh, yes. Besides lime, we've got strawberry, lemon, and now triple berry cream." The sounds of happiness coming from her favorite people caused Felicia's grin to become larger. "I think the vote is for the triple berry cream."

"Yes, please," they responded simultaneously.

59

The woman shook her head. "You're both incorrigible. Tiana, call me before you leave in the morning. I'll have yours packed and ready for travel."

"*Grazie*, Felicia. I owe you."

"A date with your Ph.D. candidate, perhaps?" The dark eyebrows wiggled comically. Both women chuckled.

"Perhaps. I think he's just about recovered from your last visit. Let me know when you can come for a long weekend. We'll figure out a way for you to corner the young man."

Ian shook his head and clucked. "I can't believe that you two beautiful women would resort to something this low. Setting up a poor, unsuspecting fellow."

"As if," Tiana growled. "He's been making cow eyes at Felicia for a year now. The only issue is that he has this stupid idea that he's not good enough for her because her family owns this place."

"Ah, that's different." Ian chuckled. "You go get him, *la tigra*."

"Thanks, Ian. You can take yours home with you, if you know which—"

Ian's mobile phone vibrated and chirped. "Excuse me, ladies." He walked off to a private area of the restaurant, as it was almost closing time. Looking at the number, he sighed. "Detective Spencer."

"Ian, it's John. We've got another one."

"What?"

"You heard me, guv. We got ourselves another body. This one is at Durward Street."

"Shit. I'll be there shortly, John. I might bring Dr. Wells with me. She and I just finished supper."

"As you say. Just hurry on down here, mate."

Ian closed his phone and headed toward the women. *How the hell had it happened so damn quickly? People are still about. Damn this killer. Damn him for not giving us some time to figure out who he is and his method.*

Ian looked at Tiana, who gripped the table while speaking with Felicia. Her eyes met his, and he knew she understood that something happened. "Felicia, can I take a rain check on the gelato tonight? I've got to go to work."

Felicia gazed at Ian. "That bad, Ian?"

"Yes. How much do I --"

The young woman waved her hands. "Don't worry on that. You're both my guinea pigs, so the meal is on the house." Hugging Ian, she spoke firmly. "Take care of yourself, Ian. I worry about you, big brother."

He kissed her forehead. "Will do, Licia." Turning to Tiana, his gaze was serious. "You were right. Do you want to come with me, or would you like me to drop you off at your hotel?"

Tiana swore under her breath. "I'll come with you. But I need to grab some things from my room before we go to the crime site."

Felicia hugged them both and let the couple leave the back way. Once out on the street, Tiana turned to Ian. "You think it's him."

"Yes."

"Why?"

Ian stopped and looked into the dark, concerned eyes of the woman beside him. "Honestly?" She nodded. "It's like you said— he means to kill, and his actions are not those of someone who is stable."

"Agreed." They continued walking. Once at her hotel, Tiana raced upstairs to her room, pulled on a pair of boots, changed her shirt, and pulled her hair back into a ponytail. Grabbing her medical bag, Tiana rushed out the door, making it downstairs in less than ten minutes. It was close to midnight. For the first time in a long time, she'd spent over two hours in the company of a man who wasn't a close friend. *Wow. And you've managed to not trip over yourself in the throes of lust. Amazing, Ti, you might yet become comfortable among men on a nonprofessional basis.*

"You're a woman, right?" Ian said with a lighthearted tone. He couldn't believe any woman could get ready in less time than a man. How many times had he heard his dad complain about his mother being unable to get ready in a short amount of time?

"That's what my birth certificate claims," Tiana retorted. "Couldn't believe I could get my stuff that quick? I'm used to moving quickly, and I'm always prepared in case of emergencies."

They got to his silver car and he opened the door for her. She stared, amazed at how clean his car was compared to her slightly messy one. "A bit obsessive with neatness, are you, Ian?"

"Right. I am a bit, actually. But considering that I'm often seen in an official capacity, I try to keep organized."

The ride to the crime scene was fairly short, though they did negotiate a bit of traffic. They both were quiet, trying to focus on what they might see ahead of them. Once they viewed the flashing lights, they pulled over near the scene. Tiana smeared menthol petroleum gel on her inner nostril area so the odors wouldn't make her sick. She offered the menthol rub jar to Ian, who also smeared some on. Tiana pulled out her latex gloves and handed another pair to Ian.

"You do come prepared."

"It's a habit instilled in me from when I spent time in Boston with my father." Tiana flashed him a wan smile as she mentally prepared herself for the crime scene. It'd been a long time since she'd been onsite.

"Okay. I don't quite get it—"

"My parents are divorced. Mom lives near London. Dad lives in Boston. I used to split time with both while growing up. I had to be ready on the fly for anything." Tiana smiled at the memory of times spent with her father. She gazed into the blue eyes of the detective and sobered more. "I'm ready when you are."

"Follow me and stay close." His eyes went to the thing she put around her neck. "You brought your badge with you. Bloody hell, you are really prepared."

Tiana shrugged and shot him a grin. "Would you rather I be inept?"

"Never. Let's go." He opened the car door and stepped out. She followed him from the passenger side. Once the car was locked up, they made their way toward the crime scene.

Tiana took deep breaths and tried to keep herself calm. Normally, she never attended the crime scene when it was fresh. Usually it was afterwards, once the body had been removed. Hell's bells, she normally never asked to be at the site. Her time came when it was time for the postmortem exam or when it was time to reconstruct the face. She only hoped her internal fortitude would be enough to get her through this. She tried to slow down her breathing as they went under the crime scene tape. *In. Out. Slow it down, Ti. You need to concentrate. Look for signs of the assailant. Focus your will to see if you can pick up some residue.*

She touched her chest, feeling the family pendant under her dark T-shirt. The reassuring warmth helped her to re-center herself. She hoped it would somehow be enough. Following Ian's footsteps, Tiana touched his back. Ian turned and brought her forward. "It's not pretty, Tiana. Her throat's cut."

Another knife-based murder. Why, oh why, gods? Why me? Tiana nodded as she stepped up next to Ian. Seeing the scene before her, bile and her stomach contents rose. "Oh, gods, not good." Turning her head away, she tried to control the dry heaving that started. Taking slow, controlled breaths through her mouth, she turned back to the young woman lying on the ground.

Kneeling in her jeans, Tiana looked at Ian. He nodded, knowing what she wanted to do. Somehow, over supper, some kind of mental connection had developed. "Have the pictures of the corpse been taken already?"

"Yes. We've not rolled her over or anything yet, though." This from one of the crime scene technicians that she didn't recognize.

"Thanks." Tiana opened her small bag and pulled out a magnifying glass as well as a lined metal probe. She looked at Ian. "Do we know her name?"

"According to the contents of the purse, her name is Maryanne Howard." The look in his eyes, she knew, was reflected in her own.

Nodding, she turned back toward the body in front of her. "Hi, Maryanne. I'm not sure if your spirit can hear me or not, but know I'm here to help find your killer, not to hurt you." Then she began checking out the wounds on the neck, jaw, and chin, while trying to avoid the pool of blood under the body. When she finished that, she looked at the naked lower half of the woman, blood covering the wounds in her groin area. She'd need space and light to look at those. Further, she'd need to have the body cleaned off.

Tiana stood up, removing her gloves and dropping them into the bag near her. Brushing off the dirt from her jeans, she tried to calm her heart, which was tripping over itself in its rapid beating. Dropping her instruments into a special containment bag, she zipped it up and sighed. Her eyes found Ian's back as she scanned the crime scene area. One crime scene tech touched her shoulder.

"Miss, we need to bag up the body so it can be taken to the coroner."

Stepping back, she nodded. "Do me a favor and place a note that this is to go to Dr. Alexander Campion only. No other. Also note that Dr. Wells was on the scene for the initial look." Seeing the nod, she thanked the man and walked to where Ian stood.

"Ian, do you have a minute?" Her voice was low, fogged with emotions. If she hadn't known better, she'd have thought someone else spoke.

Ian turned to her. "Of course. Excuse me for a moment, fellows. I need to speak to Dr. Wells about the corpse."

He walked her to the outskirts of the site and stood in front of her. "What is it, Tiana?"

She bit her lip, unsure of how to say it. Finally, she decided to blurt it out. "It's him."

"Him? The same guy from the other victim?"

Tiana nodded. "Yes. This time, he had a bit more of a struggle on his hands. There seems to be bruising forming on her jaw. I'm not sure we can get prints from it, but with the new techniques, we can try."

"Will it ruin the evidence that's there?"

"No, it helps to bring out any kind of protein. I learned it at a conference both Al and I attended last year in Boston."

Ian nodded. "Do you need to do it now? Or can it wait?"

"In situ is preferable, but I doubt it'll make a huge difference." Tiana paused. "My mobile is in your car. Can I get it so I can call Al, to warn him what's coming in?"

"Already done. He was glad to hear you were at the initial point to see her. Said something about a prelim report from you." Seeing Tiana's nod, he continued. "Then he said he expected to see you at seven, for the initial autopsy findings."

"Yeah, thought as much." Tiana hugged herself. "Means I need to get to bed. Is there any way of getting a cab from here?"

"I'll take you back. My partner has things under control for right now. Tiana, how long ago do you think she died?"

She thought a bit on the flexibility of the limbs, as well as the warmth in the forearms. "Not that long ago. Her hands were chilly, but there was still warmth in her arms and chest area. Rigor mortis hasn't set in yet. Perhaps anywhere from thirty to ninety minutes, but that's really a guess. I'd need to do more in order to give you a better time."

"That's about what I thought, as well." Ian ran his fingers through his dark hair, mussing it up. "Let's get you back to the hotel. I wish I could say we won't be calling on you again, but you're already here."

Tiana patted his arm. "I know. A good night's sleep and I'll be ready to help out any way I can." Ian opened the car door for her. She sat down, then remembered her bag. "My bag."

"I'll get it." Ian walked back to the site, returning quickly with the small bag in tow. "Here you are."

"Thanks. I like having my own equipment when I'm out in the field, so I don't take away extra resources."

"Can't blame you. Do you want me to pick you up in the morning?"

Tiana shook her head. "No, make sure you get some rest, Ian. You're going to need it more than me, I think."

The ride home was fairly quiet.

* * * * *

The man stood in the background, just part of the crowd. No one he knew seemed to notice him. Hovering on his lips were a rictus grin, radiating death and evil. *Yes, my poppet, you died just like you were supposed to, with a bit of struggle. Nevertheless, that woman needs to be dealt with. I hadn't expected her to still be around. If she interferes, I'll need to remove her, as well.* The thought made him grin further. Sliding back into the shadows and making his way to where his car was parked, he rubbed his hands together. *Perhaps they'll not get it until it's too late. Of course, that's what the guvs did last time. They never seemed to get who I was. I'm still so much better than them. I'm keeping ahead of things nicely.*

"Yes, my pretties, Jack's back, and he's better than ever. No one will ever catch me. Not even that bitch who helped release me."

Watching the car with the woman go past his parking place, the man grinned. Tapping into the mind of his host, the spirit realized just how lucky his choice of avatar was. "Perhaps I'll take you last, Dr. Wells. You can be the culmination of all these deaths. I don't need you figuring out how to stop me and put me back into eternal bondage."

Chapter Five

Tiana tossed and turned all night, her sleep even worse than the night before. Getting up before her alarm clock and the wakeup call, she tried to meditate in order to have at least some kind of relaxation. Lying on her bed, her hands cupped around the pewter pendant, she concentrated on her breathing.

"In... Out... Let my fears leave me. I need them not."

Repeating the words over and over, she felt her body begin unwinding as she slid into a light, meditative trance. Feeling almost disconnected with her body, she let her mind wander to take in all the things she'd dealt with over the past few days. Those thoughts and images were part of the reason she couldn't sleep. Somehow, during the day, she hadn't processed them through. Now she needed them gone in order for her to be able to get through the coming day and to get some deep rest. Thank gods she had learned the meanings of her dreams and how sometimes they were like a junk mail folder that didn't get emptied throughout the day.

Her thoughts flowed over the two young women who'd been killed. Instead of seeing them in a modern context, her brain was putting them in an older frame. Something before her time, perhaps turn of the century. Tiana tried to seize the thoughts surrounding them, but they slid away as the next set of thoughts came to her. *Dammit. I think my subconscious recognizes the murders as something, but why can't I pull it up? Let it go, Ti. It's not time, obviously.*

She continued to let the thoughts flow in and out of her mind as her body relaxed completely. At times, she felt herself float off to sleep then seem to come back to the trancelike awareness with a jolt. Letting herself drift off, she felt a familiar touch. It was her great-great-grandmother, one of the few who came to impart wisdom to her when it was time. It had been a long time since Tiana had felt her touch.

"Grandmother Patricia, how are you?"

"How do most spirits fare? I'm well, my child."

Tiana smiled at the old woman, her hair done up in an old-fashioned 'do. "Why have you come?"

"You're working on a case that crosses boundaries."

Tiana wondered if she looked as confused as she felt. "How so, Grandmother?"

The spirit looked away, then clasped Tiana's hands in hers. "Be careful. Have I ever told you that you're the spitting image of me?"

Tiana smiled again, hugging the spirit close. "Yes, you've often said that. In fact, the pictures I have of you show that the only difference is my hair is a bit shorter and more modern in cut."

"Then listen to me closely. Be very careful on this case. I know you're strong, but I fear that something more has happened. I'm not quite sure, but something has the other spirits buzzing around fearfully."

Tiana smiled softly. "Because you wish it, I'll take extra precautions." She then gripped the old woman's hands tightly. "I never got to thank you for that day --
"

"Shh, child. That was a long time ago, and it was my honor and privilege. You were not meant to die that day. I only helped you focus yourself enough to do what you had to."

Suddenly, a buzzing sound caught Tiana's attention, drawing her away from the trance state. "Grandmother Patricia, I love you. Though we never met, you gave me strength when I had none. Thank you."

Tiana sat up in her bed as her alarm clock buzzed loudly. The phone ringing followed that. Reaching over, she turned off the alarm and picked up the phone. "Hello?"

"This is your wakeup call, Dr. Wells."

"Thank you. Can you extend my stay here?"

"Not a problem, as we're not full, Dr. Wells. Just let us know later on how long you'll be staying."

Tiana smiled. There was a good reason why she kept coming to Brighton Square -- this would be it. The fantastic service, as well as feeling like family, kept her happy. Hanging up the phone, she threw off the covers and headed toward the shower. Stretching her body, she ambled over to the mirror and stuck out her tongue at her reflection.

"You may have your great-great-grandmother's looks, but you look atrocious this morning, dearie," she said to herself. "Go take a shower and try to cover those bags under your eyes."

Obeying her own advice, she jumped in the shower. While washing up, she pondered over the words given to her, as well as hoped that Ian was okay. There was something about him that had made her care about him quickly. As Tiana wasn't used to caring about any male quickly, it was a unique feeling.

* * * * *

Ian leaned his head forward, trying to loosen up the tight muscles in the back of his neck. Not even a hot shower had loosened up the tightness. "John, any new information?" He knew his partner sat behind him at the desk, going over all the notes.

"Nothing of value. You'd think that people went blind and dumb. Then again, it's not a well-frequented place that time of night."

"True. But no one heard anything?"

His partner scrubbed his face and sighed. "Nothing, guv. Any autopsy information?"

Ian looked at the clock and groaned. "Dr. Campion said he'd have his report ready by the time Dr. Wells comes in to do her second study of the corpse." His hand smacked his desk. "I feel for her. She's not used to seeing fresh, unwashed corpses."

John nodded. "She did well. Her professionalism, as well as her keeping to already-made tracks, surprised the others. Not many scientists know to keep to that. I think she made some good friends last night."

Ian smiled. "She's a good woman. As she said, she's half Yank, so we have to forgive her for her not quite British behavior at times."

His partner snorted in response. "Can we keep her?"

He shook his head. "Sheffield University has her. We'd have to woo her with toys and such that she doesn't have. Plus, she's also a forensic anthropology doc, not just forensic."

"Bloody hell. We need her. Go seduce her or something." Everyone nearby started snickering at John's comment.

Ian rolled his eyes and stood up. "How about I go offer to take her out to breakfast once she's done, so she'll give me first dibs on her report?"

John's eyebrow lifted. "What are you waiting for, guv? Go get the report fresh from them! Well? Go on, Ian; the report could help us more in our approach."

Ian chuckled and grabbed his suit coat. Making his way out of the office, he turned back and quipped, "Just don't change or forget the passwords to my computer this time, John. I don't feel like having to deal with our computer techs again." The whole room broke out in laughter as the blonde man blushed. Ian strolled out, feeling quite happy with that parting comment.

He considered taking his car, but the building he was heading toward was only two blocks away. Walking gave him some time to put what he knew of the crime scene in order, as well as trying to figure out a couple things. Yet, as he walked, Ian remembered his dinner with Tiana. He loved how she teased him and talked freely with him on things. Though there were times when she didn't quite speak what she was thinking, she was easy to be around. He truly enjoyed her company, beyond the work aspect. That surprised him. Ian wondered how she'd take to the little quest that he engaged in on his spare time. "Probably not too well, Ian. Don't press your luck."

Then he faced the gray building before him; a quick check of the car park told him Tiana was inside. Hopefully she and Al had some answers for him. She'd probably been there for a while now, as it was almost nine in the morning. Taking the steps two at a time, he went to find out more about the killer. Then perhaps he could convince Tiana to spend some time with him. She'd been on his mind on and off all night.

Time with him? Let's be honest here. I want to throw her down, rip off her clothes, and fuck her brains out. Perhaps slide open those thighs of hers, probing her, tasting her with my tongue while her hips keep encouraging me to touch more. Yeah, that would be nice. So would having her ride me, taking my cock deep inside her until we both come. That would work. His thoughts grew more erotic the closer he got to the building. Readjusting his hard cock, he tried willing away the erection with sedate thoughts of Tiana fully clothed with a metal chastity belt. Even that had him groaning. *Control, Ian. Fucking control your raging hard-on, mate. You're not going to win points by having this kind of reaction in front of her.*

* * * * *

"To reveal any prints, I'd recommend the method perfected by our American colleagues -- heating up superglue and placing it in a Plexiglas container with the body." She paused briefly, ordering her thoughts. "Let's overview the mutilations. Throat has two distinct cuts, one of which goes through the windpipe, esophagus, and spinal cord. The abdomen is opened from the center along the right side near the bottom of the ribs. The stomach coating is sliced in several areas, as is the stomach itself. Her mons has two wounds, as well."

Tiana paused to sip some water. It helped to clear the bile that had risen in her throat. "I concur with Dr. Alexander Campion's findings on the facial examination. I have nothing more to add in that regards, except that the bruising on her lower jaw area seems to be pressure-related. Perhaps it's from the killer holding her still while slicing her throat."

Tiana paused, checked her notes, and shivered. *I swear I've almost read this somewhere. I feel like I'm reliving a nightmare from a book or something.* "The wounds were made by a knife similar to the one used on Martha Cathridge, another victim. Single-edged, with a blunt, flat side, I'd say about eight to ten centimeters in length. With my other findings, I'm noticing the styles of the knife wounds are interesting and similar in nature. I'd recommend having a psychological profile based on the findings. I think it might help in narrowing down the type of suspect. In my estimation, he's going to keep on escalating in his violence. My professional estimation, based on dealing with these kinds of cases, is that we can only hope that he has made some kind of mistake, enough to provide us with some clues to his identity. Dr. Tiana Wells."

She sucked in a deep breath and let it out. There was a scraping noise behind her. Looking around, she saw Ian standing in the doorway, his body resting against the door. "Hi, there. You doing okay, Detective Spencer?" Her voice was low and a bit cracked with trying to regain control. Normally she kept aware of her surroundings and the door, but he was so quiet, he'd caught her off guard.

He walked over and squeezed her arm. "I'm fine. No sleep yet, but I'm doing okay. Just finished your report, I take it?"

Tiana nodded. "I did the outer aspects only, while Dr. Campion did all the other aspects, including stomach contents. We basically wanted to make sure we covered the wounds carefully between the two of us."

"I heard your overview, Tiana. You okay?"

She nodded, saying nothing, though they both knew how hard this was for her. She leaned against his arm, letting him be the strong one for a moment, while she regained her composure. "I'm as good as can be expected. We have to find this killer, and soon, Ian."

"Can I interest you in some greasy, not-quite-as-good-as-supper breakfast?"

Tiana started, then gave him a soft grin that he returned. "Pumping me for information, Detective Ian?"

He chuckled, the tone caressing her skin and her battered soul. "That was the plan. I should've known you'd see through it." He tugged on her hand. "I think you need to get out of here for a while."

"Yeah. Let me change into my normal clothes," she said, glancing down at the scrub clothes she was in. "Then we can go to the nearest place for breakfast. I still need to get back to the uni, the university."

Without waiting for his response, Tiana rose from her chair and made her way to the changing room. As she pulled off the scrubs, pausing only to toss the green clothing into a hamper, she thought on her reaction to Ian Spencer. It had been unexpected. Her heart had sped up when she'd realized he was there, and it hadn't been just from surprise. Then there was the casual conversation and teasing. Normally, she was reserved around police, due to her past experiences. Yet she felt comfortable around him. Then there was that darkness that seemed to be near him. She wasn't sure how it got there, though it was something she could relate to.

Letting down her hair, Tiana slid her feet into the gray suede loafers she'd worn today. Looking in the mirror, she decided she was presentable in a forest-green, long-sleeved tunic and dark gray pants. She wasn't out to impress anyone, but she did feel that as long as she was decent-looking, no one would notice her insecurities.

She heard a knock at the door. "Come in."

Ian entered. "You're ready already?" His smiled caused her to laugh. "Yeah, I forgot you can change clothes quicker than any woman alive."

She took his proffered arm and grabbed her purse off the hook. "Let's go eat. I'm hungry, and I need to get this autopsy out of my system."

Ian led the way, trying to figure out what she meant. He wondered how it could affect her so much when she did autopsies routinely. *Didn't she? Maybe I need to find that out.* As they strolled down the streets, his thumb lightly caressed her hand. They walked another three blocks until she was dragged into a slightly American-looking diner. Ian caught her raised brow, but said nothing until they were inside. Squeezing her hand reassuringly, he watched Tiana take in a deep breath as the scents assailed both their senses.

"This is the station's secret breakfast meeting place." He lifted her hand and kissed the inside of her wrist in a token offering of peace, though his heart began racing at her scent.

Tiana nodded and headed toward an empty booth. "Oh, I can see why. Food from home."

Ian followed her this time, impressed with her dexterity as she slid behind the table into the booth. He sat across from her, grasping her hand again. He didn't want to stop touching her. "You approve?"

"I've got myself a new breakfast place when I come to London," she replied in a happy tone. "You just don't know how much I love this."

"What did you mean by 'food from home'?" They took the menus from the waitress with thanks and continued their conversation. "Do you consider yourself a Brit or a Yank?"

Tiana chuckled as she inwardly shivered at his casual caresses across her hand and wrist. "I have dual citizenship. I used to spend my summers with my father and actually lived with him in Boston for two years while my mother was on one of her travel documentaries. Which means that I enjoy food from both homelands."

"Tell me more about your mother."

"Her last name is different. You'll recognize her, though. Jean Merritt."

Ian's face showed his surprise, his hand squeezing hers then immediately caressing away the flash of pressure. "One of the top historical documentary hosts the BBC has." He motioned for the waitress to serve them coffee. "She's like the biggest name among people who watch anything about history or archaeology. I love her attitude!"

"That would be my mother. My father is a historian at Boston University." Tiana thanked the waitress for the coffee and breathed in the scent deeply. "Where do you get your coffee beans?"

The waitress smiled. "We have them shipped from the States every three months. Sometimes sooner, if needed."

"That explains it. I think I'm in love with this place. Is the owner from the New England region originally?"

Ian watched the exchange, listening as the two ladies quickly exchanged pleasantries. Hannah was a great waitress and always kept her mouth shut when the other members of the Metropolitan came into the diner. Tiana was hot, intense about her work, and somehow turned him on more than he wanted to admit. Yet, they were colleagues. He couldn't just let lust take him over. He doubted she realized that she was tempting him. That's what made it almost unbearable -- she had no clue what she did to his body. There was a peace in touching her so casually like this, though he was ready to do something drastic, like kiss her. Once they were done conversing about the owner, Ian spoke. "Hannah, when you're ready, can I have my usual?"

"Sure thing, Ian. Two eggs over-easy, light toast, fruit cup, and a glass of juice." Hannah turned toward Tiana again. "What about you, Tiana?"

"Hannah, tell the cook I want a New England breakfast and thank you for placing heaven in London." Tiana licked her lips in anticipation.

I'd make you lick your lips if we were alone. In fact, I can almost guarantee it'd be pleasurable for us both. Ian bit back a groan, turning it into a cough, trying to not think of a naked Tiana on her knees before him. Both women rolled their eyes at his coughing fit.

The waitress giggled. "Will do. Good thing his name isn't Joe, huh?" With that, she headed toward the kitchen while Tiana laughed hard, her face lighting up with pleasure.

"Thank you so much for bringing me here, Ian. This is a treat that I've not had in ages." Tiana chuckled. "'Eat at Joe's.' I love it that she knew the old joke!"

Ian reached and squeezed her hand. "Anytime. I'm glad. This must be a taste of home for you and remind you of your father."

"Definitely. Plus, to be honest, American breakfasts are awesome." Tiana sipped her coffee, savoring the hot, strong brew. A lusty sigh emerged from her. "Oh, gods, real coffee. I think I might have to buy stake in this place to make sure I get real coffee beans."

Ian threw his head back and laughed, causing several patrons to turn their heads toward them. Again, he kissed her hand, scooting her closer to his side. "You're hilarious, Tiana. You're the first woman I've known that actually enjoys food and drink with a passion." Carefully, he brushed back a lock of her auburn hair, delighting in the feel of it. Imagining the caress of it against his naked flesh as she leaned over him, sucking on his cock.

"When you've done without and think you're going to die, you learn the art of appreciating the simple things that you take for granted. In addition, like my mother, I do not function well without two cups of good coffee. The sludge that Al claims is coffee is water compared to this."

Within ten minutes, their orders arrived. Tiana's face lit up at the sight of English muffins, two jams, two hardboiled eggs, and a small bowl of cinnamon oatmeal. It helped to distract herself with food so she wouldn't focus on how Ian's touch was making her feel. Feel? *Hell, I want to undo his pants and fuck him. Hades to high water, I've been too long without a man's touch. Maybe Jules was right—perhaps I need to start dating again. I'd love to fuck—I mean date Ian. Damn professional ethics.* "Oh, Hannah, tell the chef,

I love him and will need to negotiate regular meals, since I live a couple hours or so away."

"Will do, Tiana. I've never seen a customer so happy before."

Tiana grinned at the woman. "This is a special treat I've not had in years. My thanks to the cook."

Hannah skipped happily away. Ian turned his gaze to Tiana as she spread grape jam on the muffin, then took a solid bite. The moan of appreciation caused his cock to stand up, and his body tightened with a rush of desire. If she made that kind of sound during sex, she'd make him climax in a heartbeat. She ate her food with relish, pausing only to lick her lips for crumbs. He felt his cock press hard against his slacks. *Bloody hell, this woman has me hard. It isn't fair that she has this effect on me when she seems to be so nonchalant about things.*

He started eating his own breakfast, ignoring the need to adjust himself. Something drove him to respond to her joyous noise of the good food. Perhaps it was that he could feel her warmth beside him, or that he hadn't stopped touching her silky skin. Either way, he had to say something. Otherwise, she'd continue, and he wouldn't be able to control his actions after another orgasmic moan like that. No man on earth would be able to resist trying to make her re-create that moan while he pumped his cock deep into her sexy body. "You know, you could cause a man to try to make you do those noises for him," he said casually as he bit into his eggs.

Tiana looked up, startled. "Huh?" *Did he just say what I think he said? Oh, my gods, I think he did.*

"Those moans of appreciation. They're very sensual; most men would be tempted to be the reason you're moaning, not the food." *I want to make you moan and scream my name. I want to see your body shudder as I stroke you deeply, bringing you to orgasm.*

"Oh." Her eyes sparkled as her skin flushed in embarrassment and excitement. Please make me moan. Make me come. "What about you?"

Ian's grin grew very sensual. "I know I can get you to moan like that. There's no doubt." *Let me suck on your nipples, cause them to tighten. Let me slide my fingers deep in your pussy until they're dripping with your wetness.*

Tiana sat up, her eyes taking him in warily. Her mouth gaped slightly at him. *Is this what I want to hear? Worse, why do I really want to egg him on to see what he does or says? Duh, you're attracted, Ti. Deal with it, as mom says.* "Are you sure about that?" *Please say yes. I need you to want me as much as I want you.*

"Definitely. However, we can't do anything until the case is over or until we no longer need your services. Which is a bloody shame." Ian licked his lips, watching as Tiana took in his every move. *I hate professional ethics. I would rather throw you over my shoulder, take you to my house, and slowly undress you; lick your curves, slide my fingers over your skin, then slowly fuck you until you beg for me to go harder and faster.*

"Oh, my." *Please take me. Fuck me. You can even use the toy my sister sent me, telling me that a battery penis was better than no cock at all. Hell, take me with that and your cock. Please, oh, gods above, please, Ian. But dammit, we're fucked if we get caught. Our jobs could be compromised, but damn, what a compromise.*

She blinked, unsure where to go from there. She hadn't been expecting his response. It made him smile more. They had formed an instant friendship, but he knew she was aware there was something more between them. Something that went beyond just the physical attraction.

"I think I just shook up the unshakeable Dr. Wells." *Good, now you know how you have me feeling, Tiana.* He took her hand in his. "I find you a beautiful, attractive woman, Tiana. I know this is a shock -- it's a bloody shock to me, as well—but I won't push. We have this case to finish first, before we even consider going out on a date socially."

Tiana didn't pull back, but let her body sift through the emotions soaring in her. First was joy. He found her beautiful and wonderful, even though he knew her past. *Simply amazing.* Then there was the fact that he knew the professional boundaries and wasn't asking her to cross them. That eased her mind tremendously. How should she answer his words? Was there an answer?

"Thank you, Ian. I feel ... I feel the same way, but after the case is solved." She knew she was blushing, the breakfast they were sharing becoming an event to remember in her mind. "You're handsome and compassionate. I don't know what to say."

"Then don't. I didn't say it to embarrass you, Tiana. I just wanted you to know how much I enjoy your presence, as well as you, yourself. There were those moans, which could destroy any man's good intentions, though."

She chuckled, as did he. "I'll try to tamp down the moans from now on."

"I don't mind, as long as you don't mind the physical effects."

"Physical effects?"

He debated a moment on whether to tell her. Deciding to take the chance, Ian leaned over the table and whispered. "I've got a hard-on like you wouldn't believe."

"Oh. My. Gods." The blush flushed her skin. She knew it. When she got that badly flustered, she felt the warmth just flood under her pale skin. "I'd be more mortified, but --"

"Don't worry on it, Tiana. It's controllable. But just so you know."

Tiana tried to eat another bite of her muffin, but seeing the grin on Ian's face made it difficult. "You're an evil male."

"I don't know about evil, but definitely male." His hand squeezed hers reassuringly. "How about we switch topics so you can forget this part of our conversation. Though I enjoy making you blush, I don't think you enjoy blushing."

"Something like that."

Ian nodded. "Let's talk about the findings this morning. For some reason, the wounds remind me of something. Maybe a book I read somewhere?"

"You want to know if it's the same guy, as I stated in my report. Yeah, I do think it's him."

"Reasons?"

Tiana fidgeted under his blue stare, now just realizing how potent it was not just professionally, but personally. What was Ian trying to do—make her just as sexually aware? *Ack! It's working. Think. Concentrate, and not on his eyes or sexy grin.* For a moment, the thought of them naked together made her almost choke due to her suddenly dry mouth. "For why I think it's the same guy?"

"Yeah. I mean, I agree with your assessment; it's logical. But what elements stuck out that made you consider this was the same guy, though the wounds weren't as severe."

Tiana shifted back to her professional mode, recalling several items. "Take the wounds and the blood. Remember the blood was under her, not much on her front. He knew what he was doing. This means he's got a basic knowledge of where to kill people, as well as how to position the body so he doesn't get mussed up." She paused, trying to frame her words. "No one saw a bloody man running around?"

"No."

"See, that's the other thing. Even with the first murder, the way the victim was found is in such a way that he's preventing himself from getting splattered. I also think he's usually standing where cutting from left to right is easier for him. The two neck cuts are on the left side." She thought for a moment, trying to recall the marks without recalling the faces, frozen in time, due to horrific death.

Ian nodded, agreeing. "Anything else?"

Tiana bit her lower lip, trying to figure out how to phrase what she wanted to say. Sometimes she received impressions of the last moments of a person's life, but the jumbled thoughts of the victim didn't help her. However, she did remember the ferocity, the type of alien thinking that told her it was a male.

"Definitely a male, by the cuts. Someone with an axe to grind against women. The types of wounds suggest that he doesn't like women in any way, shape, or form." Tiana's voice shook slightly.

"Even though she wasn't stabbed as much as Martha Cathridge?"

"Yes. Look at the type of wounds. The slashed neck, as well as the stabbings near and on her genitals. He's becoming more ... adept at what he's doing. Does that make sense?" She paused. "He knows what he's doing, and his proficiency is growing."

Ian paused and sipped his coffee. "Actually, yes, it does. That doesn't bode well for us, though."

Tiana hesitated for a second, then responded. "Yes and no. I know it doesn't seem like it's a good thing. See, he's getting better at what he wants, yes. But he's also losing control. It's not been long between victims." She thought on it. "These women weren't with friends or anyone else. Thus, he's singling out women who are alone. Can we warn people to not go out at night without someone with them? I know this might make it difficult, since we're trying to downplay things; but the public can help us by following these directions, so we don't give him any more easy targets."

Ian paused and considered her words. "I'm not sure, but I'll ask my superior on it. We don't want to raise panic levels, but you're right; we've got an obligation to keep them safe after dark."

"Thanks. I know it's not always so simple. For some reason, I think that if we can keep him away from a target or two, it might help us in the long run."

Ian nodded and glanced at his watch. "I've got to head back to the station."

"I'm going to have another cup or two of this delicious coffee, then I'll head there, get my car, and do what I need to so I can get home." She reached in her purse and pulled out a card and a pen. Scribbling quickly, she handed the card to Ian. "This is the easiest way to reach me. I've also included my home phone number. Call me whenever you need my assistance."

"I appreciate this, Tiana. Let me get this, and I'll be on my way."

"Nope. My treat. Thank you for being so understanding, Ian."

He leaned over and kissed her cheek. "Thank you for being so open to working with us. I know this has been hard for you, but what clues we have are from you. We're still waiting for any trace evidence, and that's going to take a while."

"Thanks. You go do what you need to. I'm going to relax and enjoy this place a bit longer."

Tiana watched him leave and fingered her pendant. She hadn't told him everything, but she'd been able to give him something to work with. If only she could've seen the man's face. He'd come out of nowhere when he attacked the young woman. Tiana shook her head to separate the victim's final feelings from herself. Rubbing her forehead, she debated on seeing her famous mother. Would it be worth it to go harass her, or should she wait until the weekend, when she was supposed to make her monthly visit? Hmm, the choices were endless. Deciding she needed to get back to her real job, Tiana sipped on another cup of coffee while talking to Hannah and the owner/cook, Keith. After chatting with them, she promised to bring Keith her recipe for a New England boiled dinner, as well as the family New England chowder recipe.

She left a big tip for Hannah as she left. She walked back slowly; taking in the sights and sounds of this part of London was new for her. Making sure she had her purse secure on her shoulder, she enjoyed listening to the birds chirp their melodies. Part of her didn't want to leave London, especially after Ian's candid words. The other part of her wanted to run quickly and not come back for a while.

Tiana climbed into her car once she reached the car park. Though she wanted to stay, duty called. She only hoped her compatriots at the lab hadn't caused any major troubles. Okay, she hoped Kyle hadn't caused any issues she'd have to smooth over with Damian's help.

Chapter Six

Her return to the university was quiet. Damian helped get her back into the swing of a few cases they were asked to work on, including one dealing with a couple of bog people. When she asked him if they included clay models as well as the computer-generated models, he nodded, causing her to smile.

"It's not that I don't like the computer generated models --"

"It's just that the texture isn't smooth enough for you yet," Damian replied.

Tiana nodded. "Exactly." She paused, watching Kyle and Lawrence work on one skull set, plotting all the detailed points that would help shape the skull and more. "How has Kyle been doing?"

Damian lifted a brow. "You mean has he been a pain? He still thinks that a composite of many faces and skin types would help our program more, but he's not been pressing on it."

Tiana nodded as they headed into Damian's office. Once she was seated in the chair opposite his, she responded. "Good. I think honestly, that can skew the data. I know that others have used it with great results, but we're in an age where there are many mixed cultures. We can't know for certain whether anyone is just one culture or another. To do that, it could make it tougher. I liked his idea of having various features in the database, to use the minimum and maximum for the fleshy, soft tissue areas. That would give us tons more flexibility, but that's the extent. What do you think?"

"I think you're doing this to avoid speaking about what you were called to London for."

Tiana glanced at her watch. It was four in the afternoon. Closing time for the group. "I just don't want to talk much about things yet. However, I found the most awesome diner in London that serves traditional American breakfasts. Hannah was charming."

"Hannah?" The voice came from behind her. Swiveling around, Tiana saw Kyle leaning against the doorjamb.

"My waitress. She's a great girl. Putting herself through university by waiting tables. Place is called Slice of Americana. It's near London center. Wonderful food. The owner and I are exchanging recipes for some coffee beans."

"Coffee beans?" Kyle asked in disbelief. Damian chuckled.

"You know Tiana and her American coffee."

"Don't knock it until you try it. I can't get all the various flavors here that are found in the States." Tiana smiled. "He's going to get me amaretto mocha."

Damian and Kyle perked up. After Tiana's last trip to the States, they had both been recipients of that coffee and were disturbed to find out that it wasn't anywhere in Britain. "You mean you're going to share?"

"Only if you don't making fun of my coffee habit, Kyle."

"Deal."

"Where is this nirvana of yours again, Ti?" Damian asked. "I might want to drop in there in a few weeks when I get to London for that conference."

"It's two blocks south of the Metropolitan Police department. Everyone in that area knows about it. They keep it secret so they can enjoy some heavenly food and not have it overrun by tourists and such."

Both men chuckled. Kyle chimed in, "Is this your way of saying not to blab it around?"

"Damn straight. You both keep your mouth tight on this, and I just might let you in on the food that will be coming for our next departmental meeting."

Both men looked at Tiana in surprise. She hated the early morning meetings, complaining that they never had good food to help them wake up and start the day right. Normally, she dragged herself in and said very little.

"Professor Bathe made you in charge of the refreshments this time, huh?" Damian quipped.

Tiana nodded, a gleam in her eyes. "Yes, he did. He's so going to regret it. After the breakfast that'll be served with me in charge, he'll be forced to provide good food and drinks for that gods-awful early meeting."

They all laughed over the common complaint among most of the staff in the forensic science department. Their monthly meetings were held around six in the morning in order to accommodate the early classes. However, none of the teaching professors liked getting up that early. Only the lead professor, Aloysius Bathe, enjoyed it. Since Tiana got conned into doing the breakfast for the next meeting in three weeks, she had been searching for the perfect catering service. Having found out that Slice of Americana did do occasional catering, she was going to dip into her trust fund and pay out the money to do this right. The money allotted for the food expenditure could easily handle it, but she wanted this to be all hers. On occasion, Tiana could be a brat. This was one of them.

"Any news from the London Metro about the murder?" Kyle asked casually.

Tiana stiffened and motioned Kyle to sit down near her. She waited until he did as she asked. Both men looked at her askance. "There's been a second murder. Happened last night."

"Shit."

"Yeah, Damian, I know. I went to the crime scene last night. I wasn't happy. But it's the same guy."

Kyle asked, "Are you sure? Could it have been a different guy?"

Tiana shook her head negatively. "Same guy. Better in his execution, but still, there's the way he handles the knife that gives him away."

"You okay, Ti?" Damian asked in concern. She could see his caring reflected in his face. She gave him a reassuring smile, though she wasn't quite sure she was doing okay on it all.

"Yeah, I'm fine. Detective Spencer has been very solicitous of my past and hasn't tried forcing me to go beyond what I can handle. Plus, my old mentor, Dr. Campion, is there. We did confirming autopsies. I saw the victim on the scene. Trust me, it's the same guy."

"Bloody hell, that's not good, Tiana. What are the police going to do?" Kyle asked. "Do you think they'll give the public a warning?"

Tiana shrugged. "I'm not sure. Ian was going to speak to his superior on it. I'm hoping they will warn the public to be careful. Do I think it's going to happen? No idea."

The three colleagues sat back, each in their own thoughts for a couple of minutes. Damian was the first to break the silence. "You want to see what's done on the bog people skulls we've been asked to do?"

Tiana grinned. "That'd be great. What do I need to do?"

Kyle laughed. "You get to plot them all out."

Tiana leaned over and smacked his arm. "That's your job. You know I get confused without your assistance," she joked. These guys had been friends with her for the past couple of years and were the brothers she never had.

"That's what you keep claiming. Yet you always manage to get them perfect."

"Only because you're there, Kyle."

Damian chuckled. "Actually, Lawrence plotted two of them. We finished up the woman victim while you were gone. The police will distribute pictures with the front and profile views we came up with. Hopefully, they'll find out who she was."

"Excellent. How many are left to plot?"

"Just one. Wait 'til you see the x-rays and such we've got to help us."

Tiana raised a brow. "Why do I feel I'm being set up?"

Damian shrugged as he rose from his chair. The other two followed suit, going down the hallway, back toward the scanning room. They used lasers to help map all the features, including bumps, indentations, and muscle insertion points on a skull. It was something Tiana was proud to be part of. Though she was trained in various techniques, there was something inspiring in being part of a group that could get results much quicker than working with clay.

Following her coworkers, Tiana was glad to be back. She felt the lead weight that sat between her shoulders ease up. Though she was a certified coroner, she preferred using her forensic anthropology skills to her medical training. Her mother had less trouble than her father with her job choice. That could account for her not seeing Father for the last three years. It wasn't easy knowing that only one parent understood and encouraged you in your career choice.

"So tell me, how did we get involved with the peat bog people? Do we know anything, or are we going into this completely blind?" Tiana knew that the only way to get a true representation was to know nothing about the person or expectations of others. This way, doing it blind, prevented accusations of skewing the results.

"All we know is the sex of each skull image we were sent. The only other information was the location of the skulls, which were found near where the Lindow man was discovered. Otherwise, we're on our own."

Tiana rubbed her hands together. "Oh, this is brilliant. I can't wait to help work on it. Are we using the new algorithms to help with skin textures and tones?"

Kyle nodded. "Definitely. You have one, I have another, and Damian has the third. Yours is a female. If we need to see the actual bog person, we've got pictures in a sealed envelope."

"Nope, don't want any pictures to make me confuse things or begin wandering off into archaeology when I should be focusing on bringing her to life. This is fantastic. Did they come to us?"

Damian scooted over to the computer as Tiana pulled up the information regarding the bog people. "Yes. They heard of us through various sources and decided we were quite advanced considering that we're not Yanks."

"Ooh, a challenge." Tiana grinned wickedly. "I love a challenge."

"Only you would consider it one," Kyle teased. "I think this would rank right up there with solving Jack the Ripper, eh, Tiana?"

Tiana stuck her tongue out at Kyle. "Not the same. This is professional. The other is more personal. Plus, I don't think we'll truly ever know who he was. The only thing we can do is narrow down the current suspect list to a minimum and remember that it's possible Jack's not on the list at all."

Damian raised a hand. "Let's not get into the Jack-versus-today's-science debate again, you two. Let's talk about the bog."

The next couple of hours were spent tracking the points and measurements of the skulls. Since the people had been tossed into a bog, the minerals had leached from their bodies, thus causing the bones to deteriorate and become spongy, the forms to misshape. The trick was to figure out the original skull configuration before beginning the reconstruction. Those who wanted the reconstruction provided x-rays, measurements, and possible configurations, or had given them all the detailed information that they'd need to plot the points on the computer. It wasn't a bad job, all in all, sometimes monotonous when punching in numbers, but when the skulls started coming to life, it was invigorating.

At the end of the second hour, Tiana stretched, happily having plotted most of the points on the skull of the woman. Leaning back, she took in her surroundings again, feeling the sensation of home. The walls were covered in various anatomy and forensic reminders, as well as two large windows that let in sunlight during the day. The computers sat in a line along a series of computer desks that also had room for papers and working scale models. The wheeled chairs meant that often times they'd be wheeling back and forth between the computers that did the laser measuring and the computers used to create the graphic model.

She felt in control here, Tiana realized. In a way, this room, along with the others, helped isolate her from the actual violence. For her, this was how she coped with her own personal tragedy. Though she probably should get out more, beyond the consulting cases she did, she was happier when she was ensconced in a case, working on the computers, or even doing it by hand with clay. For her, it was a way to help those who weren't able to do what she did. This was her way of bringing justice to those silenced before their time.

By mutual consent, they all shut down the computers. "This was a great work session. It's been a while since all three of us have worked on a project together," Tiana commented.

"Yeah. This is nice. Especially since you get consulted a lot."

"Hey, I'm not the only one, Kyle."

"We all get asked to do consultations for various organizations. Then there are the conferences and workshops. I've got the latest forensic journal. Our article is in there."

"Bloody hell, you've kept it a secret this long, Damian?"

Damian smirked at both colleagues. Tiana could tell he was damn proud of his not saying anything until this moment. They had known the article was due out soon, but time had flown and only Damian had kept track of its imminent arrival. He retrieved the magazine and opened it up to the page in question. The three colleagues stood there, smiling at each other. Their first joint article, dealing with the complexities of forensic reconstruction using computer graphics and how to resolve certain issues, was out.

"Drinks are on me," Tiana said, her voice full of happiness. "This is just simply wonderful."

"Let's go before Ti changes her mind," Kyle joked. Tiana responded by smacking his arm again. Kyle leaned in and tickled her. She playfully smacked at his hands. Damian stood there for a moment before swinging Tiana in a hug.

"Can you believe it?"

"To the pub! I'm in need of a Guinness."

The group went to the pub to celebrate their first article. They ordered food and drink, each one taking turns reading the article.

* * * * *

Tiana felt a bit tipsy, but was able to make it home okay. Smiling, she finally felt she was justified in her own chosen field. The trip to Snaith had been short, but she enjoyed going back to her small cottage home. It had been a gift from her mother and father when she graduated. Though they had offered her a London townhouse, she wanted to be further from that city, but close enough for day trips. This was perfect for her. Snaith was almost a village, according to her father's standards, but for Tiana, it was perfect.

Parking her car, she locked it up, then unlocked her home. Once inside, she flipped on the light switch, shining light around the brightly decorated living room. The jewel-tone colors seemed even brighter and more welcoming. Looking at her phone as she tossed her suitcase to the side, she noticed there were a few messages. Some from her school chums, two from her mother, and one from her father. Then there was one from Kyrie.

She played that one first, concerned by the tone in her friend's voice. Something was going on, but she wasn't talking about it. Kyrie asked her to call at the first opportunity possible. Rubbing the bridge of her nose, Tiana knew Kyrie wouldn't phone for advice unless it was important. Doing a mental time-zone hour-change, she figured her friend would still be in the office.

Dialing the number, Tiana waited for the connection to go through. She listened to the ringing for a couple of minutes. Finally hearing her friend's voice, Tiana could sense the tension.

"Kyrie, this is Tiana. What's going on?"

"Where do you want me to start?"

"I'd say at the beginning, but due to the influence of alcohol, I'd say, how about a summary?"

Tiana listened as Kyrie told her. Overall, it seemed like everything else was going okay, but after the unbinding, it seemed it was "pick on Kyrie for everything" week. Instead of being protected, she was now finding that because she was no longer bound to a certain set of expectations, people were no longer bound to behave nicely to her in certain circumstances, either. Tiana had warned her that the unbinding could cause more complications than Kyrie realized. "So why are you staying there?"

"It's my job."

Tiana growled. She admired her friend's fortitude and determination in being a female in the largely male profession of aeronautic engineering. However, she had a problem with the risks her friend took on occasion. "Yeah, I know. What can I do for you, Kyrie?"

"Can you come for a consultation?"

"You're joking." The heavy sigh on the other end caught Tiana off guard. "Talk to me, my best friend."

Tiana could tell that Kyrie was rubbing her finger over the bridge of her nose and onto the third-eye area of her forehead. When exasperated and upset, Kyrie always did that. She used to claim it helped her to re-center and think things through better.

Listening, Tiana realized her friend was concerned beyond the norm. Kyrie was sensitive to various patterns in the world, as well as having a slight bit of precognitive ability. Sometimes it flared up and played havoc with what was and what might be.

"Tiana, I've got a bad feeling."

"About the spell, right?"

"You got it. Did you feel something afterwards?"

Tiana closed her eyes and focused on what had happened. "Yeah. There was something during, too. I figure it was the release of the binding around you, nothing more or less."

"Ti, do you think we did wrong in breaking the binding?"

"No, but there are consequences to every action, including dealing with the redressing of things. Where you once might've been protected from things, you're now feeling it full blast. But you knew that going into doing the spell." She knew Kyrie wouldn't like hearing that, but it was the truth, something they always maintained between them.

"Damn you, Tiana."

They both sat silent on the phone for a couple of minutes. "Listen to me, Kyrie. This is a transition phase and unlikely to last long. Just get through this, and make notes on who seems to have a big grudge against you, and be prepared. Find out who's pandering to you. Also, ask your grandparents which one might do a spell to protect you. You have your own inborn abilities that you can rely on to help you realize what's going on. Rely on them."

"Yeah." There was a pause and a sigh. "Maybe you're right."

Tiana blinked. Did her best friend just say --

"What did you just say?"

"Don't think I'm caving in on this, though."

They both laughed. "Never. I know this is tough for you, Kyrie. Personally, I'm involved with a case that reminds me of something, but I can't think on what it is. It's enough to drive me batty."

"What do you mean, Ti? What's going on?"

Tiana explained about the case without giving away a lot of details. She explained how the wound patterns reminded her of something, but that when she meditated to try to get things in order, she lost the strand that could show her what it was reminiscent of. "So you see, it's one of those things. I wonder if my hunches are right, even though I don't want them to be, and that's why I can't put it together."

Kyrie's voice was strong. "That could be, Tiana. To be honest, often times, I think you block out some things in order to cope, ever since you were attacked. Do these cases remind you of yours or one you helped with in the past?"

Tiana paused and digested her friend's words. Kyrie and Jules were good friends, and they had all

109

gone into jobs where science provided their income, even when magick also played a huge part of their lives. Yet, Kyrie was right. On some level, she was relating it to her own personal experience. That needed to stop. Kyrie sometimes knew her better than she knew herself.

"You know, I'm not sure, Kyrie. The concentration on the genital area does remind me of him a bit, but I know he's in prison. I was assured he's there and isn't getting out any time soon."

"How about an old case of yours? Or one of those cold cases you get once in a while?"

Tiana considered it. "Maybe that's it. I figure it's something I've seen in passing or studied."

Kyrie laughed. "At least it's not anything to do with your slight obsession."

"Bite me, Kyrie."

"Nah, that's what males are for." There was another pause. "Thanks for calling me back, Ti. I needed your steadiness and your honesty. Though I don't like some of what you said, I think it's because you're right, in a way."

"You know I'm on your side. I just think when you accept the part of you that you try to hide, you'll be the super woman I know you are. Have you heard from Jules yet?"

"No, but you know how she is."

Tiana chuckled. "Definitely. Well, I'll let you get back to work. I'm heading for bed in a couple."

They reminded each other to phone again in a couple of weeks, as was their routine. Tiana told her about the article and Kyrie whooped for her friend. After their goodbyes, Tiana hung up the phone. She debated on calling her parents. Deciding to leave it until tomorrow, she chose to indulge in a hot bubble bath.

Peeling off her clothes, Tiana ran the hot tap water into the old-fashioned tub. It was the one extravagance that her mother highly approved of. The tub was a replicated claw-foot tub, with room for two, and had an angle so people could recline back and soak while reading a book. Feeling a bit naughty and indulgent, Tiana poured in the bath salts her mother had sent her for her last birthday.

Grabbing her PDA from her briefcase, Tiana ran back to the bathroom, liking how the steam rose from the water. Sliding into the purple depths, Tiana let out a sigh as the hot water enveloped her with the scent of lavender. Her mother had definitely outdone herself in making this batch of salts to ease pain and stress. She doubted any of her mother's colleagues realized that besides Jean being a historian and great documentary host, her mum was also a practicing witch. Though she wasn't Wiccan, she was a traditionalist in the ancient wise-woman traditions of ancient Britain. Tiana smiled as she thought on her mom. She loved the woman, even if their religious practices were slightly different. Feeling the tension leaving her body, Tiana sighed happily.

Pulling up the latest books by Shelly Laurensten and Esther Mitchell, Tiana had a tough moment deciding which book to start. She decided it was time for the sexy shape-shifters that Shelly was known for. She'd save Esther's book for sneak peeks while at work. Immersing herself in the world of shape-shifting dragons, Tiana allowed the salts to do their job.

After reading one hot, sensual scene in particular, Tiana put the PDA on the counter near the tub. Oh, my gods, that was almost too hot to handle. She imagined that scene happening between her and Ian, her hands sliding up to clasp the undersides of her breasts. Closing her eyes, she imagined him stroking her body, giving in to the attraction between them.

She caressed her nipples as she gave in to the moment of imagination. As they pebbled tightly, she pulled and tugged, gasping in pleasure, imagining Ian's mouth suckling tightly around one nipple. Though Tiana rarely pleasured herself, there were things that would trigger a release when nothing else would do. After spending time in Ian's company, she needed some kind of release. That man created too many emotions within her. Her body always felt tight and aroused near him. Reaching over to a drawer, she pulled out the small, waterproof vibrator that Kit had bought her a year back. She never thought she'd break down like this, but after the time with Ian, she— no, craved—release.

Running her fingers down her softly rounded belly, she ignored the scars that ran across the area, dipping her fingers in her auburn curls. Feeling the nub strain toward her fingers, Tiana caressed in the way that pleased her most, causing her body to shiver. Then she slowly rubbed the vibrator over her clit, pressing the button, starting the vibrations. She gasped as her clit quivered, her hips arching for more. Giving in to the need, she imagined Ian touching her as she pleasured herself.

Ian's hands slid under her slick wet skin as his cock butted against her entrance. "Let me in, Ti. I want you."

Allowing him access to her hot, wet pussy, she moaned as his long, thick cock slid in hard. When he was buried deep within her, she moaned, loving the feel of his hands over her breasts as he began rocking slowly, pulling out of her only to thrust deeper into her sheath. He lifted one of her legs onto his shoulder, while the other limb hung over the side of the tub. "Oh, baby, you're so open like this."

"Ian, please. I'm going to come!"

"Not yet. I'm not done with you quite yet. Don't you dare come 'til I say so." His voice was harsh and clipped with passion as his fingers parted her ass cheeks. One finger caressed the rosette of her ass, and he moaned against her breast. *"Does this feel good, Tiana?"* His finger entered her anus slowly as his cock thrust deep and hard in her pussy.

Her inner muscles clenched, trying to keep him deep inside as the sensations overloaded her. *"Ian, I can't --"*

"Come for me, Tiana. I want to hear you moan like you did in the diner!" He thrust hard and deep, continuing the penetration both of her pussy and her asshole, deep and undulating in time.

Tiana screamed her climax as her body shuddered at the daydream. Slowly, she came back to her senses, as her heart started to slow down, her panting slowing down as well. Sliding under the water, Tiana allowed the lingering warmth of the water to caress her face and hair before she pushed up, sucking in the air. "Ooh, that feels much better. Granted, I hadn't thought I'd --" she whispered to herself, then heard the ringing of the phone.

Grabbing a towel, she wrapped it around herself and padded into her bedroom, grabbing the receiver. "Hello?"

There was no sound on the other end of the line.

"Hello? Anyone there?"

Nothing. She hung up the phone and wrinkled her nose at the weird phone call. They weren't that common, though at times she did get them. Nothing to complain about. Some people were shy, she supposed.

Tiana went into the bathroom to finish washing up, taking the time to give herself a facial, something her mother brained into her through the years. It was her way of relaxing and treating herself to something special, even when she felt the most stressed.

The phone rang again as she entered her bedroom. "Hello?"

"Tiana? This is Ian."

"Evening, Ian. Everything okay?"

"So far, it's been quiet. Things okay with you?" Hearing his voice made her smile. In a way, she'd missed him, though she was happy to be back where she belonged. She could get used to his voice easily ... perhaps too easily.

"Definitely. The article that my colleagues and I wrote is out. I've got an interesting reconstruction on the table, and I just took a soothing, hot bath. Granted, I'm still a bit damp, but overall, I can't complain on how the rest of my day went."

Ian groaned. "Tiana, that brings some very naughty thoughts into a man's brain when you speak like that. I wish I had been there for the bath."

Tiana whispered under her breath, "Oh, you were," then said normally, "Well, perhaps once this case of ours is done."

"That reminds me on why I'm calling you. I wanted you to know that my superiors and those who deal with press relations are debating on telling women to be careful. As you know, it's the risk of public uproar versus protecting them."

She sighed, knowing he was right, but also feeling that warning people was the right thing to do. "Can't they just say, with these two unsolved cases, we'd just like to remind people to be careful and be more aware of their surroundings?"

"I'll try to see if they'll use something like that. No guarantees. I just wanted to let you know." He hesitated a minute. "I missed not having you here to talk to tonight. Nothing new on the information front, but it'd have been nice to have someone to share my gelato with."

Tiana smiled. "You brat. You know I forgot to pick mine up."

Ian chuckled. "Yes, I do. Felicia told me. Said if I spoke to you before she did, to let you know that she was going to overnight you some and to expect her about two weeks from Friday."

"Great. I'll let Lawrence know. He'll be in a panic and excited to know she's coming." Her amusement was evident in her voice and she knew it. "I know it's mean of me to be so damn happy over his misery, but honestly, he's deluding only himself. She wants him. I'm thinking she might not give him a choice in the matter."

Ian laughed. "Sounds like her brother. He was the same way once he made up his mind."

"I think they get it from their mother," Tiana chimed in. "Isabella doesn't wander around the mark."

"No, she doesn't. Well, it's late. I best let you get some rest. We'll talk again soon, Tiana. Something besides work next time, I promise. Sleep well."

"Dream sweet, Ian. Keep me updated on things. If you need me, you know how to reach me."

Tiana hung up the receiver and grinned. Climbing into bed, Tiana snuggled under her favorite lightweight summer quilt, happy to be home.

* * * * *

He watched her move from the bathroom to the bedroom, only able to see her shadow as she moved through her home. The more he thought about her, the more he realized that Tiana Wells couldn't live if she ever caught onto his plan. There had been a moment when he thought she'd picked up on his slight change of tone. She was smart, and part of the reason he'd been released. He had to control the blood lust burning in him right now. It wasn't yet time to deal with her. *Soon though. Soon.*

First things first. Let the fervor die down a bit in London, then go back and visit a place in particular and make his mark, letting Tiana know that she was a threat and that he knew her every move.

Sliding back into the darkness, the man walked away from the cottage. Once in his car, he headed for home. In time, nothing would stop him and his reign of terror. Not even the unusual Dr. Wells.

Chapter Seven

The next three weeks went fairly quickly for Tiana as she worked on the clay models of the bog people. The computer reconstructions were finished. The clay models would allow the company to have physical components to go with them. Ian called her every couple of days, but while some trace evidence was found on the victims, they had no way of knowing if it had been picked up on the street or from the killer. Tiana felt as frustrated as Ian did. They'd met up a couple times in London when she staffed her consulting office for dinner, developing a solid friendship. Nevertheless, it was too damn early on Friday morning, and Tiana had to get to the staff room to let Slice of Americana set up the breakfast.

Tiana stepped out from the shower and smiled at her reflection in the mirror. She noticed that lately she was feeling more relaxed and a bit more confident. Even when facing her mother's wrath for refusing the monthly Sunday brunch last week, Tiana felt her own private strength again. Drying off, she took a realistic look at her body. Though rounded and considered a bit overweight by some, she felt healthy and strong, especially since she kept up her workouts in weight-training and kickboxing. Tiana didn't mind much about her looks except the scars.

After dressing in a forest-green silk shirt with nubby black silk pants and jacket, Tiana felt almost ready to face the forensic department head. Putting together the finishing touches, she smiled at her reflection in the full-length mirror that stood opposite her dresser. The last thing she needed was her favorite lipstick, but she'd put that on when she was there. Grabbing her briefcase, keys, and purse, Tiana left the house.

"Too bloody early in the morning for my ass to be up and going to work. If Bathe doesn't like the meal today, I wonder how hard it'd be to put him six feet under?" Tiana wondered as she got in her Aston Martin.

The drive from Snaith to Sheffield University was only about twenty minutes on a bad day, but since it was way too early for anyone sane to be up, Tiana made it to the sprawling university more quickly than she'd expected. When she pulled into the parking lot near the administration building where the monthly meeting would be held, she saw the catering van.

Grinning, Tiana knew she could get her coffee fix instantly, once she went inside. Walking quickly, Tiana got to the door and saw Hannah's long blonde hair.

"Hannah, if you love me, you'll tell me that you've got coffee brewing," Tiana called out with a slight whine as she entered the room.

The young woman chuckled. "Yes, Tiana. I've got coffee, including amaretto mocha, as you've requested." The waitress handed Tiana a mug with Slice's logo on it. "Go get yourself a cup of the good stuff. We've got regular, decaf, and the mocha."

"*Bendithion*, blessings, Hannah. I think I might need to marry your boss." Tiana poured herself a cup of coffee, added a dollop of cream, then sipped the ambrosia with a sigh.

"You say the sweetest things, Tiana," Keith said as he hauled in the omelet-maker and set it up on the side table. "Thanks for the recipes. The consensus is that they like your New England clam chowder recipe rather than mine."

Tiana chuckled. "That'd be because mine is authentic. I'm glad it's going over well." She offered to help them set up, but they refused, saying she'd interfere with their routine.

As she watched them do the finishing touches and start making omelets, Tiana placed her order.

"Make it good, Keith. Just no mushrooms." She made a face. "I don't do fungi."

"But if you hum a few bars, she might sing it," said a voice from the doorway as Damian stumbled into the room. "Coffee. I need coffee before I expire from caffeine withdrawal."

"Lazy sot. The coffee is next to the beautiful Hannah. Hannah, Keith, this is my coworker, Dr. Damian Collins. Damian, this is Slice of Americana's owner, Keith Tucker, and his wonderful assistant, Hannah Chapman."

Damian gratefully took the mug from Hannah. "It's amaretto mocha, Dr. Collins." Tiana watched as Damian sipped it, giving a growl of happiness before dropping to his knees in front of the young woman.

"By the gods, this is ambrosia and you're Aphrodite. Marry me and keep me in this, and I promise that everything I have is yours. And call me Damian." Everyone laughed as Damian got up with Hannah chuckling.

"Had I known how popular the coffee was going to be, I would have brought the one-kilo bags for purchase," Keith quipped.

Tiana waved her hands negatively. "Ixnay on the offeecay."

"You sell this?" Damian said appreciatively. "Do you ship? If so, I'll give you the money and my address now."

"Deal, Damian. I've got some sheets in case anyone is interested in any of our shop-from-home products. So take one, fill it out, and give it to Hannah or me. We'll ship it out today or tomorrow for you."

Damian grinned at Tiana. "You know, I think this will be the best meeting ever. Food that tastes wonderful, coffee made for the gods, and coffee being shipped to my house. I don't see how it can get better."

Kyle Mortimer entered the room. "It just got better. Bathe is late and I'm here before him."

The other professors chuckled at Kyle's words as he grabbed food and some amaretto mocha coffee. "Oh, it's the ambrosia brew team. Coffee shipped to me, too. I think finally we might be able to break Tiana's grip over our department with her miserly sharing of the good stuff."

Tiana rolled her eyes from her seat. "If you'd give me some money, I'd share more of my stash; but 'til then, nope."

"Hey, I cough up money on occasion," Damian protested while sipping on his second cup. "Well, when you prod me about it."

At that moment, the head of their department, Professor Aloysius Bathe, entered. Once he'd gotten some food and drink, he sat at the head of the table. Tiana silently thanked the coffee gods for the burst of caffeine in her system to get her through the morning, as the head went into drone mode. Damian elbowed her on occasion to make sure she stayed awake.

When they got to other things, each professor took a turn discussing some concerns as well as accomplishments within the new curriculum changes. Damian and Kyle also presented the article to the group, surprising many who hadn't realized the group had prepared the article. "Well, what do you know, you three finally decided to be part of the publishing members of the university."

Tiana lifted her brow. "Actually, Aloysius, that's not quite true. We already were part of the publishing aspect, such as my manual regarding edged weapons and wounds, or even Damian's technical book on the adaptation of various computer graphic interface programs for forensic reconstructions. It's just that you're not used to those being considered as important as other features. But that's okay, you know. We're not up to your standard; it's something to gear for in time."

She knew only Kyle, Damian, and a couple of others caught the subtle snub she gave the head professor. Though not a radical, Tiana didn't care much for the whole "publish or perish" way of scholarly tenures and such. It was something she fought against on a local, national, and international level. She was for scientific literacy for the community, often holding programs for the public to learn the latest developments and what it meant on a personal level for people.

"Well, yes, you're right, Dr. Wells. It's something to aspire to. In fact, my next book will be out in two years, dealing with the history of forensic science and its use in the legal system."

Everyone politely applauded while Tiana glanced at Hannah, sharing an eye-roll with her. They both stifled giggles. At the end of the meeting, everyone complimented Tiana on her catering choice. When Professor Bathe asked for the bill, Tiana took great satisfaction. "Aloysius, I've taken care of the bill personally. But here is the price breakdown for everything that was here today."

The older man was surprised, but she could tell he was happy. Not only had he had third helpings, but she'd noticed he'd squirreled away some for later. "That was generous of you, Dr. Wells."

"It's the least I could do since I wanted to try this new caterer. I think they were a hit; what do you think?" Tiana grinned, knowing she had him right where she wanted.

"The others seemed to appreciate their fare."

"So did you. I noticed you had a particular fascination for the apple strudel, which I agree was perfectly divine."

"Ah, yes. Do you think perhaps that they might consider doing this monthly for us, dear?"

Tiana turned on her brightest smile for the older man. "Why, Aloysius, what a wonderful idea! You do know that the leftovers they've put on the side table were included in the price. Isn't that nice? We get leftovers to pick through for the rest of the day."

She watched the man go from a bland expression to a happy grin. "Now that is jolly good of them, Tiana. Which of them is in charge of the business portion?"

Tiana took care of the introductions, watching the professors start to leave without their mugs. "Hey, everyone, those mugs were a gift from Slice of Americana, to thank you for having them here today. So take those mugs with you." She watched as everyone grabbed his or her mug again, with "thank you" and "bloody good" tossed in the mix. Winking at Hannah and Keith, she left them to handle the new client business, while she scampered off with some more strudel and another refill of coffee.

Catching up to Damian, Tiana grinned. "So?"

Damian's return grin was as huge as hers. "So what?"

"You know. What did you think of the food?"

"You mean, what do I think of the ambrosia, known as coffee, served by those people?" Damian held up two bags of coffee beans. "I got a gift from Keith. Coffee for our department area."

They both laughed as they talked about the day's work as well as Aloysius Bathe's reaction to the food and drinks. "I think you made a sale for Slice, Ti."

"I hope so. They've been working really hard on the diner and their catering. As Keith told me, there are many Americans who live in Britain and want an occasional treat of home."

"I concur. I know your yearly retreat to meet your school chums always gives you a boost when you need it most."

Tiana smiled and then frowned. "Kyrie called. Something is going on with her, though she couched it so I didn't quite get it all."

"Is she okay? I like her, even if she's a bit flakier than most," Damian responded.

"Yeah, she's okay physically. But emotionally, she's bothered by her reactions and what she's picking up, though I'm not sure I completely understand why." They entered the building that housed their department area, heading down the corridor to their ragtag break room.

Once there, they waited for Kyle, who probably was talking to Eileen Wilkins, another professor in the forensic department, about the book they were working on together. Damian and Tiana exchanged some ideas for a follow-up article to the one they'd published, as well as their joint book explaining computer graphic forensic reconstructions for laypeople. As they jotted down the basic points they wanted to get across to people, Tiana wondered what was taking Kyle so long.

"He's being difficult, isn't he?"

"He who?" Damian asked, looking up from the notes.

"Kyle."

"Stress is probably getting to him. He and Eileen haven't heard back from the publisher yet about the book. It's been over eight months, and you know how he gets when he doesn't get his answers right away."

"Yeah. It's just weird—"

At that moment, Kyle entered the room, his slightly wavy dark brown hair rumpled, a thoroughly happy expression on his face, and in his hand, a bag of coffee beans. "Ha! I've got amaretto mocha."

The three shared a laugh together as Tiana held up her two bags. "Amaretto mocha and orange hazelnut."

"Ooh, nice. What about you, Damian?" Keith asked as he put his marked bag in the refrigerator.

"I've got mocha and Jamaican Blue." Both Tiana and Keith swiveled to look at Damian, who had a shit-eating grin on his face. "What? I admit I paid for the pleasure. More importantly, I'm willing to share."

"You better share, you sot," Tiana teased.

"I'm not a sot; that's only when we're out drinking." They all laughed and headed to the computer room to see how things were going with their graduate student. Talking shop, they entered the room, seeing Lawrence already hard at work.

"The first two skulls are cut for clay modeling, Tiana."

"Great, Lawrence. Thanks. Up early this morning?"

Holding up a cup of coffee, Lawrence nodded. "Couldn't sleep. I had a couple of ideas in regards to handling the problems of the crushed-skull issue, as well as with the bog people. I could be wrong, but since it's part of my thesis, I thought I'd try out the variables and see how it goes."

The day settled down nicely for Tiana. Though she missed seeing Ian, this was her life, something that she thoroughly enjoyed.

* * * * *

Ian walked into the precinct, his eyes a bit blurry with the lack of sleep from the last two nights. Though the one case was going cold, he was also balancing two other homicide cases, one that had been solved in the early morning hours. "Coffee. I need coffee," he bleated tiredly.

John handed him a cup of the steaming brew. Sipping it, Ian made a face.

"Hey, I know it's not great coffee, but it'll wake you, guv."

"It'll kill me if I'm not careful, you mean," Ian quipped, nodding his thanks as he carefully sipped on the coffee wannabe. This wasn't the good stuff like he had at his flat, but then again, he wasn't sharing his coffee with the others, either. It wasn't his turn.

"Heard the Babbinger case went down last night. Things go alright?"

Ian sat in his chair and leaned back, looking over the rim of his mug at his partner. "Yeah, things went down fine. Where were you last night? There was no answer at home or on your mobile."

"My wife was hit by a car when she was coming home from the market. I was at the hospital all night with her."

"Shit. How is she?" Ian asked. Maggie was a good woman, one who kept John on the straight and narrow. She was the light of his partner's life, and the idea of her hurt made him angry. "Did they get the guy who did that to her?"

"Calm down, Ian. She's got a fractured arm, bruises everywhere, but otherwise, she's fine. The guy turned himself in this morning, which is why I'm here. The paperwork has been filed."

"Good. Tell Maggie I'll bring her some goodies so she won't have to worry on cooking."

John grinned. "You do realize you're going to spoil my wife."

Ian chuckled. "That's the plan. Then she'll come running to me, so I can have the happiness the two of you share." Clapping his partner on the shoulder, he realized that was true. He wanted happiness like his friend, but he wasn't sure he'd ever get it. Not with the cloud sitting over his head like a wet blanket. Sometimes the sins of the father— in this case, great-great-grandfather—are passed down the family line.

"Dream on, my friend. The woman is mine, though she's been asking about you. Said she's worried you might be working too hard and not taking the time to play."

"I'm fine, and I'll reassure her tonight when I bring over food from Arrabiata's."

"You're an evil man, Ian Spencer. That's one of her favorite places."

Ian dialed a number from memory and spoke in fluent Italian to the woman that answered. After ten minutes, he hung up the phone. "Done. Supper will be delivered to your house every other night for the next two weeks."

"Thanks, mate. I know it'll ease Maggie's mind while her arm heals."

"Anything for Maggie. Both she and I can't stand it when you don't get your dinner and you're so bloody fussy."

John chuckled as he tossed the paper at Ian. "You see this? Seems someone among the press wants to know why there are no updates regarding the two murders in Metro London."

"Because there are no further clues? Because there have been no more murders since we've asked the public to keep aware and not to be out at night alone?" Ian responded a bit sarcastically. "Why on earth do I keep seeing a similarity in these murders and a set I can't remember? Must be from working too many homicide cases." He sighed.

"Down, guv. You and I both know that's it, but for this reporter, they've taken up a crusade. Which means we'll be getting the heat turned on us if people consider this a major crisis."

Ian sighed and ran his fingers through his unruly dark hair. "I know, John. Thing is, honestly, how the bloody hell are we supposed to find this guy when the trail is cold?"

"Good question. Wish I had an answer."

They continued their work, typing up reports and getting things done with the one case they had finished. Ian's thoughts occasionally strayed to Tiana. He missed her laugh, but he hadn't had a chance to call her, considering the break in his latest case. She listened to him as he talked about the things he could easily speak on, and respected his privacy when he couldn't. It was nice sharing his day with her.

Moreover, his knowledge was growing as she shared her work with him, as well. Beyond the forensic autopsies, he got to hear about her passion, forensic reconstruction, and the cutting edge of using computers to help with the reconstruction. Her passion for her work rekindled his own passion for his job.

Ian recognized that they had bonded as friends. Perhaps there was more. Every night after they talked, he had to take a cold shower to accept her limitations that they couldn't be together until after the investigation, or at least her part, was finished. He respected that limitation, but sometimes it made it hard when all he wanted to do was drive to Snaith, lead her to the bedroom, and have mad sex until their brains and bodies were fried. Part of him wondered if this attraction was due to the circumstances by which they met, but he knew that had they met any other way, they'd already be lovers. His body tightened at that thought, and he casually repositioned himself.

They'd made plans to meet next weekend, during Felicia's visit. That way, they could get Lawrence to join them without feeling any pressure. Tiana was slick in knowing the graduate student's mind. Plus, being away from London would give him a much-needed break, something Ian realized was essential. The thought of seeing her that weekend improved his humor.

133

* * * * *

That night, he met her for a rendezvous. This was the first time he'd pre-selected his victim, but it was one that would shatter the woman who was giving him fits and starts. She still kept her interest in the case, he knew, but beyond that, he wasn't sure what all she knew.

Feeling a touch on his back, he turned around and smiled at the young woman. "Hello, luv," he said as he leaned in to kiss her cheek. "Thanks for coming out here to meet me."

"I've never been out here before." She turned from him and pointed. "Look, you can see Whitechapel church from here. Isn't that neat?"

"You know about the church?"

The dark-haired woman nodded. "I'm studying modern crime. I want to be a lawyer. Right now, we're studying the police procedures done in the Whitechapel murders." Seeing his look, she explained. "Jack the Ripper. One thing some of us students noticed was that all of his crimes took place within the limits of the sanctuary."

"Really, how interesting. How did you all come to know about that?"

He felt the woman warming up to the subject. "I also love medieval history. All major churches in various areas were designated as sanctuary areas. Whitechapel was one. Though a lot of it was forgotten, it was something that hit my brain. I don't know if Jack the Ripper knew about that part, but it was interesting to see that of the canonical victims, they were all within the realms of sanctuary."

"Fascinating. You're enjoying your study of Jack the Ripper?" His voice was low as he stood next to her, his hand on her arm.

"It's interesting. I mean, I love law and order, but it's intriguing to see what went wrong among the police force that allowed a serial killer to walk free."

"The police were stupid and unable to piece together the information," he growled.

She turned toward him. "They were not. Granted, they didn't have today's advances, but they did the best they could. But there were errors made that shouldn't have been."

"Bitch, they were stupid!" Then he hit her. The shocked look on her face when she saw the glint of his knife made him smile. She tried to scream, but he stopped that. "Trust me, I know, my dear. Jack knows the stupidity that got the police, then and now. No one will hear you scream. No one will know that you, too, are a victim of Jack the Ripper, reborn."

With that, he hit her once more, before re-creating the next murder. She struggled, which made it even more pleasant for him; and in the end, he had his way. As he walked away from the broken body of the young woman, he imagined the horror on Tiana Wells's face when she heard about the next victim. Ah, yes, he'd scare her before making her his fait accompli, before his new terrorizing would occur. The thought made him shiver in evil pleasure.

Chapter Eight

The phone shattered Tiana's sleep. "Hello?" she uttered groggily, trying to catch the time. Six in the morning, on Saturday. *Who the hell—*

"Tiana, it's Ian. I need you to come down to London." The tightness in his voice woke her up quicker than a cup of coffee.

"What's wrong, Ian?"

"Just get here, Tiana. He's struck again."

"Fuck. It's worse than before, isn't it?"

"How long will it take you to get here? Al wants to know and so do I."

Tiana thought on things. "I need to get dressed, grab a coffee, and I'll be on the road in twenty minutes or less. Depending on traffic, I should be there by nine, I think."

"I'll be at the lab waiting for you." There was a pause before he spoke again. "Tiana, I need to warn you, this victim isn't pretty. He really cut into her badly."

"Okay. I'll be prepared, Ian. Just be careful. I'll be there as quick as I can without getting stopped."

"I'll get your room for you at Brighton Square arranged."

"Thanks." She hung up the phone. Ian sounded hurt. Like something in this case had become personal. There was a feeling in her gut that whatever happened wouldn't make her happy. That it might just shatter the world she'd created to keep herself safe. Taking slow, deep breaths, Tiana brushed away those dark thoughts.

Within twenty minutes, she was in her car and on the road. Besides her usual accoutrements, she brought some of the Ripper work that she'd been doing the night before. The article she was working on with Hamish was due in a couple of weeks. She had been going over some of the inquest information, as well as the postmortem results, correlating data while trying to plot positions and times on a map Hamish had created for her. He was a good, if slightly obsessive, friend.

Dialing her mobile, she notified Hamish that she was going to London on a case and wouldn't make it up to Edinburgh for a while. Informing him that she'd emailed him a copy of the article stuff she'd put together already, she told him to call her if he had any questions. Hanging up, Tiana sped toward London, hoping that whatever had Ian upset wasn't as bad as she feared it might be.

* * * * *

Pulling the necklace badge over her hair, Tiana grabbed her briefcase and locked the door of her car. Quickly, she raced up the steps of the gray building, which now seemed to hold a hint of menace. As she walked through the doors, Tiana spotted Ian. Walking to him, she spared one of the guards a nod.

"I'm here, Ian." Hugging him, she looked at his eyes, seeing the pain and haunting deep within them. "What's going on?"

"Tiana, we need to talk before you go in."

She followed him down the stairs to where the forensic unit was housed. When they walked into the changing area, she shed her clothes while glancing back at Ian. "Talk, Ian. What's going on? I've never seen or heard you like this before."

"It's about the victim."

Pulling on the scrub pants, she tied them at the waist. "What about the victim? You said she was badly injured. We know he prefers knives. It won't be easy, but I'll do my job."

"It's not that, Ti."

139

"Then what?" She pulled on her top and waited. "Well?"

Ian grabbed her hand. "I don't know how to do this without causing pain." He closed his eyes, then opened them. Tiana could see the pain radiating in them. "Ti, the victim is Hannah."

She pulled away from him. "No! That's not possible." Shaking her head, she denied the truth she saw in his eyes. "Hannah said she was being careful. That she wasn't taking any risks. There's no way it can be her." Crying, she slid to the floor, the cold wall offering little comfort. "No, no, no, no!"

Ian gathered her in his arms. "I'm sorry, luv. I'm so sorry. I know you've been helping her with her studies."

"Oh, gods, she can't be gone. She was coming up with Felicia. We were going to con Damian into coming along—" Tiana sobbed, tears spilling down her cheeks, her body wracked with shudders. "No, please tell me you're lying, Ian. Please."

"I wish I was, Ti. I wish I was." He held her and rocked her until the sobs stopped. Wiping the tears from her face, he leaned forward, his lips brushing softly against hers. "We'll get this bastard, Ti. For Hannah."

"For Hannah." The lump in her throat was still there. "I've got to do this for Hannah." Steeling herself, Ti clung to Ian for one moment, letting his warmth fill her body. "Let's do this," she whispered brokenly.

She mechanically washed up, her brain shutting down the emotions that threatened to overcome her once again. *Control. I need to keep control. The bastard is going down for this. He touched mine. Oh, Hannah, why did this happen to you?* Tiana pushed the thoughts away as she dried her hands. Gloving up, she walked into the autopsy room. Already there were Ian and Dr. Campion.

"I'm sorry, Tiana. Ian told me that you both knew the victim."

Tiana nodded sharply. "I'd taken her under my wing, Al. She was going into criminal justice, with a specialty of police procedures." A hiccup emerged, swallowed down as Tiana bit her lip, controlling the emotions she knew played across her face. "She was so bloody smart. She'd have been an asset for any police force."

"I'm sorry, my friend. I've already made my initial report. It's not pretty. I've got the crime scene photos if you need them, to see how they found her."

Tiana inclined her head. "Later. Let's just get this over with." As her mentor pulled down the sheet, he revealed long blonde hair lying limply on the table. When Hannah was fully exposed, Tiana turned and ran to the bathroom, barely making it to the toilet as her morning coffee came up.

She felt a cool facecloth pressed against the back of her neck. Tiana knew it was Ian. "Thanks. I knew it was bad, but ..."

"He brutalized her, Ti. We need to find this bastard, and quickly."

"Yeah." She looked up from her bent position. "Give me a moment, okay? I'll be right out. It just took me by surprise."

Ian left the room. Tiana took gulping breaths as her hands fiddled with the pendant. "Family, help me. Give me the strength to handle this. Elements guide my hands, my focus. I call upon you for help in this time of crisis." As always, the pendant gave her warmth and helped her to re-center herself. "Thank you," she whispered as she emerged from the bathroom.

The pale walls felt like they were tight against her, but she felt the cool air being circulated around. Without a word, Al handed his report to her as well as the crime scene reports. Reading them quickly, she noted various pieces of information. With a determined gleam in her eye, she made mental note of what was found. Taking her position back at the body of her friend, Tiana whispered, "Hannah, I swear we'll catch him. I'll make him pay for what he's done. I swear."

She began her observations, including the notes from her mentor. Something about the recitation recalled something else that tantalized her memory, but wouldn't come into focus. Biting back the rolling nausea, Tiana began the recitation of injuries.

"There are old domestic violence wounds, which are included with this report. The victim left an abusive relationship just recently. There is an abrasion on the head of her ring finger, yet there aren't many defensive wounds beyond this. It's possible she knew her attacker."

Rubbing her forearm against her cheek, Tiana's eyes burned with unshed tears. However, she knew it wasn't yet time to cry. Right now, it was time to take care of business. She felt her heart in her throat, but she had to make sure that every detail was noted. She was here in regards to the wounds. Concentrate, Ti. Do this for Hannah. She needs you to do your job. "The shortest throat incision runs from the front of the throat and terminates on the right side. The longest throat incision completely encircles the throat, running along the line of the jaw. There are two clean and distinct cuts on the left side of the spine, parallel to each other, and one-and-a-quarter centimeters apart."

She continued onward, detailing the worst part, the abdomen area. "According to the crime scene reports, the small intestines and part of the abdomen lay above her right shoulder. A small portion of the belly wall including the navel is missing. The uterus and its appendages, with the upper portion of the vagina and the posterior two thirds of the bladder, have been entirely removed. No trace of these parts could be found, according to crime scene technicians. This was done in one clean cut of the knife, which therefore must have at least twelve or fifteen centimeters in length."

Tiana continued giving depth, angle, and length measurements in detail. At the end, she stated. "I believe that this is the same man who was also responsible for two other deaths. The violence is escalating and so is the severity of the wounds. Though the first victim was more stabbing than cutting, the assailant shows a proficiency in slicing and removing organs. I'd look for someone who has some kind of medical training, or someone who knows how to slaughter animals. Dr. Tiana Wells."

She set down the medical instruments, turned away, and walked toward the changing area. "I need to get out of here." The panic in her voice was apparent, even to her. "Now."

Ian grabbed her arm as she walked into the changing room. "Okay, let's get you to the hotel." She watched him gather up her clothes, briefcase, and purse. She followed him wordlessly as he headed toward another set of stairs.

"Where does this go?"

"Directly to the parking area. This is only for those who work here, but in this case, I think you need out of here more than you need to leave the normal way." Pushing on the doors, he led her outside, where the fresh air assaulted her.

She took in the sweet, clean air and started to shake. Ian realized what was going on. "Come on, luv. Let's get you to the hotel. You need a shower and to relax." Nodding, she took his proffered hand and went to his car. He opened the door and slid her into the passenger seat. Before she realized, Tiana had her seat belt on and Ian was in the driver's seat, starting the engine.

She didn't remember much of the trip to the hotel or even checking in. Ian handled everything. After opening the door, he started the shower, helping her remove the scrub clothes and easing her into the hot, steaming water. He helped her rinse away some of the grime she felt in her soul. Then he left her alone in the shower to weep for her new friend. She knew he was just as badly affected, but hid it much better than she could. When she was done, she wrapped a towel around her body and stepped out of the bathroom.

His eyes took in her body and her expression. She looked better than the shocked state she had been in. His body tightened as he watched a trail of water hug the slope of her breast and slide under the towel. He tried to smile, but instead stepped forward and said in a raspy voice, "Let me see you, Tiana."

She stepped closer and, with a twist of her fingers, undid the knot in the front of the towel. With a slight flourish, the towel fluttered to her feet, leaving her body exposed to Ian's gaze. They both needed something, something that only being together on this level could provide. Life, they needed to feel alive.

"You're lovely. So bloody lovely," Ian purred as he knelt before her. His fingertips lightly traced the scars from her ordeal. At that moment, he knew without a doubt that this woman was as strong as he was in will and temperament. She'd never let anyone bowl her over, even if they were friends. She had survived too much to let anyone treat her as a fool. Tiana tried to move away from him caressing her scars, but he wrapped one arm around her, pulling her closer against him.

"Don't move. Don't be ashamed. These are badges of honor, luv." He paused as he kissed one scar across her rounded, soft abdomen. "You're more beautiful because of them. "

Tiana gasped. Ian smiled at her and went back to administering light kisses across her abdomen as his free hand slid between her thighs, parting the slick lips of her labia. As Tiana arched against him, Ian slid his fingers back and forth, spreading her wet warmth as his mouth kissed its way down where she was ready for him. Slowly, his fingers opened her wider so he could see the glistening nub waiting for him. Lowering his face against her most intimate part, his tongue swirled around it as her hands fisted in his short hair. Licking her from front to as far as his tongue would reach, he went slowly, deliberately, teasing her body. Her knees felt weak, but he wrapped his arms around her, holding her close against his face.

His fingers parted her further, exposing her dusky pink flesh to his gaze. His tongue darted out and flicked her clitoris. She gasped in pleasure as her fingers buried into his hair. "Tell me you want more, luv."

"Ian, please," she hissed. "I need—more. Oh, gods, I need more."

"Your wish is my command." Sliding a finger between the nether lips, Ian spread her wetness, carefully not sliding into her entrance. Tiana wiggled, her breaths coming out in soft pants as he continued to tease her, stroke her velvety wet skin. Her moans and muttered threats amused him as he continued to blow lightly across her clit while his fingers stroked around both her pussy and her puckered ass. "You need something, Tiana?"

"Ian, please, I need you to make me come. Please!"

"And you do beg ever so nicely, Miss Tiana," Ian whispered against her clitoris. With a quick motion, he suckled hard on her clit as three fingers slid deeply into her pussy. Her body bowed back as her climax rolled through her. Her natural fragrance shifted to a more erotic scent as his fingers kept plunging deeper and harder, coating themselves with her juices. Then cautiously, he slid one finger deep into her back canal as she moaned his name over and again.

The sound of her voice calling his name was addictive; he wanted to drown in it. His cock throbbed in time with his fingers as they fucked her in both areas. This woman was so damn responsive. He needed her as much as she needed him. Blowing lightly across her clit, he licked it, letting his teeth rasp it gently.

"Ian!"

He pulled back, his gaze hot upon her. "What, luv?"

"Love me, Ian. Help me to feel something, anything."

Ian stood up, his hand cupping her chin. "Are you sure, Tiana?"

"Yes. I need you in me, thrusting deep. I need to feel alive."

He scooped her up into his arms and took five steps toward the bed. Setting her down lightly, Ian unbuttoned his shirt, having taken off his jacket earlier. Then he undid his pants, letting them fall around his ankles. Toeing off his shoes, he quickly removed the rest of his clothing.

She caught her breath. He was beautiful. From the sculpted muscles that delineated his chest, down to the dark trail that led to the thatch of hair surrounding his cock, Ian Spencer was like a Celtic god. Her hands lightly traced a couple of small scars on his chest. "How—"

"Shh, let's not talk on those. I need to kiss you, Ti."

Then he did, deeply, thoroughly, ravaging her mouth with his. She softened at his touch, taking him deeper as her mouth suckled on his tongue. Her fingers were soft against his chest, caressing his nipples as his hands palmed her breasts, his thumbs flicking over her peaks. Gasping, she arched her head back, allowing him to kiss down her throat, lavishing love bites and soft, healing pressure after. When he reached the top of her breasts, she heard his growl and felt comfort, not fear. This man made her feel safe when she was with him, something she hadn't felt in a long time.

Suddenly, thought stopped as his mouth claimed one nipple, as his fingers began lightly pinching and pulling the other. "Oh, gods, Ian," she groaned as she lay back, her legs wrapping around his hips. His tongue laved her dusky peak, his teeth lightly rasping the tender areola, causing her to buck against him in need. He lavished the same attention on the other nipple, letting his mouth suck and tease her to a tightness she'd not felt, ever.

He started down her abdomen, when she stopped him. "No," she whispered huskily. "My turn."

Ian shook his head. "No, luv. Let me love you. I need to taste you once more as you come." His mouth lightly caressed the auburn curls that surrounded her womanhood. Sliding his hands under her thighs, he lifted her legs easily onto his strong shoulders. With his long fingers, he parted her open, his eyes glittering in the light.

"You're so delicious, Ti. So bloody damn delicious." His mouth claimed her center. As his tongue probed into her sheath deeply, she grabbed the coverlet on the bed, her moans growing loud in the room. She gasped as she felt one, then two fingers slide deep in her.

"Ian, yes," she hissed, rocking her hips upwards.

His fingers played her, sliding deeply within her and then out, the rhythmic rocking increasing as her counterthrusts rose in tempo. She couldn't believe the murmurs pouring from her lips as Ian's mouth paid homage to her ultimate femininity. Feeling pressure, tightness, and oblivion coming, she threaded her fingers through his dark hair, urging him deeper. "More, please. Ian, please."

He complied, sliding a third finger in, curling his digits slightly within her. Ian's mouth suckled hard on her nubbin as she climaxed. It felt like heavenly oblivion as her heart beat in time with the waves of completion. When her eyes fluttered open, she looked down and saw his darkened blue eyes looking back at her. Her breath came in short pants, but as he slid up her body, she inhaled deeply, smelling his essence.

He kissed her, his mouth tasting of her and him. Something better than any coffee, she thought mindlessly. She wrapped her arms around his neck, feeling his cock against her hip. Raising her legs up, she wrapped them around his slim waist, urging him to enter her.

Reaching down, he slid something out of his wallet. Ripping open the silver foil packet, Ian made sure they were both protected; Tiana could've told him there was nothing to worry about, but that he took that much care in protecting her made her feel gooey inside. Something in her heart broke open, but she wasn't ready to figure out what it was. Not willing to admit that it could be more than the need of the moment.

Kissing each nipple, Ian then smiled down at her. "Look at me, Ti. I want to see your lovely eyes when I take you."

Green met blue as one hard, deep thrust connected them on more than one level. Ian paused above her, giving her time to acclimate to him. She licked her lips, then claimed his as her body rocked against his, urging him forward.

Giving into the sensations, Ian began sliding in and out of her, each thrust met by her willing warmth. She felt like heaven, something that he hadn't felt before. Tiana was special to him. Somehow, he had connected to her on a level unlike anything he'd ever felt before. Pulling himself almost fully out, he loved hearing her whimper for him. Bracing his arms on either side of her shoulders, he flexed so he entered her even more deeply than the last thrusts. Her eyes widened as he picked up the pace, each thrust going deeper, harder into her.

Her cries of pleasure fueled his desires. "Oh, luv, you're so beautiful. So giving. I love how you feel beneath me, Ti. Satin against my skin. Your sweet wetness surrounding me, making me want to take you more."

"Yes, Ian," she moaned as her hips rocked hard against him. "Please. I want you, need you harder, deeper." Her voice broke as she begged. "Please, Ian, I need release."

"Me, too, my love. I need you, too."

Their lovemaking became feverish as their panting breaths matched each other, the kisses making promises neither was sure they could keep, yet ones they wanted to, deep in their hearts. Finally, at the pinnacle, Ian growled Tiana's name as he came hard inside her. She followed him, his name tripping off her lips repeatedly.

His body pressed against hers, his lips lightly kissing her face as he tried to recover his breath. "Tiana, Tiana, Tiana. You're so wonderful, my love."

She smiled at him, her heart starting to slowly return to normal. "You're better than that, Ian." A blush caressed her skin. "I've never reacted like this before."

He caressed her cheek with the back of his hand. "Me, neither, luv." Deftly, he rolled onto his back, pulling her across his body. "Rest on me for a while. Let me hold you."

"Yes, I'd love that," Tiana said, as sleep overtook her thoroughly sated body.

Chapter Nine

Morning came too soon for Tiana. In the middle of the night, Ian had woken her up, murmuring about skeletons that had to be held out of sight and finding the key to showing there were no skeletons. Somehow, she managed to get him calmed down before falling back to sleep. But right now, her mouth felt dry and there seemed to be a huge lump in the bed, something Brighton Square wasn't known for. As she wiped the grit from her eyes, she remembered that Ian hadn't left. Rubbing her head, she let out a sigh. Things had changed for them both. This meant something, but she wasn't sure what.

"Morning, luv."

"Morning, Ian." She looked at the lightly tanned expanse of chest and gave him a small smile. "You being here is proof that I wasn't imagining anything after we left the office, right?"

Ian gathered her against him and kissed her deeply. His hard body slid against hers, showing her how much he still wanted her. "What do you think?"

Giving him a slightly bashful smile, she responded, "Well then, you're the reason for the slight headache I've got. That bottle of wine was potent." After a long nap, they'd ended up spending the day in the room, ordering room service and making love a few more times. Times that had been punctuated by occasional nightmares from them both. Hers about Hannah, while his were about family skeletons. "And you're right, I do like that birthmark of yours."

Ian laughed hard, and Tiana enjoyed the sound of his laughter as it surrounded her in warmth. "You only like it because you don't have one."

"Well, yeah, duh."

Ian kissed Tiana again, sliding her body over his "birthmark." She couldn't help her moans as he slid into her sheath. "Hmm, I don't think I have one of these, though," he whispered as she began rocking on him.

"Guess this means we've both got something the other enjoys." Tiana increased the rhythm slightly. Leaning forward, she kissed Ian's lips. "You're wonderful."

Their rhythm carried them cresting to another high that neither could've reached without the other. After they both reached their completion, Tiana lay across Ian, grinning. "One might think this is excessive use of the police to maintain sanity."

"Use me, luv. Use me a lot." His hand caressed her cheek. His eyes turned serious. "Unfortunately, I have to work today. I wish I didn't, but I took yesterday off, and with John's wife having problems—"

"I know. I think since I'm here, I might go see my mother. Last time she said she had something for me, but I could only get it in person. So I'm going to go see her today." She looked at him, hesitating for a moment. "Do you think that I'll be needed today?"

Ian shook his head. "Probably not until tomorrow. Depends on what the trace evidence is and such. You still need to sign off on the report, right?"

"Once it's transcribed, yeah. That usually takes a while."

Ian kissed her again. "Shower with me."

Tiana lift a brow. "But your birthmark might attack me, and I'll end up dirty again." She couldn't hold the smirk from her lips.

"You know you like being dirty that way."

She smacked his chest lightly. "Brat."

"Bloody hell yes. I learned from the best."

* * * * *

By midmorning, Tiana found herself at her mother's home. Looking at the three specially brewed coffees, she only hoped they were enough to tame the savage beast known as her mother. Though many people considered Jean Merritt a wonderful host, as well as a witty, intelligent woman, none knew her like her daughter. Unless her mother was already up, this would be a two-coffee welcome, one to wake up her mother, the second to bring out the civilized side.

Carefully carrying the coffees, Tiana rang the doorbell. After ten minutes, she withdrew the set of keys from her purse and opened up the townhouse. "Mother? I'm home. Where are you?" Her voice rang out through the rooms.

The brightly colored house reflected her mother's love of sunshine, as well as her love of history. There were reproductions of various famous pieces, as well as some original archaeological finds that had been handed down through the years. Tiana smiled at the quality reproduction of Tutankhamun's funeral mask that framed the doorway to the kitchen. "Only my mother would think that death leads to afterlife in coffee nirvana," she chuckled.

Setting down the coffees, Tiana peeked in the refrigerator. Inside, she found what had always been there -- various fruits, vegetables, and the makings of any omelet she could come up with. Taking out the ingredients, she began preparations as she heard movement from upstairs. "I'm in the kitchen, Mum!"

"Don't talk to me, you ungrateful child!"

"I brought your favorite coffee!"

There was a pause in movement upstairs. "You good, wonderful, loving child. I'll be right down!"

Tiana smirked as she continued making breakfast. She doubted that anyone knew of the famous Jean Merritt's penchant for flavored coffees and omelets for breakfast. Sometimes, Tiana wondered what it would have been like to not be the child of a famous television star, but overall, she couldn't fault the fact that she was allowed to study anything she wanted because of it. Finishing one omelet, she went on to make her own for breakfast.

Tiana heard a noise to her left and glanced up. Anyone seeing her mother would realize where the auburn hair came from, if they didn't know that Jean had been a platinum blonde in her younger days. Matching smiles showed them to be mother and daughter, though Tiana was taller than her mother by three inches. Putting down her spatula, Tiana gave her mother a hug, then handed her one of the coffees. "Blue Jamaican. The second one is mocha supreme."

"You are the only one who loves me."

"Right. What about Kit?"

"Your sister is excavating in Alexandria. She hasn't brought me coffee. Thus, you're the only one who loves me."

Tiana and her mother chuckled as Tiana slid the omelet in front of her mother, who sat at the kitchen table. Grabbing the other omelet, Tiana joined her mother. She sipped on the coffee marked with her name on it.

"I'm sorry I didn't come up last week, Mum. Things have been a bit hectic."

"I do understand. However, I came across some stuff that could help you in your research. I'm not sure how, but it could."

Both mother and daughter looked at each other. When Tiana and Kit were young, their mother had sat them down and discussed magick, paganism, and abilities with them. She never discouraged them learning. It was part of her family legacy, something Tiana maintained more than Kit did, though both believed and practiced paganism.

"What did you find?" Tiana's curiosity piqued. "And for what research?"

"Jack the Ripper, dear," her mother said patiently while opening up the second cup of coffee. "I found your great-great-grandmother's journals."

"Patricia?"

"Yes. Remember those trunks up in the attic that were collecting dust and causing us to trip over them when we'd go up there?" Seeing her daughter's nod, Jean continued. "Well, I finally took a week to go through them to see if they were worth keeping, or if they'd have better use elsewhere, like for old-fashion costumes, etcetera. In one of the trunks, I found

Patricia's journals, her wedding gown, and some other things of hers. They're all yours, if you'd like."

Tiana blinked back her tears. "Really?"

"Really." Her mother gave her a smile that millions saw every week, but only Tiana knew came from the heart.

"Thanks, Mum. I'd like that."

Lifting one brow, Jean sat back. "Now, we need to discuss why you're here. I thought you weren't coming to London."

Tiana sighed, knowing her mother had gone from loving to inquisitor mode. The second coffee must not be completely drunk yet. "A forensic case, mum."

Jean nodded. "That brutal slaying of the young woman, I take it."

Tiana mirrored her mother's eyebrow lift. "What makes you say that?"

Counting out on her fingers, Jean responded drolly, "One, you're a knife-wound specialist. Two, it's the only major event that could've dragged you out of the woods. Three, you came up for a knifing a couple weeks back. Common sense."

Tiana blinked. Sometimes her mother could catch things that others didn't manage to put together. Even knowing her mum like she did, there were times when she was caught off guard. "Mum, I can't go into details, but based on what you've read, what do you think?"

Jean gazed into her daughter's eyes. The brown depths were like caramel coffee and filled with warmth and compassion, unless angered. "I think you're in danger, Ti. Bad enough having Kit out doing whatever it is she's doing, but something deep inside me says you're in terrible danger."

"Oh, boy. Is this one of those bone feelings?"

Jean nodded. "Yes and you best get over your fears, my dear. I'm telling you this straight out. From the couple of visions I've had, you need to be able to handle yourself again. The past is past, Tiana Marie Wells. What counts now is that you're able to do what needs to be done."

Tiana's fingers gripped her coffee cup tightly. She and her mother often butted heads over the past, but never like this. "Mum, the past isn't so easy to dismiss. You, of all people, know that."

"There's a difference between you and me, Ti. I accept the past and its lessons to continue moving forward. You haven't. Until you do, you'll remain in deep danger."

Tiana stood up, taking away the empty breakfast dishes. "I don't want to fight."

Her mother sighed deeply. "I don't either, but this is reality. You're in danger. I fear this greatly, Ti. I can sense his evilness trying to caress you. It scares me, but it's all up to you in the end."

She hugged her mother tightly. "I promise to be careful. I'm not too sure about taking back up edged weapons, though I do admit I miss them a bit."

"Try for me, please?"

Tiana looked at mother. This was the first time her mother had ever asked her to do that. It used to be that her mother harped on her fascination for ancient and current edged weapons and it being unladylike. This was a complete turnaround. She wouldn't have asked unless it was really important. "For you, yes."

Her mother smiled and headed to the coffeepot. Opening the cabinet above it, she looked. "What flavor do we want for our next batch?"

Tiana looked over her mother's shoulder. "Hmm, I'm partial to anything chocolate, but I just had that. What about Orange Spice?"

"Lovely choice. I'll go put a pot on. You run up to the attic to where the trunk is. It's the one with the light blue trim on it."

Obeying her mother, Tiana raced out of the kitchen, up the stairs to the end of the hallway, where there was a small closet door. She opened it and followed the stairs up to the attic. The lights came on when she was halfway up the stairs. *Ooh, mum got in the motion-detecting lights. Nice. However, it means no more late night explorations for Kit and me.* Once in the attic, she spotted the trunk right away.

Tiana knelt beside the trunk, lifting the lid. It was definitely designed during the Victorian age. She recognized many things from that period. Though Kit, her sister, was the historian of this generation, Tiana knew enough to keep her head up without causing any major shame. Thoughts of Kit made her realize that her sister hadn't come home in over five years, except for brief visits to her. She knew Kit and their mum had fought about what happened to her, but still, that shouldn't keep her younger sister away. Kit had lived with their dad and only came over during holidays and in the summer. It was the only thing that really hurt about their parents' divorce; the two sisters, although they were seven years apart, had been close until that time.

Lifting out an ivory dress, Tiana gasped in amazement. This must've been Patricia's wedding gown. It was beautiful in the classical Victorian style. Her hands brushed the silky fabric and smiled. Kit would demand that this be given to a museum to showcase the fine clothing from the Victorian age. *Not for a while, my sister. I want to possess it a little bit longer.* Setting it on a nearby stool, Tiana resumed looking in the trunk.

She saw the journals with the dates stamped on them. Tiana stroked the one numbered 1887-1888 and felt a cold tingle. Now she realized why her mother said it might be relevant. If she had felt that same tingle, it was an obvious sign of information needed. Taking out a dark blue box, she opened it up and blinked a couple of times. There was no way she could be looking at what she thought she was.

Taking out the body of the handheld machine, she saw the insert and busted out laughing. "Oh, my gods! I can't believe it!"

"Can't believe what?" Jean stood behind her daughter.

"Grandmum Patricia had a ... vibrator," Tiana giggled. Jean sat next to her and took the machine from her.

"That could explain why those pictures show Patricia always smiling."

"Gives a new meaning to 'hysterical' in our family," Tiana teased.

"This is true. Did you find the journals?" Jean asked, handing back the vibrator. Tiana nodded as she put aside the ancient medical device. "Good. The dress is yours unless you want to donate it to a museum. Patricia packed it very well. It's in excellent condition."

"You mean hide it so Kit doesn't find out I own it."

Jean chuckled. "I didn't say that. However, yes."

Mother and daughter looked through the trunk at some of the papers that were there, as well as through the jewelry box. "Are you sure you don't want these pieces, Mum?"

"They're yours. In fact, the only piece that I had from that collection is yours now, the pendant."

"Patricia had the pendant?"

"Yes, it goes to the oldest daughter of the matrilineal line on their sixteenth birthday."

Tiana hugged her mother. "Thanks, Mum. I best head back soon."

Jean nodded. "It's good to see you. You're coming in a couple of weeks, before I leave for Egypt, correct?"

Tiana lifted a brow. "You're going to Egypt without me, and you want me to visit so you can gloat?"

"Yes."

"I'll be here. Maybe I'll bring a friend for you to harass."

"Male?"

"Perhaps."

"Brat child."

"Take after my mum, you know." Tiana kissed her mother's cheek. "I love you, Mum."

"Love you, too, Ti. Just be careful, as I've asked."

"Promise." Tiana dragged the trunk to the stairs. Her mother lifted one end as she took the other, carefully negotiating the stairs. Once down on the first floor, Tiana grinned at her mum. "You know something, it'll be interesting to see what Patricia has to say regarding the Jack the Ripper murders from that time. She was in the upper middle class, right?"

"Yes, her father and brother had a small shipping business. She took part with the Salvation Army in helping others until she was twenty, if I remember our family history correctly."

Tiana grinned. "If Patricia is anything like the rest of the family has been, she was a wild child and full of radical ideas."

Jean nodded. "This would not be surprising. I think my mother always said I took after Patricia."

"Grandmum Shirley said *that*?"

"Yes."

Tiana chuckled and hugged her mother. "Well, I think it's a good thing. Look at all the good you've done for other young women. I love you, Mum."

"Take care of yourself and call me if you need anything."

"Will do." Tiana took the trunk to the car and packed it in the back. Part of her couldn't wait to start reading the journals. As she drove away, she had a strange foreboding that her mother had indeed felt something that Tiana herself had tried to ignore. Making a mental note to be more open to things, Tiana headed back to Brighton Square.

* * * * *

Once back to the hotel, she snagged a bellman to help her take the trunk to her room. After tipping him, Tiana sat cross-legged on the floor, her eyes gazing at the chest. Her mother was right; there was some kind of information that Patricia had about Jack the Ripper that might've gone unnoticed. If things were documented properly, then it could do something to help solve the age-old mystery of who Jack had been. That within itself would be magnificent.

Her mobile phone rang. Picking it up, she answered hollowly. "Hello, this is Tiana."

"Ti, where are you?"

"Damian? Oh, shit, I'm sorry. There was an emergency call this morning. I forgot to call you."

"As long as you're okay. I was worried when you didn't call or show this morning. What's going on?"

Tiana closed her eyes, imagining her dark-haired friend standing and pacing. "Damian, sit down."

"How did you know?"

Tiana smiled ruefully. "I just know you well. But sit down, please."

"Sitting."

"There was another victim, Damian. It was ... it was ... Hannah Chapman."

The silence on the other end of the phone was telling and deafening. "Damian?"

"I need to go, Ti." There was a small sound. "Are you sure?"

"Yeah, I'm sure. I did the follow up on her yesterday. It hurt badly."

"Yes, I bet it did."

Tiana grunted. "Listen to me, Damian. We're going to nail this bastard. I promise. He won't get away with this. I promise."

"You better. If I find him before the police do --"

"Damian Collins, you listen to me, and listen to me closely. You know how I'm different. Don't you dare interfere or investigate. Let the police and me do what needs to be done. I know how you felt about Hannah. If it helps any, she felt the same way. She was going to come up with Felicia to be around you."

"Bloody hell, Ti!"

"I'm so sorry, Damian. I'm so damn sorry. I should be home tonight sometime, unless a break comes up in the case."

"We'll talk when you get back."

"Definitely. And Damian, I know this hurts. Trust me, I know."

"I know, Ti. Just keep safe."

"Right, will do. Talk with you later."

She hung up the phone and sighed. Lying against the back of the bed, Tiana relived the phone call, seeing what she'd messed up on. There had been no easy way to break the news, short of being there in person; and knowing Damian like she did, he wouldn't have wanted her to see his reaction. This sucked beyond anything she'd ever dealt with before. She really hated this. How could she do anything when there were no clues?

Getting an idea, she grabbed her phone again and dialed a number that had become memorized just recently. Hearing his voice, Tiana cut in. "Ian, this is Ti. I need copies of all the files on the cases so far."

"You want what?"

"All the notes compiled on the cases so far."

"Why?"

"I'm helping out."

"No."

Tiana sat up straighter. "Excuse you?"

"You're not getting any deeper involved than you are now."

"Listen up, Ian Spencer. I don't plan on doing any kind of interviewing or anything else. What I want is what you all have already done. As someone who was a victim at one time in her life, I might spot something that could be telling, but that you all might not get. That's all. I want to be kept current on things. That's all. This isn't about you and me having sex. This is about the case."

There was a hesitant moment. "Promise? I know we didn't plan to get involved, but we are. I don't want that to change, but I don't want you any deeper than you are now as a consultant only."

"Yes. I don't want to pretend to be the big, bold female detective. That's not me. What I want is access so I can see everything that's been found, all the evidence as well as the pictures of the crime scenes, autopsies, and forensic reports. That way, perhaps I'll see a pattern that no one else has seen. It might not work, but I just told Damian the news, and I'm feeling worse than helpless right now. Business is business, and our private lives are private, but I want to help catch this creep."

"As long as you don't give out the information, I'll see what I can do. You're part of the investigation team as it is, even though it's as a consultant."

"Thanks, Ian. I'm at the hotel. Saw my mum and got a Victorian trunk filled with goodies from an ancestor. I'm going to read one of her journals for a while. I'll be here if you need me."

"See you later tonight, then. Take care of yourself, Ti."

"Until later, Ian. Ta ta."

Hanging up the phone again, Tiana opened up the chest. Delving under the gown, she grabbed the journals that most interested her. She only hoped that the sensation playing around her fingertips was a true one, not a false alarm or something caused by her wanting there to be something about Jack the Ripper.

Before getting into the journals, she called for room service and changed into a T-shirt and shorts. Thanking the man who brought up the food and drink, Tiana made herself comfortable on the bed. Opening the journal to the date of September 29, 1888, she read what her ancestor had written, hoping for some kind of information.

Chapter Ten

25 August, 1888
Dear Miriam,

I'm beyond scared right now, and I daren't tell my father what happened tonight. Since I've no one else to turn to, I'm writing this to you. Perhaps with it being out on paper, I'll feel better and realize I'm being silly. Well, one can hope, right? Let's start at the beginning.

As you know, I help with the Salvation Army down in the East End of London. Though Father doesn't much like it, he does agree with me that the people there need some help and should be encouraged to try to improve their lot in life. Luckily for me, Father knows the priest who serves at Whitechapel. I often speak to him on various matters while waiting for my carriage to come take me home. Since I work into the early evening hours at times, it's the only way Father would let me continue to go to

the church, especially after those brutal murders by
that man, Leather Apron.

Today, I spoke with Catherine and a couple of
other women. I strongly counseled them against heavy
drink and to try other means of earning money.
Though I can't completely understand their
circumstances, I do know if they continue in this
manner, they'll end up dead from disease. They are
nice women, even if they are poor. Catherine showed
me a gift she got from her new guv. She insisted on me
calling her "Kate." I told her that her given name was
a beautiful name and much better than mine. She
laughed and called me "Patty" instead of Patricia. She
left me about 5 p.m. or so. I told her I hoped her new
guv would keep her safe, with the mayhem happening
out there. When she smiled and turned away, I tried
to give her the witch's blessing, but somehow I could
feel it wouldn't take.

I helped do some cleaning and organizing in
Whitechapel while waiting for my father's coach. The
father and I resumed our discussion about women's
roles in the Bible. It was quite interesting, though I do
disagree with him regarding his dismissal of the so-
called Apocryphal books. But that's neither here nor
there. As I stood in the vestibule talking to him, I
decided to look out the side window to check for the
coach. It was ten minutes late.

It was then—

It was then when I saw the face. He was grinning at me, his teeth gleaming by the streetlights. There was something inherently evil in his look. I backed up two steps, my hand clutching my heart, while my other slipped around the pendant that my mother left me for my birthday a couple years past. As suddenly as I saw him, he left.

Not more than five minutes after, the footman knocked at the church door. With him was my brother's friend, Simeon Tucker. They escorted me into the carriage. I could still feel that evil man. Yet, nothing happened. That is a good thing, considering that I'm to go back to Whitechapel tomorrow. I'm feeling foolish. It probably was someone who was trying to see if he could sleep in the vestibule of the church without being caught.

Simeon looked a bit peaked himself. Like me, he's sensitive to certain vibrations and the feelings of evil. He's been concerned about me being in the East End, considering the murders. I've told him that I can take care of myself. He still doesn't seem to believe me. Oh, well, he'll see. I can handle myself quite well.

Patricia

P.S. I've been thinking and remembering. I'm enclosing a drawing of the man as I remember him. Though the glass distorted his features, could it be possible that he's really who I think he is? I mean, the East End is no place for a man like himself. But I admit, the more I consider it, the more I realize who the man looked like. I hope I'm wrong.

* * * * *

30 September 1888
Dear Miriam,
Father has come to me, forbidding me to go to Whitechapel anymore. There has been a double murder and everyone is in an uproar. I fear the worst. Could that man I saw have been the evil man himself? I've seen the paper with the letter that's supposedly from this man who calls himself "Jack the Ripper." Such an awful name. I do hope those ladies are safe.
Patricia

* * * * *

2 October 1888
Dear Miriam,
It's the worst. Catherine is dead. They say that this "Jack the Ripper" did two in one night, killing Elizabeth Stride, as well. Nevertheless, something tells me that he didn't commit the first murder. I'm not sure. Father and Thomas have been discussing the case, though I'm not allowed to chime in. They are wrong to assume the women have asked for it. They are only trying to keep a roof over their heads. I

*almost asked what was different from Catherine and
her friends, and the women I know that my father and
brother have on the side. They think I don't know,
but considering I'm the one who does the ledgers, I'm
more aware of the money spent than they'd suppose.
Men!*

*I've contacted Libby. We must meet with as
many of the others as we can. Hopefully by doing the
ritual, we can stop this murdering beast before it gets
worse. There has to be a way to bind him and make
sure he never does this again.*

Patricia

* * * * *

10 November 1888

Dear Miriam,

*Well it's done. Hopefully our actions will help
slow or stop this killer. Father is determined to marry
me off. I know whom I want to marry, but I don't
know if he'll be allowed to come calling for my hand.
Would it be too much to ask for a man who makes me
happy? If you need to find the information regarding
the ritual used, you can check the grimoire for the
information. Everything is there, and it's hidden
where we had decided a long time ago. Thank the
gods for parents who have some respect for privacy.*

Patricia

Chapter Eleven

Tiana gasped over the revelations she'd read so far. Enclosed were various newspaper clippings of the articles published regarding Jack the Ripper, including the "Dear Boss" letter. Fingering the ancient, well-preserved clippings, she wondered over her ancestor's comments. There was more, including some private speculation regarding who the murderer was. Not once did Patricia ever use a name, though she often used other descriptives.

The only thing not in the journal was who the others were that Patricia had gathered together. There was a later reference, after the Mary Kelly murder, that the girls gathered together for something special. But there was nothing listed on what was said or done.

"What the hell was my ancestor thinking, not even bothering to leave me clues on what she and her friends did?" Tiana asked herself out loud.

"Because she feared someone would read her journals?" A male voice asked behind her.

Whipping around, Tiana stopped when she saw Ian. "How did you get in? You startled me."

He hugged her. "I got that impression. You also didn't shut your door all the way." He looked at the journal in her hand. "Been busy reading, huh?"

Tiana nodded. "Yes. Seems that my great-great-grandmother happened to be alive during the time of Jack the Ripper and, in fact, possibly saw him."

"You're kidding," Ian said, his voice taking on an odd note. She shot him a glance, but his expression was one of curiosity only. Perhaps she'd imagined the weird tone.

"Nope." She handed him the journal. "Take a look at this." While he read the journal entries in question, Tiana got up and repacked the case. When he was done, she turned to him. "Well?"

"Does she say who he is?"

Tiana shook her head. "Only by description. Plus, I can't find the picture she made of the man. It's not in this journal or the ones that come after. The only thing I can think of is that she had a second, more private journal that she used for things of a more private nature."

Ian paused, thinking. "What is this group that she was part of?"

Now it was Tiana's turn to hesitate. It was time to explain some things to him that he might not like. She sat next to him on the bed. "How open are you to things that are unexplained?"

Ian's gaze met hers. "You mean like paranormal stuff?" Seeing her nod, he continued. "Pretty open, why?"

"Our family lineage includes witches, Ian."

"I see. Were any burned at the stake?" He chuckled. Seeing her serious look, he stopped. "You're serious."

"I'm a witch, too. As are my mother and sister." Her tone was flat and unassuming.

"Define witch."

"We follow the ancient pagan beliefs. Kit actually walks both the witch and the Druid path. I'm an earth-based practitioner. Think Practical Magic."

Tiana waited as Ian digested her words. She knew it wasn't easy. Not many people wanted to understand the neo-pagan movement, considering it to be an affront to others. However, when she pointed out what religion was there prior to Christianity, it shocked many people into really thinking. Her mother called her the Instigator for good reason. Her one and only television debut on BBC channel four had been when a person claimed that a series of murders were done by Satan- possessed witches. Tiana had lost her temper and demanded that her mother put together a special on the truth about pagans and Christianity, going through history. It was the show that truly brought her mother fame, but only she and her daughters knew that Tiana's anger was the reason behind her mother's surge of success.

"I don't know what to say."

"It's okay. I do understand." Tiana scooted away from Ian, only to be caught as his hands gripped her arms.

"Don't move away."

"You need time."

"To adjust. I'm not turning away just because you're a pagan and I'm Protestant." He hugged her and kissed her deeply. "It doesn't change how I feel, just means I need to know more about what things you do." His brows rose. "You do celebrate birthdays, right?"

Tiana chuckled. "Yes, I do. Why?"

"Your birthday is coming up in a couple of months, and I have a gift idea. I'd hate to scrap it just because you don't celebrate."

"Oh, Ian, you're too funny. Yes, I do enjoy birthdays. I have eight major holidays that I indulge in. Then there are some minor ones, usually god days. But those are just acknowledging them usually."

Ian nodded as Tiana explained about the beliefs she had. It felt wonderful for her to be able to share her soul with another person. There was part of her that hoped Ian accepted her and her beliefs. Though she wasn't a devoted witch, not like Kit, she was thankful for the things she'd been taught.

"So, you're a coffee witch, just as your mother before you, right?" Ian teased.

"Brat!" Tiana tried to pop him on the arm, but he pinned her beneath him. She arched against him, wrapping her arms around his neck. "Thank you for not walking away."

"You being you isn't something to walk away from. However, it does help explain some of your pet phrases." Tiana gave Ian a quizzical glance. "'Oh, my gods,' for example."

"Oh. I hadn't thought on that. I don't even think most people hear the difference."

"I did and I wondered. But it's good to know." He kissed her cheeks, her chin, then her lips. He whispered softly, "Do you think you could deal with a slightly abused Protestant who doesn't know too much about paganism?"

"Yeah, I think I can. Let's order something to eat for dinner, and we can talk."

Ian shifted his position and kissed her again, his tongue mating with hers, his hands caressing her body, pulling her against his hardness. "How about we play, then we eat and talk?"

Grinning, she started unbuttoning his shirt. "Why Detective Spencer, I think you've got a hell of an idea."

"Thanks," he gasped as Tiana's mouth latched onto one of his nipples. "Yessss."

Tiana decided that she'd pleasure him. He was the first beyond her good friends to accept her for what she was. It made her happier than she thought possible. Could she be falling for Ian? Would it really be that easy?

Pushing away those thoughts, she concentrated on tasting Ian's slightly rough, tanned skin. He wasn't your typical Brit, as he had dark hair, blue eyes, and a ready smile. His fluency with languages was surprising and well-enjoyed. Many times they had played "Stump the Bobby" while trying to find a language in which he wasn't partially conversant. Whispering in Egyptian Arabic, she wasn't sure he was familiar with, Tiana made her way down his body, her mouth punctuating each phrase she uttered.

"*Oreedok, habibi.*" Her mouth trailed between his nipples. "I want you, beloved."

Her tongue caressed around his belly button, dipping in and out. "*Ahtaggo elayk*, Ian." Her voice was hoarse with desire as she began unbuttoning his black slacks, sliding them down his hips. "I need you."

As she eased out his erect penis, her tongue flicked across the tip, causing Ian to shudder as his hands fisted in her hair. Her green eyes twinkled at him. "What do you want, Ian?"

"You. I want you, Tiana."

"Good." Her lips sank around him, taking him fully into her mouth. His taste was pure male mixed with salt and musk. Tiana groaned in appreciation as she felt him swell beneath her touch, her fingers stroking as her mouth moved around him.

She felt his muscles clench as his hands gently urged her to pick up the rhythm she had going. Tiana lightly rasped her teeth on the underside of his shaft, grinning slightly as his moans filled her ears. Sliding him in and out of her mouth at a quicker pace, she could taste the warning that her ministrations were getting to him. Pulling her mouth off of him, she smirked. "One might think you're wanting more or something."

"Tiana," Ian growled, the sensations washing over him. "I'm so damn close, woman!"

She chuckled huskily, her own breath coming out in pants. "Are you now? I wonder if I should stop, then. I'd hate for you to go over without company." She bent her head back to the task, this time letting her tongue glide up and down the length of his cock. It twitched at her touch, and she could feel it pulsate beneath her fingers as she slid them up and down in time with her tongue. Rasping her teeth lightly over the purplish-red head, she chuckled as his hips arched upwards.

Suddenly the room spun around as Ian rolled her on her back, moving aside her baggy shorts and underwear. With a sharp plunge, he entered her easily. "Oh, you're coming along for the ride, luv. I wouldn't dare leave you behind."

Ian thrust deeply into Tiana as her body softened around his. He loved the feel of her sheath clenching his cock. This woman was so warm and giving that it amazed him that no man had claimed her before now. Anyone who had tasted her sweetness or loyalty would know that she was special.

His mouth captured hers for a loving kiss. Yes, he loved this woman. Though there were things he'd yet to share with her, he would, and soon. Though she was amazed at his acceptance of her private beliefs, he wasn't sure that she could handle his hidden secret. Not with her interest in Jack the Ripper.

He moved slowly, leisurely, while Tiana grabbed his shoulders, her body arching and joining his. "Oh, Ian, you feel so good," she whispered as her mouth kissed his jaw, his chin, and eventually his lips.

"You feel better, love," Ian retorted, his hand cupping one breast, drawing it up to his mouth as he slid into her welcoming body. She shuddered as the first series of orgasms raced through her, making him even harder. He loved that he could make her body react so quickly and deeply with his touches.

Her nipple tasted of something sweet and sultry. His mouth fastened on it tightly, suckling on it, feeling it expand in his mouth. Ian's tongue rasped against it roughly as his teeth gently nipped it. Laving his tongue against the taut peak, he switched his attention to the other nipple. Treating it with equal abandon, he felt Tiana's nails rake his back as her legs wrapped around his hips.

"Ian, please. I'm coming... Ian!" Her words were almost drowned out as he groaned while thrusting hard into her, their bodies becoming one in that moment as he joined her. His release complete, his heart opened itself to include the woman that lay beneath him.

As their racing hearts and lungs tried to regain their equilibrium, somewhere deep inside Ian, he realized that he was falling in love with Dr. Tiana Wells. Something he felt wonderful over. His only hope was that she'd understand his past and the possible sins of ancestors. Not all ancestors were worthy of respect.

Chapter Twelve

A knock at the door interrupted their romantic moment. Tiana scrambled out from under Ian as he tried to find his pants. She tried not to giggle but lost as she reached the door while wrapping her robe around herself. "Do something," he mouthed at her as he tried pulling on his slacks.

Tiana watched him bend over, admiring the tight backside of her lover. *Damn, he's hot. Can I get the nerve to tell him that one day? Probably not.* Another round of knocking on the door brought her attention to the reason she stood at the door. Carefully opening it, she saw Felicia standing there with one of her waiters.

"Felicia, what are you doing here?"

The Italian woman's grin was nothing short of wicked. "Well, I'm delivering the dinner I sent over with my waiter. He said there were noises inside but no one answered the knocking." Wiggling her brows,

Felicia continued. "So, I came to lend my service to make sure you and Ian ate food and don't subsist on other forms of pleasure."

"Brat." Ian's voice floated to where they stood. Laughing, Tiana looked over her shoulder to see Ian sitting in one of the chairs. She opened the door fully, letting in the waiter and Felicia.

"But you know you love me."

"*Te amo mi cara, perro no*, Felicia. So there," he responded with a kiss on the young woman's cheek. "What did you bring us?"

"Well, since you don't love me like you do your dear, then perhaps I shouldn't feed you," Felicia sniffed.

"Yeah, yeah, yeah, ducky. You know I love you." Ian pulled the woman down for a hug. "So what did you bring us?"

Felicia slapped his hands and smiled. "I brought you some veal fettuccini, while Tiana has one of her favorite fish dishes." She pointed to Tiana, who had taken her plate from the waiter and was opening up the dish, picking out pieces of zucchini. They all looked at her.

Tiana grinned. "What? I'm hungry."

Felicia snorted. "Things are okay with you both, yes? You know Madre is wondering about the two of you."

Ian chuckled. "Of course she is. What does she want to know?"

"Are you two an item?"

"Officially, no. Unofficially but privately, yes, indeed," Ian stated with no hesitation.

"Is this true, Ti?" Felicia asked the woman who was biting into a piece of sautéed fish.

"Uh huh." Tiana swallowed the piece and moaned appreciatively. Her eyes met his and she smiled in thanks. Then she turned to her "sister." "This is fantastic, Licia. Have I mentioned how much I need you to start making me food to freeze, so I can just heat it up and eat it whenever I want it?"

"Ti!"

Tiana grinned. "Yes, we're dating; I guess you can call it that. Tell Mama I'll come and talk to her before I leave London. However, make sure she knows I've got gelato coming to me. I'm not leaving the city without it this time."

"Sí, will do." Felicia kissed each of them on the cheek. "You catch this bad guy who hurt my new friend. Then we shall have a huge celebration for you both." Shooing her waiter, Felicia and the young man left, leaving Tiana and Ian alone once again.

They looked at each other and laughed. Tiana commented, "She's taking more and more after her mother as years go by."

Ian bit into the fettuccini. "Yes, she is. She's a sweetheart. No one realizes that there's a shark beneath those sweet waters, though."

Tiana agreed and started eating her meal. It was one of her favorites, one that her mother also enjoyed. "Tell me what's going on with the case."

"Let's wait until we're done. I hate to ruin this wonderful meal because of ugliness. Why don't you tell me more on the article you and your fellow Ripperologist are working on?"

Tiana eagerly went into the article, discussing the various factors they were dealing with, as well as how they wanted to take a new look at some of the photographs. She regaled him with some of the antics of various serious Ripperologists, as well as some of the weirder theories out there. As she went into describing some of the wounds on the victims that linked them together, Tiana stopped cold. *It can't be that, could it?* Her mind raced over some passages she should be able to recite from memory.

"Oh, my gods, that's it!" She left the table and went searching through her briefcase. Pulling out some printouts, she scanned through them and grabbed a red pen, circling certain passages.

"I think I figured out what about the murders was bothering me, Ian," Tiana said excitedly. Handing him the papers, she pointed to the names. "Those are the victims, including one non-canonical victim. Notice the types of wounds for each one. On top of that, look at where the murders occurred."

Ian pushed aside the last bit of his meal and took the papers. As he began to read the autopsy overviews that Tiana had printed up, he felt a bit lightheaded as some pieces began falling into place. Had he not seen it for himself, he'd not have believed it. "This is—"

"Spooky, beyond weird? Any other description you want to use?" Tiana picked up a book that dealt with all things Jack the Ripper and opened it to a map that had the murders plotted out. "Notice the positions of the bodies in relation to today?" She took out a map of Metropolitan London for comparison.

"Yes, I see it. Hannah was found on Hanbury Street." Ian tossed down the papers and his gaze met Tiana's. "We've got someone trying to match Jack's killing spree, don't we?"

Tiana sat down, fingering a page in the book. "Yeah. I hate to be the one to say this, but this guy has done his homework. He's gotten details that are hard to find. Most of these are not easy public knowledge. They take some digging to find." She tapped a page in the book. "See, the only thing he's not done was to do something to get the attention of the police and the newspapers. If he does that, then all bets are off. People will try to capture 'Jack.' This isn't good, Ian."

"Bugger! What the bloody hell am I doing, dealing with this? A man who has a need to re-create Jack's murders?"

"Well, it depends, Ian. The next thing that's up is the double-header. I don't know if he can pull it off, or if he'll do both."

Ian blinked and his voice dropped. "You mean the Elizabeth Stride and Catherine Eddowes murders."

She reached over and squeezed his hand. "Yes. Thing is, depending on whose view he's taking, he either will attempt the double homicide, or he'll only kill one."

"What do you mean? I know somewhat about Jack the Ripper, but I'm definitely not as up on the theories as you are."

Giving him a rueful smile, Tiana shrugged before explaining. "It's one of those fascinating things. History's mystery and all that. A serial killer that hadn't been caught. Now having read Patricia's journal, I'm thinking that she did, indeed, see Jack the Ripper. My poor ancestor could've been his victim." Sighing, she sat back. "See, some theorists believe there was no way that Jack killed Catherine and Elizabeth that night. Others have spent years trying to prove it was possible."

"What is your opinion?"

"I always felt the timing, especially in regards to how far apart the murders were discovered and the viciousness of Catherine's death, suggested that he wouldn't have had enough time to do Elizabeth and Catherine. Plus, there's that whole thing about him being interrupted. The man knew what he was doing; there's no way he couldn't have sliced Elizabeth, had that been his intent. Then there's the fact of her ex-husband knowing she was murdered before she'd been identified. Jack might've considered her a target, but somehow, I don't think he killed her. When you look at her wounds, they're not at all in the same league as the others."

"She's the one where they thought Jack was interrupted?"

"Yes. But think on that. Elizabeth's body was discovered at one in the morning. According to various accounts, she was seen with a man around eleven or so. Some claim that Louis Diemschutz, a jewelry salesman, interrupted the murder. Yet, how can that be, since it was dark, there was no noise, and the body was already on the ground?" Tiana got up and paced the hotel room. "That is another of the aspects of the case that often puzzles scholars, along with the time span. Yes, those women would sleep with anyone who gave them money. But when you consider going far from a tavern and out of sight, when everyone in the East End knew about Leather Apron, it makes little sense, unless the woman had seen the man and somehow trusted him a bit."

"That makes sense. Then you think that Elizabeth wasn't a victim of Jack's?"

"Well, we know that this person selected Martha to be Martha Tabram, who has been on and off the canonical list of victims. From that, we can see that he's already decided that he's done something other than the original, canonical list. For me, no, Elizabeth was killed by someone else." Tiana paced again, flipped to another page, and placed it in front of Ian. "Catherine Eddowes was mauled by Jack. Why? Some people claim his anger was unassuaged by his interruption of Elizabeth's murder. Yet, look at how far they were apart. Could Jack have taken the time to have gotten Catherine's trust, to take her down that quickly?"

Tiana picked up her ancestor's journal and opened it up to the page in question. "I think Patricia's insight is remarkable, Ian. I think, not only did she see Jack, but also she had a valuable clue. Jack picked out his victims ahead of time. A new guy had given Catherine a gift and was meeting her that night."

"Wasn't Elizabeth found with something, as well?" Ian asked, flipping through the pages of the book.

"Yes, flowers and a packet of cachous." Seeing his confused expression, Tiana explained. "Cachous were breath sweeteners, usually used by smokers. However, of all the information, no one knows if she was a smoker. She was a known heavy drinker and the cachous would have hidden the alcohol smell on her breath."

"What about Catherine? Do you think she was Jack's victim?"

Tiana sat on the edge of the bed. "Yes. When you consider this information from my own relative, it makes it more conclusive. I feel for her. What if she did see Jack the Ripper? I can only pray that I find that missing grimoire or journal that holds those pictures. It'd be nice to know who she saw."

Ian moved to her side and sat beside her. "I'll need to notify my superiors of the link we've found. You do realize any Jack the Ripper fanatic will be considered suspect."

Tiana lowered her head. "Including me."

"Well, I don't think you have the skill or capacity to have dealt a killing blow. Plus, we know for a fact you were in Snaith the night Hannah was murdered."

"True. I don't know how this is going to help us, but maybe it'll be a way to protect others. If he goes according to plan, we're looking at a horrific murder of one woman, possibly two. He's gone to great lengths to recreate the stabbings and cuts, Ian. He's either been getting the information how most of us have done, through the Internet or from Jack the Ripper books. There are some books that go into detail regarding the wounds, though there's no one book that has it all." Tiana shook as the realization hit her. "Oh, gods, he's going to re-create the Mary Kelly murder." Her eyes looked at Ian. "We have to stop him before that. We have to!"

Gathering her in his arms, Ian rocked her gently. "Shh, we will, Ti. I promise. We'll get this information out and make sure that no one goes out at night alone. The Jack the Ripper tours will just get a kick out of all this."

"They best get it in their minds that this man is sick. We don't know if Jack really stopped for some reason, or moved on and continued doing his deeds in a worse fashion," Tiana swallowed the end of her sentence. "He was a brutal killer who knew what he was doing, Ian. Same with this guy. This guy has some medical training; I can almost swear it."

"Shh, no more. Let it go for right now. I need to call my superiors and let them know what we stumbled across. Where can I get this information to show them?"

Tiana handed him her sheets. "I can reprint these from various sources. If you want a quick confirmation, including some autopsy overviews, you can go to casebook.org. They're the best online site dealing with Jack the Ripper. You can email the Webmaster and ask for more information that might not be listed yet."

"You're a dear to do this for us. I know it's hard for you, but I swear we'll get this Jack wannabe."

Tiana leaned into Ian, his warmth and the warmth of the pendant helping her to re-center. "Thanks, Ian. I know you'll get this guy. I'm just afraid. It's like a vision of my past coming back to face me."

"It's not. That man is still in prison. I checked on it since you and I originally talked. He isn't going anywhere anytime soon." In response, Tiana kissed Ian deeply, her arms winding around his neck.

"Thank you, Ian Spencer." Letting him go, she looked at him. "You best go down and show them this stuff. I'll go through my other things and see what else matches what's known about Jack the Ripper."

The ringing of a muted phone caught both their attention. Tiana dug out her mobile phone, flipping it open. "Hello?"

"Ti? This is Kyle. Did you come into work today?"

"No, I'm in London. Why?"

"Shit. Hold on then. The lights are on in your office."

"What?" She waited as Kyle put down the phone, and told Ian what Kyle had said. Heavy breathing hit her ear as Kyle picked up the receiver. Before she could think, her body began shaking in undisguised fear. *My office? Why?*

"Ti, you need to come back home. Your office is completely and utterly ransacked. What the hell is going on?"

"I'll be there soon. Call campus security as well as the local police force," Tiana said quietly, hanging up her phone. Without looking at Ian, she responded dully. "My office has been ransacked."

"You think by the same guy?"

"Yeah. I know my name has been used in connection with Al's in regards to the autopsies, though Al is the only one who was at the inquests." Tiana took a deep breath in, then slowly exhaled. "I bet he was searching for information on the cases. I keep nothing at the university office."

"Where do you keep your notes then?"

Tiana pointed to the laptop on the dresser. "That's the only thing I keep information on. When each case is resolved or I'm removed, I erase it completely or I give whatever documentation I have to the officials in the case."

"Do your colleagues know about the case?"

"Nothing beyond the headlines and that I've done two autopsies and a preliminary onsite examination with follow-up. I don't share details. It's one of those things that it's better to have gone through blind, not with extra knowledge. If I need their opinion, it's best if it's without any knowledge that I could give them. That way it's not tainted."

"Like double-blind studies and such."

"Exactly. After a case is over, we might talk on it all or we might not; depends on the results. Or if we're working a case together, then we'll discuss it. But with this, I've not said anything to anyone." Tiana hesitated. "I take that back. I told Damian about Hannah's death."

"That's public knowledge. Best he hears it from a friend." Tiana nodded in acquiescence. Ian continued. "I'll make sure that Metro gets the information from the break-in. Anyone whose fingerprints we should expect to see in the office?"

"Dr. Damian Collins, Dr. Kyle Mortimer, and Lawrence Tanner, our graduate student. Beyond that, perhaps the cleaning staff, though they normally leave my stuff alone, except on Fridays when I leave the door unlocked for them to clean."

Ian noted everything down on one of the pieces of paper that held information about Jack the Ripper. "I want you to keep this room. I know you'll be needed for a statement, but I'd prefer you to come back here afterwards. Who knows if the guy found out where you lived."

Tiana shuddered as she grabbed her small purse from her briefcase. "I'll stop home, get some things, and come back here. As it is, I'll be in London this week doing some consultations."

Ian knew that Tiana came to London every so often to help various police communities develop their computer reconstructions. Though forensic artists do well, with the new computer forensic reconstruction programs, you could get quicker results, which was why she'd branched out, to help make sure the science did the job just as well as artists did. She was a leading proponent in using computer graphic technology to help identify criminals and reconstruct crime scenes in order to get an accurate portrayal of what happened. He was so proud of her commitment to helping apprehend criminals however possible.

"I'm going to get this information to them. When can I expect you back here at Brighton?"

Tiana looked at her watch. It was now five-thirty at night. Counting up the travel time as well as the time spent talking to the police, she sighed. "Not until after midnight or so."

Ian pulled her into his arms, his hand cupping her chin. He slid his mouth over hers, his warm lips caressing and coaxing open her mouth, his tongue teasing hers. She moved closer against him, wanting and needing more. A small whimper erupted from the back of her throat. Her mouth sucked against his tongue, creating a more intimate caress. Finally, they both stepped back, trying to catch their breaths.

"You could easily convince me to wait until morning, Ti."

Her response was a knowing grin. What she wouldn't give to not go face this mess that awaited her. He was so good to her, so understanding, and always at her side. Like a knight in shining armor. *I could fall in love with you deeply, Ian Spencer. I really could.*

"Feeling is mutual, Ian." She picked up her purse. "Escort me to my car?"

Taking her hand, he walked down the stairs with her. "You've got your phone with you?"

"Yes."

"Call me when you get to the university and again at your home. Then call me before you leave, so I know when to expect you back at the hotel."

"Being a bit protective, aren't you?"

Ian nodded, his blue eyes stormy. "He knows who you are and is trying to find out how much you know about him. I don't want you left unprotected, but I can't do anything until I get this information to my superiors." His free hand clenched and unclenched in anger. "I would rather be going with you, but somehow I think that's not a possibility tonight."

"I know. I'm just teasing a bit. If I don't go and take care of this situation, I feel like something is trying to take over my life, something I won't let happen if I can help it. I won't let another bully run my life, Ian. I can't do that."

He took her keys from her and unlocked the door. "I know. Just be safe. Call me as I asked, okay?"

"Sure. You be safe, too, Ian. I'm not the only one in the spotlight."

He kissed her swiftly, then shut her car door. He knocked on the window. "Go," he mouthed.

Obeying him, she started the engine, flipped on the headlights, and headed home. She only hoped the damage was only to her private stuff and not the university's equipment.

* * * * *

Ian walked into the station, his serious demeanor taking many of his fellow detectives by surprise. At his query, he was told that their superior was still at his desk. Pulling out his personal family folder, Ian glanced from the notes he had to the ones given to him by Tiana. There was nowhere near as much information, but like Tiana had said, you just had to know where and how to look. You'd think he'd have more, but there hadn't been much time once he made detective. He hadn't ever seen many details regarding the killing blows, beyond the old pictures, but looking at some of the autopsy photographs, he saw the similarities. Shoving his folder back into his desk, Ian made his way to the office and knocked on Bernard's door.

"Come in!"

Ian entered and greeted his boss, Bernard Edwards. "Boss, I've got some news on the cases I've been working on."

"Sit down, Spencer. What have you come up with?"

Ian went over the various pieces of information, checking with the current autopsy reports and showing how the wounds seemed to correlate. As he put together the information in a logical manner for his boss, the growing sensation of darkness gathered at the edges of Ian's mind. *Now I know why this sounds so damn familiar; but still, there's so much more to worry on. And this time, it's not whether my ancestor was a serial killer.*

"This is damn good fieldwork, Spencer. You and Dr. Wells did a great job on this. Now we know a bit more on what this maniac is using as his basis." Bernard's face was serious. "The question now is, what does this mean for the general public? Last thing we need is for our killer to follow Jack exactly and send notes to the press."

"I know, sir. I'm not sure that he's going to do that. If anything, he might just keep quiet." Ian looked his boss in the face. "There's been a break-in at Dr. Wells's office at Sheffield University. She's gone back to see what was done and will be filing a police report with the local authorities."

"Do you think she's a target?"

"I'm not sure. But it's well known that Dr. Wells is a Ripperologist on the side. It wouldn't surprise me if this maniac learned it and wants her to not realize what's going on."

"Yet, that's the case. You both picked up on it."

"After we started talking about the Ripper case, sir."

"Do you think this incident is related to our case?"

"Definitely."

"She's going to be coming back to London, correct?"

"Yes, sir. She's staying at Brighton Square."

Bernard nodded and looked at the various pieces of information. "We'll have to call Scotland Yard and see if any of their people have any ideas on how this guy will work his next move. If you and Dr. Wells are correct, his next victim will be murdered at Henriques Street and another at Mitre Square. We can post extra patrols of those areas to deter our killer."

"That would help. What about the public, sir?"

"I'm not sure. I'll talk to the commissioner, and we'll make a decision from there." Bernard took the papers and placed them into a file folder. "Type up your official report on the information you've just correlated and then—"

The ringing of the phone startled both men. It was rare for the phone to ring this late in the evening. Picking up the receiver, Bernard barked into it. After listening, he spoke quickly and then hung up. "Where's the telly?"

"Sir?"

"You need to see what's just been announced." Both men walked into the main room, where only a couple of detectives were working. A couple detectives were straggling in from the break room. Walking into the dull, pale, beige-colored room, they found the men watching the news.

"Tonight's headline news is out of the history books. The known gravesites of Jack the Ripper's victims have been desecrated. In fact, according to mortuary officials, two of the skulls were put together to show what happened to Jack's victims. Now back to Sheila Evans."

Bernard and Ian shared a look. Neither said a word, though both were horrified on what it could mean. Though the cemeteries were in London, they weren't in the Metropolitan London area, which would put it out of their jurisdiction. Ian rubbed the back of his neck and tried to think on how to handle the media coverage.

"This is going to make it worse, if we go public."

"Think that was the killer's intention? To make it almost impossible for us to go public with the information?"

Ian considered his boss's words carefully. A half-formed thought filled his mind. "I'm not quite sure, sir. I think he's trying to distract us all from the next murder. I'd still recommend increasing patrols in Mitre Square, as well as Henriques Street. Beyond that, I don't think we can go public with this information. From the reaction of the media, this will make it even worse if we bring up the Jack the Ripper similarities."

"Agreed, Spencer. When the good doctor returns, let her know I'd like a full report in the morning. I'm going home to try to get a couple hours of sleep, before my wife decides I'm expendable."

"Tell Emmy I send my best wishes."

"Will do. See you at eight in the morning." Bernard picked up his things, locked his office door, and left the building. Ian watched as his boss left, the man's shoulders seeming to carry a weight not their own.

Ian went back to work, trying to put together the information in a logical, coherent picture. Tiana could probably do a better job of it, he thought, but she was traveling and wouldn't be back until much later. Contenting himself that the killer had come back to

London and wasn't at Sheffield University, Ian started typing.

* * * * *

Tiana drove as fast as the speed limits allowed, plus a bit over. "How dare that creature attack my office? Did he think it would scare me away?" She seethed with barely restrained fury. Pulling out her phone, she dialed Damian's number. As she cruised, Tiana needed to make sure things were really okay.

"Hello?"

"Damian? This is Tiana. Did Kyle tell you what happened?"

"Yeah. Your home is okay and untouched. I've not been at the office yet. Do you need me to show up?"

Tiana smiled at her friend's compassion. "Would you? I know you've got other things to do, but I'd appreciate having someone else besides Kyle there."

"What is it between you and Kyle, anyway? I've always meant to ask, but until now, had no reason to."

Tiana sighed. *How to explain it? We're like siblings who could easily kill the other if left alone too long?* "Honestly, it's a simple matter."

"Then how come I've never been told?"

"Because it makes me, and him, look childish," Tiana admitted with a low chuckle. "Kyle knew of my

Jack the Ripper interest, and he's always made it a point to say that Jack was helping out the population by ridding the world of those lower-class prostitutes who might've been infected with syphilis and were drunks."

"And you went off on the sanctity of life, I take it."

"Correct. Of course, this was before Kyle knew about my own personal experience with mad killers. When he and I went at it one time, while you were on holiday, I lifted up my shirt and told him what kind of crappy-ass person he was really defending. Since then, we've been at quiet loggerheads."

"I see. But still—"

"You're also my best friend, Damian. I'd like you there. You know my stuff as well as I know yours."

"When will you arrive?"

"Should be there in about sixty minutes or so."

"See you then, Ti. Just be careful."

"'Til then, Damian. Ta. Thanks again." She closed her phone and placed it on the passenger's seat. Feeling better about Damian being there, as well as the police, Kyle, and the university security staff, Tiana felt some tension leave her.

Now she just had to figure out why the killer had targeted her office. Somehow, she felt like there was something missing.

Chapter Thirteen

Tiana took tentative steps toward the building that housed the forensic computer lab and her office. Part of her dreaded seeing the mess her office would be in. Lights were on and there were various official vehicles in the parking lot. Seeing Damian on the steps, Tiana strode forward, glad that her friend was there.

"You okay? You look really pale."

"There's more going on than you realize. The case I'm helping with has crossed lines in many ways, Damian."

"You'll explain that comment after. Let's go get this dealt with first."

Hand in hand, they walked down the corridor. Damian's firm grip kept Tiana from letting her imagination and fear get to her. As it was, she was worried on how big of a mess her office would be and if there was anything else damaged. As they neared her office, they could see flashes of bright light and people standing around outside.

"Excuse me, I'm Dr. Tiana Wells. May I ask what's happening?"

One tall gentleman announced himself first. "I'm Detective William Much. My partner is taking photographs of the scene, and we've started dusting for prints. If you'd be so kind as to answer a few questions, I'd appreciate it, Dr. Wells."

Tiana nodded and led the man to the break room. Damian followed, since Tiana refused to let go of his hand. When they all sat down at the table, Tiana spoke first. "Can you tell me if there's been any damage done to the computer or other equipment?"

"There were books cut and thrown around, and your desk was emptied, but it doesn't look like anything else was touched." Detective Much took in Tiana's startled glance. "You expected more damage?"

"Yes." Tiana looked thoughtful as she considered her next words. "They knew what they were looking for, then."

"Seems to be that way. We know you're working on a case for the London Metropolitan Police. Any chance this is related to that?"

Damian interjected. "Too bloody likely. The police department never considered that mentioning her name might put her at risk."

Tiana patted Damian's hand. "It's okay, Damian. That's part and parcel of our jobs. Sometimes we get publicity, some good, and some bad. This time, it was bad."

"Correct, Dr. Wells. I know that they wouldn't have said anything if they suspected something like this would've happened. Any ideas on why?"

Rubbing her forehead, Tiana tried to consider how much to tell and what to withhold. At that moment, her phone chirped. Giving a look at the officer, Tiana answered it. "Hello?"

"Why didn't you call to tell me that you were okay?" Ian asked.

"Because there hasn't been time. I'm in the middle of speaking to the lead officer on the case."

"Put him on the phone. I need to speak to him."

"Righto." Tiana held out the phone to Detective Much. "Detective Spencer from the London Metro would like to speak to you."

She tried to piece together what was said by Ian, but the other police officer was circumspect in what he responded to, keeping everything vague or grunting. Shooting Damian a look of frustration, Tiana massaged the pendant to try not to lose her temper. When pushed, she knew she could be quite volatile. This was ranking up there as one of those moments.

Finally, the detective said goodbye and closed the connection. "Detective Spencer was a great help to the investigation. Everything we find will also be sent to London Metro."

"I see. Do you have any other questions, Detective?"

The detective asked her a few more questions regarding who had been in her office and who had keys, as well as access to her computer. Tiana answered to the best of her abilities, trying to remember anyone who'd been in the office since she came home from holiday. When she was done answering, the detective nodded and jotted down some notes. "That's all I have for now, Dr. Wells. I do appreciate all you've done to be cooperative. My partner should be done, and then we'll be able to let you go in and see what's missing and what's not."

At that moment, a tall, blonde woman, wearing a dark brown pantsuit with a badge at her waist, entered the room. "Will, everything is completed."

"Great, Sarah. Dr. Wells, would you come with us and see what's missing?"

Tiana and Damian followed them to her office. They stepped aside and Tiana entered, the feeling of violation growing, against her stern control. Her desk chair was sliced and torn apart, and her books were everywhere. Pages were ripped and sliced out. The contents of her desk were overturned onto the floor. This was almost as bad as being raped, in Tiana's eyes. Her professional world was slowly crumbling before her very eyes. *Don't give in, Ti. Go on. Find out what has been taken. You know something doesn't look right.*

Tiana knelt near her bookcases and started straightening up the books that were scattered on the floor. As she tried to place the books back where they belonged, her brain started the tally work on the cost of replacing those that were damaged beyond recovery. Getting the small three-shelved bookcase organized, she turned to the detectives and named three books that were missing, unless they were under the rest of the papers.

Damian entered the room. "Let me help. I'll get the papers together and hand you books, Ti." Quietly and swiftly, they worked as a team as the others watched in amazement at how unemotional Dr. Tiana Wells was over this intrusion of her life. Damian knelt next to Tiana, handing her the books, but said nothing. She gave him a slight smile, thanking him for his help.

As she finished each shelf, Tiana listed the titles of each book missing. From each shelf, there were at least two books missing. Then she got to her collection of Jack the Ripper books. Mentally, she catalogued the books she'd taken with her, then tried to piece together the books that were missing. *Too fucking many of them are gone or trashed beyond compare. Dammit all to bloody hell!*

"I'll have to type up the list of books missing on this shelf. This is my private research shelf, with books dealing with a specific topic."

Detective Sarah Swentiboldt grinned. "Dr. Wells, I've read your work on that topic, if you're also known as 'Bones and Groans.'"

Tiana glanced at the female detective. "Why, yes, I am. And you?"

"I'm 'Evidence and Fax' on the message boards."

"Ah, good to finally meet you in person." Tiana grinned. "I'll call out the titles. Most of them are on the suggested reading list."

Damian looked at Tiana. "What the hell are you two talking about?"

Tiana tried not to sigh at Damian's question. "Detective Swentiboldt and I are part of the same online message boards that talk about Jack the Ripper."

"Oh. She's as bad as you, you bloody Ripperologist?" Damian teased. "Does she rope people into listening to her latest ideas?"

"Nah. She is a great moderator, though. Even better, she keeps a lot of us from forgetting methodology when we start getting a bit fanciful."

"You don't seem to be affected by that as much as others though, Dr. Wells."

"Tiana, please. Well, I guess it's my training. It's so ingrained into me that I sometimes think I do things according to the scientific method because I can't break out of the mold." She chuckled. Calling out titles of books, she grimaced over other books that would need replacing. Lucky for her, she had gotten duplicates of most of the books in her office. They were either in her home or in her car. The killer couldn't know about her private collection, as she always said her books were in her office when she visited the message boards. Not even Damian knew that she had a second set of the missing books. There were a couple she hadn't managed to get copies of, but with time, she could replace them.

When she was done, she turned to the detectives. "That's it on the books. I'll have to look at the desk stuff and see what was taken."

"Seems like he was mostly interested in destruction."

"Definitely." Moving her mouse on the mouse pad, her computer logged into the system and turned on. Tiana was amazed because she always turned off the office computer. "The killer tried logging onto the uni system. I turn my computer off daily. I hadn't used it on Friday, so it shouldn't have come on."

"Did he manage to get in?"

Tiana pulled up the history and the spy program she'd put on her computer to monitor use. "Not into the uni mainframe, but he did try searching files on my hard drive. He wiped out three files, but I have those backed up and locked away. However, all of my Jack files are missing. According to my program, he copied them onto disk and then wiped them out. I can recover them as I make backups, but it'll take a while."

"Methodical and meticulous, Dr. Wells. That will make it easier for you to get things back in order." Detective Much noted down what she said. "Anything else?"

"Nope. That seems to be all. Why such a fuss over my private research? It's not like I know who Jack the Ripper is. Bloody hell. At the most, I can only get rid of a couple of suspects."

"Really, Doc? Definitive proof?" Detective Swentiboldt asked.

"Yes. Not just timelines, but also physical evidence. Hamish McGowan and I have a couple of articles we've been putting together. The first one comes out in next month's journal. The second one is in the works."

"I can't wait to read it. You and Dr. McGowan do great work. Even Peter can't refute it when you get into your expertise."

"But he does try. He's so into his theory that he doesn't see how the evidence proves him wrong. But that's a human failing. We underwent a huge review on the upcoming article. People were beyond picky on it. I think a lot of that ended when I finally gave in and told them where I got the evidence, as well as sent them the letters of verification."

"This will be a doozy of an article, then. I can't wait. I wish we could've met under different circumstances, Dr. Wells, I mean, Tiana."

Tiana shook the officer's hand. "Me, too. Perhaps once things calm down, we can go out for lunch and spend some time talking shop -- Jack the Ripper, that is."

"I'd enjoy that." The detective handed her a card. "Here's my number and email address. Contact me when you're free, and we'll arrange something."

"Thanks. You can email me or call me." Tiana handed her one of the cards that hadn't spilt onto the floor. "It's nice to finally put a face to the name. Hopefully, this is nothing more than just a prank by someone who wants Jack the Ripper to be unsolved forever."

Tiana didn't believe what she said, but she smiled at the detectives. Inside, she was still trembling and needed to release the built up tension at seeing the mess of her office. When she turned, she saw Damian finish putting the papers in various piles on her desk.

"You can come back and do this another time. At least the worst of the damage is cleaned up. The rest can wait until later."

"You okay, Tiana?" Kyle Mortimer stepped out of the small crowd that was still there.

"Where were you?" Tiana asked, a shiver going up her body that she couldn't explain or control. Something about the way he looked at her made him seem menacing, though his words were mild.

"Been talking to another detective on what I found, where, etcetera. You know how that goes."

"Oh."

Kyle's eyes swept over the room. "You're missing things."

"Yeah, my books about Jack the Ripper and some others."

"Told you that it wasn't worth digging into the past to find out answers that weren't meant to be."

Damian interrupted. "Shut up, Kyle! Ti doesn't need this from you right now. How would you be feeling had it been your office that had been vandalized?"

Kyle bowed his head, his face flushing. "You're right, Damian. I'm sorry, Ti. What can I do to help?"

Tiana sighed. "Nothing right now. It's as clean as I can get it. I need to head back. I'm due to be in London all next week for consultation work."

"That's right. You've got two talks you're giving, plus you're doing some other stuff, right?" Kyle asked.

"Yup. I should be back here Thursday or Friday. I might take one day to go to my mum's house."

Damian slipped his arms around Tiana and hugged her. "That might be a good idea. Isn't your mum going on a trip soon?"

"Yeah. It'd make her day if I go and spend time with her so she can gloat she'll be seeing Kit before me."

"Have your mum give Kit a hug for all of us," Kyle injected.

"That I can do." Tiana sighed and shut down her computer. "Okay, I need to head out again. Kyle, thanks for keeping a heads-up and noticing what happened."

"Anytime, Ti. I just wished I'd have seen the guy who did this."

"Well, I'm glad you didn't. He could've killed you and I'd have been devastated."

Kyle hugged Ti. "Just remember to keep yourself safe. You're going to be at your office in London this week, right?"

"Yeah. It'll be the easiest way to get in touch with me if you can't reach me by phone."

"Take care of yourself then, Ti. See you when you get back." Kyle walked out, leaving Damian and Tiana alone.

"Ready, Ti?"

Tiana watched Kyle leave, feeling something cold swirling around her. It was like a whisper of a thought, a cold, dark idea. Something she couldn't quite put her finger on. Turning to Damian, she flashed him a small smile. "Yeah, let's go to my place so I can get more clothes together for my London stay."

"Good. Then I can quiz you about the Detective Spencer who is being very protective of you."

"Umm, butt out, Damian."

The dark haired man shook his head. "Hell no. This is too great. I think you found someone you can trust enough to protect you." His eyes took in Tiana's blush. "You're blushing. You like him!"

"Bugger! Come on, Damian. Follow me in your car. I'll explain things while I pack, okay?"

"Done."

* * * * *

At Tiana's place, Damian asked questions while Tiana packed. She placed a couple of phone calls, letting people know where she'd be, as she answered him. Making sure that she had everything needed for a week in London, she faced her friend.

"Well?"

"Well, what?" Damian asked, a smile playing on his lips.

"You know you've got a comment somewhere you want to make." Tiana tapped her foot impatiently. "Just make it. I can take it."

219

"You're in love with Detective Ian Spencer."

Tiana's jaw dropped open. "I am... I am... not!" Damian's chuckle caused her to stamp her feet. "I am not in love with him. Just some major lusting."

"You're going to take him to meet your mother, the Grand Dame Witch, and you're denying you're in love with him? Who are you trying to fool?"

Tiana slumped on her bed. "I don't know if I am. I do love him. He makes me feel things I haven't felt in a long time, Damian. However, being in love? I'm not quite sure yet."

"How so?"

Tiana waved her hands around. "It's hard to explain. I know he's hiding something in his past from me. Occasionally, he's talked and mumbled in his sleep about a family skeleton that he's got to keep hidden. I've not dared to ask him about it yet. He doesn't trust me like I trust him."

"Well, ask him. Maybe he needs help in revealing it. Perhaps what he considers a family skeleton is, in fact, nothing of the sort."

Tiana considered what Damian said. Could that be the case? She wondered. Could he be hiding it because he thought his family's past would be a barrier between them? She'd told him her deepest secrets; he should realize that nothing in his family's past could make her run away from him. What's past was past; it didn't affect their lives now.

"You might be right, Damian. I'll think on it and see what to do."

Her home phone rang, causing them both to jump. They looked at each other in surprise. Who'd be calling her now? Picking up the phone, Tiana answered. "Hello, Wells residence."

"Dr. Wells? This is Inspector Frederick Saducci."

"This is a late call, Inspector. Are things okay?"

Damian's eyebrows lifted. "Inspector?" he mouthed.

"Scotland Yard," Tiana mouthed back. She lifted her hand upwards and signed the letter J. "Interested in Jack." Damian nodded his understanding.

"You've not yet seen tonight's news?"

"I'm sorry, Frederick, but I had a break-in at my office, so I've not had time to watch the news."

"Are things okay, Tiana?" The inspector's voice filled with concern.

"I'm fine, and the things broken can be replaced. What was on the news that would make you call this late at night?"

"The victim's graves of Jack the Ripper were disturbed, Tiana. He unearthed and placed two skulls side by side. We don't know which belongs to which grave."

"Bugger!" Tiana thought about the implications of that move. "What is going to happen to the remains?"

"That's why I'm calling. Remember our phone call a couple of weeks back? I spoke to some others and asked if this wouldn't be the best time to do as I had wanted, to make plaster casts of the skulls and do reconstructions of what they looked like, so we can honor their memories."

"And?"

"The skulls will be brought to you as soon as you wish."

Tiana rocked on her heels, shock warring with fascination. "Have them delivered to Dr. Damian Collins at Sheffield University. I'll be in London this week, giving talks. But as soon as he has made the casts, he'll bring me both the skulls and the casts to work on."

"Do you know how long the process will take?"

"The cast-making takes a couple days, as the lasers must measure everything. Then once the numbers are checked and rechecked, the copies can be made. Then come the parts I excel in. I'll do a clay model, while Dr. Collins does the computer version. That way, you'll be able to see both for comparison."

"That would be more than acceptable. Do you have time to do this?" The inspector must've known of her involvement with the London Metro police.

"Yes. I'm only on call for Metro. Plus, for something like this, I'd make the time. We can start at first light, if you wish. Dr. Collins is here and I'll give him the basics."

"Thank you so much for your cooperation, Dr. Wells. Security will be maintained?"

"No one will know who the skulls are, if that's what you're asking. In addition, we have a special vault that only Dr. Collins and I know the combination to. Therefore, it limits who can go in there."

"That'll reassure my superiors, Tiana. I'll have the skulls ready. Dr. Collins will need to sign for them with some identification."

"I'll make sure he's aware of the process. Thanks again for this opportunity, Frederick. I'll do a good job, I promise."

"I know you will, Tiana. Thank you for taking this call so late at night."

"Good night, Frederick."

"Good night, Tiana." He hung up his end as she hung up hers.

Quickly, she related all the necessary information to Damian, without telling him details that might skew his perception of the computer reconstruction he'd be doing.

"Once the reconstructions are done, what then?"

Tiana knew the answer. "The remains will be reburied in their proper graves. That's the whole purpose, to give a face to those who were mauled by Jack the Ripper."

"Sounds good to me. You want me to keep the skulls in our special safe, then."

"Yeah, that way no one is tempted and no one knows who they are. I don't like that my Jack stuff has been touched. The graves of his victims have been ruined, and the skulls are at risk if anyone decides to do more damage, you know? They said that it'll take a while before they can get everything back in order, and they'll be waiting for confirmation from us on which skull belongs to which victim."

"Yeah." Damian looked at his watch. "You best be heading back if you hope to return to the hotel before one in the morning."

"Ack! You're right." Tiana tossed some other things into her suitcase, including some items she normally would've left at the house, but with the increased risk, didn't want to take any chances. "I need to get another set of copies of the ruined books, as well as the missing ones. Good thing I always buy duplicates."

"Bloody good thing. You're being awfully calm over all of this, Ti. Are you sure you're okay?"

Tiana nodded. "I know I need to cry and scream, but not right now. Later, when I'm alone in my room and can let the adrenaline slip away."

Damian hugged her, whispering that he'd be there if she needed him. Tiana hugged him back, letting his warmth imbue her with strength to get back to London.

"Thanks, my friend. I'm not sure what I'd have done without you being there, Damian."

He took her suitcases to the car and packed them in the trunk, as Tiana locked the door and activated the security system. Sighing in relief that her home hadn't been touched, Tiana gave her friend one last hug. "I'll ring you in the morning. Okay?"

"Sounds good. If I don't answer, I'm at the lab. Be careful driving back to London, okay?"

"Always."

They hugged, and Damian kissed Tiana's forehead. She watched him leave in his car, then followed him to the major highway. When she was on the road back towards London, she called Ian. After telling him the latest in updates, she turned on her Clouseau CD and let the music fill the car, helping her to let go of the emotions that had built up in her. "*Altijd Meer en Meer*," she sang with the song, as she flew down the highway.

Chapter Fourteen

Her phone rang insistently as Tiana buried her head under the pillows. "Go 'way," she mumbled as she tried to will the phone to shut up. It kept ringing. Reaching for it, she flipped it open and growled, "What do you want?"

"Hey, is that any way to treat the person who had chocolate waiting in the hotel room for you when you arrived?"

"Ian?"

"Who else? Still sleeping, sweetie? It's almost noon. You want to meet me for lunch at Arrabiata's?"

"When?"

The chuckle on the other line let her know that she was quite amusing. "How about around one, since you probably need a shower as well as some caffeine. There's a carafe of chocolate mint on the table for you."

"Bless you. I might let you live for waking me up." Tiana sat up and stretched, a yawn emerging. "When did you leave this morning?"

"Six-thirty. I had to be in for an eight o'clock meeting. Are you doing any better?" His comment reminded her of how she fallen apart in his arms over her destroyed office. The lovemaking had been soft, gentle, and reaffirmed that there were more important things than possessions. She needed to feel loved and cherished. Somehow, Ian knew that and made sure that her pleasure came before his. Her love for him had grown at that moment, when he asked her if he could be inside her, asking for permission to take what she offered him freely. A smile crossed her lips in remembrance.

"Much better. I think you drugged me. I never sleep this late."

"You needed it, after the miles you drove and all you went through. Have you heard from Damian yet?"

Tiana looked at her mobile and flipped through the messages. "Nope, not yet. He'll call me once he gets the package."

"Let me know if he needs any help. I can see about sending someone down to protect him."

"Nah, I got connections I can rely on, if that's the case. Plus, I've got money to buy him a bodyguard."

"Rub it in, why don't you?"

"Only if you're willing to rub back," Tiana teased, her voice turning husky with desire.

"Evil woman, you know I can't leave work right now. One o'clock at Arrabiata's?"

"You're on. I'll have our booth reserved." Tiana hung up, dialed another number, and spoke in Italian to the woman on the other line. Within minutes, things were taken care of. All she needed to do was shower and change into clothes for lunch. Tiana headed for the shower. First things first; the coffee would be welcome once she had her eyes opened correctly.

* * * * *

Pouring a cup of chocolate mint coffee, Tiana groaned happily at the aroma. She sipped it cautiously, the coffee still deliciously warm. Sending a mental note of thanks to the coffee gods and Ian, she began dressing. Between sips, she managed to dress in khaki pants, a royal-blue shirt, and khaki ankle boots. After brushing her hair and putting on minimal makeup, she felt almost human.

Her phone rang just as she packed her small purse. "Hello?"

"Ti, Damian. The package has arrived. I'll start the process tonight, with Lawrence's help. I should be able to give them both to you come Tuesday. You'll be at your office?"

"Righto. Works for me. Make sure it's to arrive after one in the afternoon. I've got a morning talk with University College of London's anthropology department."

"Will do. Talk to you later, Ti."

That one detail taken care of, she left a message for her mother and then headed out to the Italian restaurant. Though things weren't as bleak as they'd seemed last night, she knew they were still not the best they could be. Yet, unlike five years ago, Tiana felt that no matter what happened, this time she had people to turn to, in case she needed them. People like Damian and even her sister, Kit, were support systems that she never considered before. Things seemed a lot more together. For that, she knew she had Ian to thank.

Reaching the doors of the restaurant, she felt like she was being watched. Looking around, she saw nothing out of the ordinary. *Just leftover crap from last night, that's all. There's no way he'd know where you're at, or stalk you. Calm down, Ti.* She walked into the cool, slightly darkened room.

"My daughter, you are here," Isabella said, hugging Tiana close. "I heard the good news about you and my son dating. This is a good match. I had thought on introducing you both, but this is so much the better. He makes you swoon, yes?"

Tiana put up her hands in surrender. "If I promise to tell you everything, can we go sit down and wait for him? He's coming to lunch. I'm here a bit early so I can explain things before he arrives, and to place our orders." She shot her adopted mother a wicked grin.

"Ah, you want to make sure he gets what you wish for him to eat."

"Yes. I want *cannelloni alla parmigiana* for him and *salsiccie e fagioli* for me. For dessert, how about *budino di ricotta y grostoli?*"

"*Bene*, daughter. I think he'll enjoy that, as he's never had those dishes. I'll tell Felicia and the other chef."

"Thanks, Madre." Tiana sat back in the booth, waiting for Isabella to come back. She knew that the woman hadn't gotten all the information she wanted yet, and Tiana hoped that by ordering those dishes, she'd get a bit of respite. It wasn't that she didn't want to tell her anything, but it was still too new for her to just bare all.

Sure enough, the woman returned. Tiana answered some of the questions, occasionally exclaiming, "Madre!" in a slightly shocked voice over the woman's comments. At one o'clock, Ian strolled toward the back of the restaurant. He spotted Tiana at the same moment she saw him.

"Ian, over here."

He kissed Isabella's hand. "Madre, you look beautiful today."

"You are a scoundrel, my son, but a gracious one."

"*Grazie*. It's Papa who encouraged me, you know."

"*Sí*, I know. Your meals will be here shortly. I hope you enjoy them and the dessert that follows."

The woman left them alone. Tiana sipped on her juice as Ian drank from the water goblet in front of his plate. "Our meals are already ordered?"

"I took the liberty this time. That way, neither Madre nor Felicia could come up with something to keep us here for them to question us at their leisure."

"Smart woman." His eyes raked her from head to toe. "You look a lot better today."

"Thanks. Damian called. The delivery is made. I should be getting the skulls by Tuesday night."

Ian nodded. "That's good. You know, my boss would like you to speak on the case to the other officers involved."

Tiana blinked and frowned. "Why? You know everything I do."

"Because you're the expert; I'm not."

"Ian—"

"I know, Ti, but he's right. It'll help if you come in and give a short, sweet lecture about the similarities and what to look for. We both know that the guy will

231

strike again. Patrols in the crucial areas are increased, but the odds are in his favor, Ti."

She sighed. "You're right. When does he want me to come in?"

"This morning. But since I explained the circumstance, how about tomorrow morning?"

Tiana rubbed the bridge of her nose, trying to think. "I've got a talk in the morning at ten. It'd have to start at eight and go no longer than nine. I need to get to that talk at University College of London."

"Understood."

The waiter arrived with their food then. Digging in with a relish she hadn't realized she possessed, she almost inhaled her food. The flavors exploded on her tongue as she enjoyed her meal. It'd been a long time since she had the traditional Italian dish of fagioli. It had been one of her favorite comfort foods when things went bad.

"This is fantastic, Ti. Thank you. I've never had this before." Ian resumed his eating.

Neither of them spoke much as they enjoyed the food and the low Italian music playing in the background. The aromas of fresh Italian cooking wafted their way every so often. When they both pushed their plates away, Tiana grinned.

"I've not eaten like that for a while. I guess the case has been getting to me more than I realized. I almost overdid the comfort food. This means I need to go for a walk later."

"Just be careful. I'd prefer you to wait for me."

"It'll only be at my mother's. I'm going to see her today, before her trip. While I'm there, I'll probably wander her gardens a bit."

"That's okay, then." Seeing her look, he explained. "I worry about you, Tiana. You're important to me, and that this maniac knows who you are... I don't want to put you at risk."

"I understand and appreciate it, Ian. Just realize that I'm not used to it. Be patient with me, okay?"

He kissed her cheek as their dessert was brought out to them. The cream cheese custard was decadent and rich, while the crisp cookies were a light, airy counterpart. They dug into the custard and sighed as the chocolate flavor rippled across their taste buds. "This is a dessert for gods," Ian moaned.

"Uh huh. Indeed. It's why I asked for it. It's creamy, chocolatey, and made for this moment."

When they were done with their dessert, Ian leaned against the back of the chair. "I think I might explode."

Tiana chuckled and poked him lightly. "Ate too much, dear?"

"Oh, yes, but it was so hard to stop."

"Naptime?" Tiana wiggled her brows.

"I wish. I've got another case I'm working on, besides this one. I have to head back, but I needed this break with you." She smiled at him, coating him with her love.

"You're wonderful to have thought this up."

Ian placed money on the table as they headed for the door. Isabella nodded from her seat and waved goodbye to them both. Tiana grinned. "You know you're the only person who can get away with that."

"Yes, and I do it every time I'm there." He headed back towards the hotel. "How are you doing on your article and such?"

"Haven't given it much thought in the last twenty-four hours. I'm going to bring the journals to Mum and see what she says."

"Think she might know about the lost journal?"

Tiana nodded as they entered the hotel and walked up to her room. "Yes. She would've been the original recipient of knowledge, so it's a logical assumption that she'd know about the lost journal."

"Makes sense to me. Anything I can do to help you out?"

"Anything from the trace evidence unit?"

Ian shook his head. "Some trace fibers, maybe a hair, but otherwise, nothing major."

"Dammit. There's got to be something that will help give us an idea of who it could be."

"They're working on it. There was something embedded under Hannah's nails, so they're hoping the information pans out."

"Great. Hannah's killer needs to be put away for life, if not killed," Tiana grated between teeth. "Do we know when she'll be buried?"

"Keith says it'll be this Saturday. You're going to go?"

"Yes." Tiana opened the hotel room door and swiftly stuffed a couple of books and papers into her backpack, as well as a chamois bag. Opening a small box on the dresser, Tiana removed a small metal rod and put it in her purse.

"Ready to go to your mum's?"

Tiana nodded, her eyes scanning the room to see if she'd forgotten anything. Feeling ready, she turned. "The quicker I get out there, the quicker I can get back. Tomorrow is going to be an early day for us both."

"Let me guess—breakfast at Slice of Americana?"

"Yup." Tiana waited for Ian, then closed her door, listening to the lock click into place. Checking the knob, she nodded. "Let's go."

Ian walked her to her car. "You sure you don't want company?"

Tiana chuckled. "What excuse would you give your boss?"

"Bugger, there is that slight problem." Ian kissed her. "Be careful, Ti. I'll see you tonight. I should be in by eight."

"I should be home by then. Mum will want me to stay for supper. Plus, it's the night of the full moon, so we'll probably share in a moon ritual together."

"Ah, then that silver metal thing was your wand?"

Tiana looked at Ian in surprise. "Yes, it's my metal one. I didn't bring my oak one with me. How did you know?"

His grin lit up his face. "I've been doing some research into your beliefs, to understand things. Samhain has just passed, so your next holiday is Yule, right?"

"Correct. You get a gold star." She kissed him and caressed his cheek, reveling in the strength within him. "Would you like to celebrate it with me this year?"

"I'd love that, Tiana. You've got your coat with you?"

"Definitely. I've noticed that our warm weather has gone and left us." Tiana pointed to the duster that lay on the back seat. "I hate coats, but it's a necessary item here in Britain."

"See you tonight, luv."

"Ta ta, Ian." She pulled out of the parking lot and glanced in her rearview mirror, his image stamping itself in her memory. Waving, she pulled out onto the road and sped off toward her mother's home.

"Here's hoping that Mum has some idea on where the damned grimoire is. It might help us with this blasted case," Tiana muttered as she negotiated traffic.

* * * * *

Knocking at her mother's door, Tiana was surprised when her aunt Trisha answered the door. "Trisha!" Hugging the older woman, Tiana walked inside. "What are you doing here?"

"It's a full moon tonight, Ti. Surely you didn't think that your mum would do her rituals alone."

Tiana smacked her head. "I forgot. Where is she?"

"Where is who, dear? It's good to see you, Ti." Her mother walked down the stairs and hugged her daughter.

"You. I've got questions to ask you, and I need answers." Looking at her aunt, then at her mother, she saw her mother's almost imperceptible nod. "It's about Patricia's journals."

Trisha ushered them into the kitchen, where the woman efficiently began brewing coffee for them and tea for herself. Tiana grabbed the mugs for them and brought out the creamer and sugar. "What about them, Ti? Jean told me that she'd given them to you."

"Did you know that Patricia saw Jack the Ripper once?"

Both women stared at Tiana, giving her their full attention. "What did you just say?"

Tiana pulled out one of the journals and opened it to the bookmarked page. "See, great-great-grandmother Patricia saw a man in the window the night that Elizabeth Stride and Catherine Eddowes were murdered. She, in fact, thinks that it was Jack the Ripper." She left unsaid that their ancestor thought she had recognized the man.

Both women read the journal entries in question as Tiana poured the coffee and the tea into the proper mugs. Stirring in milk and sugar, she sat back down. "Where is the grimoire that Patricia refers to, Mum?"

"I don't know, Tiana. Trust me, if I did, I'd have given it to you with the trunk. If it was the coven's grimoire, you and I both would've seen it."

Aunt Trisha looked pensive and thoughtful. "I wonder—"

"Wonder what, Aunt Trish?"

"Remember as kids, we were taught to keep a private journal, the mirror book, to only be used rarely? Could this be the book Patricia is talking about? Something she'd only share with the closest of friends? Those who also worship the God and Goddess?"

"Good questions, Trish. You're the one named for Patricia. What do you think she'd have done with the book?" Jean asked, reaching into a nearby drawer and taking out paper and pens. She began doodling as they all talked.

"She'd have put it somewhere safe. It was only to be shared in the direst of needs. If she made one to stay close to her friend, Miriam, then it would've been sent back and forth between them, so it'd have to be in code."

"Bugger. So it's possible that Miriam's family might possess the book, right?" Tiana asked, sipping her coffee and watching her mother. She knew her mother had fallen into a trance state, and didn't want to break her concentration.

"What does Patricia say in her last journals, Ti? Have you looked to see if there's further mention?"

Tiana blushed. "No, I hadn't gotten that far." She handed one of the journals to Trisha and took the other. They started reading through various entries. Tiana remarked at one point, "You know, Grandmum Patricia was quite a woman."

Trisha laughed. "Yes, she was. Ahead of her time in some ways, and yet, a throwback in others. Depends on how you want to look at it. Hmm, in this one, she says that she's received the book back from Miriam and was glad to add to it, but it couldn't be this journal, as there's no correspondence from Miriam."

"So that confirms the theory of another book being used between them." Tiana skipped to the last journal with the dates 1913-1914 on it. As she skimmed over the writing, Tiana stopped and dropped the journal. "No. Please, no."

Trisha placed her hand on Tiana. "What is it, Ti?"

"She saw her own death. The last entry is written the night before she died." Tiana closed her eyes, trying to regain her balance. "Patricia wrote to Miriam that the book was where it could easily be accessed but not seen on sight" She inhaled and exhaled slowly. "She also named that her death would be avenged by one of her descendants."

Trisha gasped. Jean opened her eyes and handed the picture she'd drawn to Tiana without looking at it. "Like this?" Jean said, her eyes full of compassion.

Tiana glanced at the picture and pushed away from the table. "Yes," she hissed. "Mum, how did you—"

"You know my gift doesn't include me being able to direct things to that strong of a degree."

Tiana lowered her head to the table, Trisha caressing her hair. "It'll be okay, Ti. Remember, this is in the past. Whatever it was, Patricia went to her grave knowing that her family would always remember and honor her."

Tiana handed the paper to Trisha. "Tell that to someone who wasn't named in the damned journal or by this paper of mum's. According to Patricia, the one who helps solves her murder is also the one who recaptures Jack the Ripper, which isn't fucking possible!"

"Language, Ti!" Jean snapped.

"Mum, with all due respect, I don't care. Jack the Ripper is dead and gone. There's no way on this earth that he can be alive again."

"Are you so sure, Ti?" Trisha asked, her brown eyes scanning the picture that Jean had drawn, comparing it to the description that Patricia had put in her journal entry. Turning the page, Trisha gasped. "You know, Miriam wrote an appendium to the journal, Ti?" She handed the journal to Tiana.

Dear Patricia's descendants,

You're probably wondering what happened to her after her vision. It came to pass that when she left for Cornwall, she disappeared, only to be found the next day, just as she predicted. In this journal, she doesn't name the man, but she and I both know that he was Jack the Ripper. Now, you must know the truth regarding what was done those many years ago.

Patricia, I, and others are witches. Though it's not looked highly upon in this time, we haven't forsaken our heritage, though we've combined it with some Christian rituals. Yes, you've probably read how the occult has made a comeback, but it's not a true renaissance to the true path. When Patricia saw Jack the Ripper that one night, we decided that we had to do something. Our group tried to stop Jack the Ripper when he was at the height.

Did it work? According to this journal, no. He was tormented and moved locations, which protected us all; but at the end, he killed my best friend in the world. I sit here looking over her child, Margaret, and I worry on if this all will last into the next generation. Not having her mother will cause her problems, but I believe her father will ask me to help. Patricia and I swore an oath when were children that if anything happened to either of us, we would never forsake the children. All would be trained in the ways of the witch.

I share in your sorrow. Patricia said that one day, one of her descendants will release her from the darkness that killed her, and also stop the entity called Jack the Ripper. If this is you who are reading this journal, know that you are strong and can defeat him. Bind the dark energy as you'd bind anything that needs to be put away. Use the binding spell that is in the grimoire, either the coven's or the private mirror book. The mirror book has not been moved from where Patricia said she left it. I will never touch it again in this life.

Blessings be upon my best friend and her descendants. May the Lord and Lady look after you always.

Miriam

Tiana laid the journal down and rubbed her head. "Is this even fucking possible?"

Jean read the entry upside down. "You mean possession? Yes, you've seen samples of it at various times in your life. Why?"

She knew the look she gave her mother was one of pure misery. "Because if your picture is right, I'm in deep shit, and worse, the killer isn't imitating Jack the Ripper—he *is* Jack the Ripper."

Jean sat up and tilted her daughter's chin so their eyes met. "Get over it, Tiana. We all get asked to do something beyond what we can handle. We don't know for sure that this is Jack the Ripper you're fighting. All you do know is that this crazy is re-enacting Jack the Ripper crimes. There is no other evidence."

Tiana sighed. "You're right, Mum."

"Of course I am. I'm better than that. Now listen, it's about time for the full-moon ritual to be started. We'll make a light supper; we'll talk on other things, and perhaps even on receiving wisdom; then we'll begin the ritual. You will stay for the ritual, Ti."

She nodded, part of her mind thinking on the picture that her mother had drawn. Jean didn't often go into the trances that produced automatic writing or drawing, but sometimes when they happened, they were very accurate about things that had happened or were about to happen. Tracing some of the lines, Tiana looked at the brutal picture. Though the face of the man was obscured, the picture was detailed in the murder of their ancestor and then Tiana being attacked by the same man.

On the left, Patricia was being slashed from behind. She was fighting well, but she knew she was losing. The glint of the knife was before her, and she knew it was the end. On the right, Tiana was fighting off someone with a knife, as well. The description in the journal was an accurate portrayal of Tiana, something that she couldn't deny. Letting out a deep breath, she put the picture away in the journal.

"I need to find that missing journal."

Trisha smiled and stood up. "You will. It'll come when it's ready to be found. Now let's make some lemon drop soup for supper."

Tiana and Jean shared a look. "Trisha, why do you always cook for us on ritual days?" Tiana asked.

Trisha gave her a grin that showed that Trisha and Jean were sisters. "Because I'm the chef of the family. Do you think your mother can really cook anything beyond the basics?"

"You have a point," Tiana chuckled softly. "I'm going to walk in the garden for a bit, then I'll come help with food preparations. Okay?" Seeing both sets of eyes on her, she added, "This will also give you two time to consult without me being here, and you can amaze me with your wisdom."

"Smart ass," Jean retorted, pushing her daughter out the back door. "Go walk the garden. It's not much during the late fall, but there is still some beauty left."

"I know, Mum. I do love you." Tiana hugged her mother and then, grabbing her mother's coat hanging by the door, she went outside.

Bundling up, Tiana felt the air getting chilly. Perhaps this was a sign that England would receive its first snowfall of the year.

The garden still had some late blooms in it, and in the waning sunlight, Tiana enjoyed the bursts of color amid the greens and browns. Her mother had always had a way with plants. Kit and she could kill plants without a problem, but their mother had a talent for making them flourish. As Tiana walked the small path past the flower entry, she inhaled the clean, crisp air, and then released the tension that had been building in her since reading those last journal entries.

Her mother's garden was a place of gathering energy. In the spring and summer, it was the height of power. Now was the time of the Crone, thus a time to gather energy inward for the darkness that might gather around. To learn from the year and look forward to the spring. Touching various plants along the spiral route, Tiana felt energy build while tensions melted away. As she neared the center of the spiral, Tiana found the small bench and sat there, meditating over everything going on. Her mind flashed a picture of Ian, and she smiled.

"Oh, Ian. How do I explain this all to you? Can I explain this?" Tiana asked softly into the waning day. She saw the glittering of the stars as they started winking in the sky. "Perhaps it's best to not explain everything yet. Just as you have your secrets, I think I need to keep this one."

Finding a sense of peace in the garden, Tiana stood up and retraced her steps back out of the garden. A sense of peace and acceptance came over her. Whether Patricia's vision, or her mother's, was true or not, panic wouldn't help. Accepting that it might happen, and being prepared, was the best way to be. Making the mental resolution to begin preparing herself physically for what might come, Tiana strolled back to the house.

As she opened the door, the first snowflake landed on her face. Tiana smiled up into the night sky. Though she wasn't a fan of snow, the first snowfall of the year was one of her favourite moments. "Thank you, Cerridwen and Arianrhod."

The delicious smell of lemon drop soup beckoned her into the warmth of the house. Tiana hung up her mother's coat and rubbed her hands together. "What can I do to help?"

Jean and Trisha stood next to each other in front of the stove. Jean responded first. "You can set up the living room with the candles and such."

"You don't want help with cooking?"

"No. Go set up for the ritual. Then you can come back in and tell us about the man that you're wanting me to meet."

"Mum, you so need to stop that."

"Stop what?" Jean grinned with a slightly mischievous tilt.

"Picking up surface thoughts."

"It doesn't happen often. Deal with it. Now go do as I say."

"Yes, Mum." Tiana walked past the two sisters and headed into the living room. Once in the great big blue room, she grinned. When her mother had redecorated this room, creating an outdoor scene around all the walls and the deep-green carpet, many people had wondered what she was thinking. Tiana had realized her mother was bringing the outdoors into the room. Even the furniture looked as if it belonged, each representing something found in nature—a stone chair, a billet of leaves, even a bush with flowers. It gave Tiana a sense of peace each time she spent time in this room.

Opening up the cabinet next to where the television was hidden, Tiana pulled out the candles and holders for the night's ritual. She also gathered the pinecones and the incense burner. Placing them at the cardinal points sacred to both belief systems, Tiana felt a sense of peace and purpose begin to build in her. Now she understood her mother's pushing her to do this.

After setting the last candleholder in place and putting the silver candle inside, Tiana smiled. Everything was ready for the ritual. The altar was in the cabinet below the television. Taking advantage, she pulled it out and set it in the center of the working circle area. After checking that everything was there, including the family grimoire, Tiana headed back to the kitchen.

"All done. Anything else I can do for you both?"

Trish pointed to the kitchen table. "Have a seat. It's quiz time."

"Can we skip this part?"

"Nope."

"Who is this Ian person?" Jean asked without preamble.

Tiana raised her brow. "Now, I know you don't have that kind of information, Mother."

"Ha. I keep tabs on you. You've been seen talking with a Detective Ian Spencer, Metropolitan Police. What's between you and him?"

Tiana turned towards Trisha for help, but found that her only aunt had sided with her mother. "Yes, tell us more about this man. Is he a good man? Does he practice the old religion?"

Cupping her head in her hands, Tiana moaned goodnaturedly. "You won't leave me alone or let me eat if I don't fess up, huh?"

"You got it, toots. Come clean, and I'll make sure you're fed," Trisha teased.

Tiana spent the next fifteen minutes or so answering questions about Ian and her feelings for him. When she mentioned that he was holding back things from her, she admitted she was worried that it was something that could hurt them both.

"But aren't you also holding things back, Ti?" Trisha asked.

"What do you mean?"

249

Jean interrupted. "You're not going to tell him what Patricia's journal said, or about the picture I drew."

"No, I'm not. He's just now learning to accept some things. He's not quite ready for the full force of these things."

"What if his life, and yours, depends on him accepting it?"

"That won't happen, Mum. We both know that."

"You best learn to see with your eyes wide open, Tiana. What you're doing right now is fooling yourself. Do you want him to be killed because you refuse to let him know?"

Her mother's words stabbed at her. Could she be taking that kind of risk, by not sharing? The whole thing sounded farfetched. Perhaps if things begin turning into something more, she'd tell him. Until that time, she decided it was best to not tell him.

"I'll tell him things as it becomes necessary. I want this to work, Mum. I do love him. Losing him because of being able to do things, like calling forth the last memories of dead people when I touch their skeletons, or the fact that sometimes I get visitations from people, isn't something I can easily share."

"I know, Tiana. I've taught you to be circumspect in your dealings with nonbelievers. If this Ian is that important to you, you need to tell him some of these things, so he won't be completely freaked out when you go into a trance, or you scream because you're watching how someone died."

Tiana closed her eyes. "You're being rude."

"No, I'm being damn honest here, Ti. I love you, but there comes a time when you need to let that person in and trust them to not leave you."

"Like with Dad."

Jean sighed. "Your father has his own abilities. He just couldn't accept that I don't use my abilities for the betterment of myself, but instead use them for helping others."

"Is that really why you and dad broke up?"

"You were only ten when we divorced, Tiana. Kit was only three. What do you remember of the two years before we moved to England?"

Tiana thought on it. "I remember fights, screaming, and crying. There was one time, Dad cut my thumb and captured the blood in a cup for something."

Jean nodded at her daughter's memory. "That was his last try to bind me to him. He knew I had the talent to do what I'm doing now. But for all your father's goodness, he had a blind spot when it came to being told no."

"Yeah. I learned that over the years. I love Dad and he's mellowed out a lot since Lori came into his life."

"This is true. But he tried using yours and Kit's blood that night to bind me to him and to keep your gifts from being your own. I broke that spell midway through and took you both that night. Later on, when forced, I had to give up Kit to your dad. By then, Lori had come into his life. That was the only reason why I let Kit leave us."

"Kit wondered why you let her live with Dad. She knew you loved her."

"Kit and I talked this out about three years ago. Her powers are like your father's. I couldn't but give her the basics of those gifts. She needed to be trained by him to learn control. Kit has strong psi talents, Ti. So much that they sometimes overwhelm her. It's why she deals with dead people, doing excavations."

"They don't speak with her?"

"No, that is your gift. For her, they speak in other ways, but not where they overwhelm her." Jean glanced at the clock. "Time to eat. Then we can each take a bathroom and wash up. Ti, your ritual things are still in your room."

"Thanks, Mum." Tiana clasped her mother's hand. "I want you to know, I'm glad you forced us to see Dad after that first year. Sometimes, he had scared us, but it was because he didn't have a teacher to help him with things, did he?"

"Your dad's parents didn't realize that sometimes abilities skip generations. No one had seen his abilities in over two generations. They'd forgotten the training. Luckily enough, Lori was trained and able to help break some of the wrong habits that I couldn't." Jean ended the conversation by bringing out the bowls and scooping the soup into them.

Tiana inhaled the delicious aroma, sending Trisha a smile. "Thanks, Aunt Trisha, for being here tonight."

"Anytime, Ti. I'm glad that some things could be cleared up. Personally, I think that we're in a crucial time. Even in my meditations, I've felt tremblings of power being shifted. Just be careful over the next couple of weeks."

"I will, I promise."

"Take up your edged-weapons practice again."

"Trisha!" Jean snapped.

"Jean, I won't hush on this." The woman looked at her niece. "Listen to me; I know how you feel about holding weapons again, but something in me says you need to do this. It's time to get past what happened and to go back to using those weapons and keeping up your skills in edged-weapon combat."

Tiana felt the world tighten around her as her heart began tripping over itself. "Aunt Trish --"

Two hands gripped hers, bringing her back. "I know that's a hard concept, Tiana. But I honestly think that if there's any truth in what your mum has seen, as well as what I feel inside, you'll need any edge you can get. And you promised your Mum you'd try, but you've not done so. You need this, Ti."

Tiana nodded. "Okay. I'll try. I can't guarantee anything, but I'll try."

"Good. Now eat your soup."

The women ate their soup while staying away from loaded subjects. Once they were done, they adjourned upstairs to change for the ritual. Tiana wished Kit or Kyrie were around to talk to. Though Trisha was six years younger than her mother, they were still part of the same generation. Sometimes, they just didn't understand her life or the parts of her that had changed since she almost died.

Taking off all her clothes, Tiana slipped on the silver velvet robe. It amazed her that her mother hadn't told her to take all of her stuff home with her, but she was glad. Though she had a set of robes and the like at home, it was nice to know she had things here if she ever needed anything. She went to the closet and lifted down a small cedar chest, and after putting in the combination, lifted the lid.

Inside sat Tiana's ceremonial dagger, as well as a silver cord. Taking both, Tiana slid the cord around her right wrist, tying it securely. The dagger, in its sheath, went into the deep pocket on the left side. She sat on her bed and said a small prayer to the gods. As the waft of cinnamon, cloves, and sage hit her nostrils, Tiana knew it was time to descend.

Chapter Fifteen

Descending the stairs, Tiana met up with Trisha, dressed in a similar robe, but dark gray in color. "I thought you were the mother tonight?"

Trish snorted. "You're home. That makes me, though younger than your mum by a couple of years, the crone."

Tiana shook her head. "Sometimes I don't understand how the two of you can easily switch faces of the goddess between you."

Trisha's arm went around Tiana's shoulders as they descended the last stairs together. "Many years of practice. Just as you and Kit did before you went off to uni."

"Ah. Whereas we've stopped due to distance, you two have continued on."

Trisha inclined her head. "But of course. You have the role as maiden."

"At least I don't have to be a literal maiden for the role," Tiana smirked.

"Yeah, then none of us would qualify." They both entered the living room, where the candles, altar, and incense were ready for the ritual. Jean entered the room from the kitchen, bearing bowls of water and flowers. She placed them on either side of the main cauldron. Jean nodded to Tiana and Trisha, each who took up residence at the northern quarter of the circle.

Using her lighter, Tiana began the first part of working the circle by lighting the chocolate-brown candle that represented Earth. "I call upon the element of Earth to attend our workings, lending us potency and stability for what we do."

Trisha followed Tiana as they went widdershins—clockwise—to stand before the blue candle in the eastern quadrant. She lit that candle, speaking, "I call upon the element of Air to attend us, lending us comprehension and discernment."

Jean joined them as they stopped at the crimson candle in the southern position. She lit it and spoke, "I call upon Fire, that which is sacred to Brigid, to attend our workings. Guide us and aid us with strength and power."

The three women then walked to the western quadrant, where the turquoise candle waited. Tiana lit the candle. "I ask Water, that which leads to Otherworld, Summerland, and Avalon, to attend our work. We ask that it grant us intuition and mental clarity as we do our ritual."

Together they spoke. "Tonight we celebrate the full moon, ripe as a mother's womb, shining brightly in the night sky. For the moon symbolizes our other self, the shadow self that isn't easily seen, unless you know how to look."

They approached the altar together, Jean in the middle. She lit the first candle, a pure white one with figures carved on it. "We call upon our Patron deities to guide us and watch over us as we work. Bless our ritual and be welcome here."

Trisha lit the yolk-yellow candle. "Today is Sunday, a day that represents hope, beauty, creativity, and guardianship to all workings, the oak moon of November."

Tiana lit the candle that had swirls of various colors running through it. "This candle represents us, the petitioners, that our workings will be heard, and is the focus for our work." She moved to the side, allowing her mother full use of the altar. She grinned as her aunt did the same.

Jean spoke as she took a piece of paper out of her robe pocket, along with a dark green oil crayon. "The full moon sees many things that were hidden and are now visible. We ask that Selene and Nut, goddesses of the full moon and sky, help us in revealing where we can find the answers to our questions."

Trisha took the paper and crayon. Writing quickly, she spoke. "I wish to know where the best source of protection for my niece Tiana is. I fear this case of hers, and I wish for her to have protection."

Jean passed the paper to Tiana. She blew her aunt a kiss. "I wish for my mother to have a safe trip when she goes to see my sister. I also ask for knowledge that might help me right the wrong done, if it's in my power."

After adding her request, she handed the paper to her mother. Jean wrote and spoke. "I ask that Selene and Nut help bring understanding to my daughter as she walks this path. Though the end is unknown to many, I know that she has the skills to do what's needed. Please guide her and Kit, as they both seek knowledge and understanding."

The paper crinkled as Jean put down the crayon and held the paper over the petitioner flame. "Let our requests be heard, let knowledge be ours. Just as many consider the oak tree sacred, let this time of the oak moon bless us as well. I give our requests over to the elements to be considered and duly acted upon with the deities."

The paper caught on fire. Jean dropped it into the waiting bowl. As it burned to an unrecognizable crisp, Jean placed her fingers in the bowl of water, then let the droplets fall onto the burned ashes. "Air to carry our magick, water to clarify."

Trisha dropped a couple of dew-covered flower heads onto the ashes. "Earth to bring stability."

"Fire to bring about cleansing and to further the power of our magick," Tiana concluded, lighting the sage incense.

"So as our will pushes our words to magick, so let the elements and deities guide us as well," they all said simultaneously. "Full moon, shining bright. Lovely lady of the night. We work not for personal gain. Our goal is to right wrong's covering stain."

"I am Artemis, the young huntress maiden, whose light is bright," Tiana invoked, taking out her silver wand and holding it up in the air. "I am the crescent moon that lights your way in the dark."

"I am Selene, mother goddess of the full moon, who shines brightly tonight." Jean held up her pale ash wand that seemed to twinkle in the candlelight. "Your way is now clear for you to see."

Trisha held up her darker wand, not quite as bright as the others. "I am Hecate, the crone goddess of the dark moon, in which energies are worked in secret and are re-energized. In accordance to your request, I shall reveal what has been hidden."

Each of them sat down, in their own thoughts, allowing the power of the magick they built to envelop them and see what insights could be received at this moment in the circle. For Tiana, it seemed that pieces of the puzzles started moving in ways she hadn't expected, including some movement of friends and family. She watched as overlays of Patricia and herself meshed and melded together. At that moment, Tiana felt her great-great-grandmother's spirit meld with her own. "*I'm with you, Tiana, my child. Know that the journal is within your reach, in a place you've seen but not touched.*"

The swirling energies slowly seemed to work to a point, and then calmness descended. Tiana nodded toward her mother. She was prepared. She had to be to face what was ahead. She bowed her head in thanks to those who helped her tonight with their insight.

Jean stepped forward and said loudly, "We thank you for answers and for the revelations of this night. As tokens of affection, we leave you the flowers, the spring water, and feathers from a falcon. Gracious ladies of the moon, we thank you."

Tiana walked to the western candle, blowing it out. "Thank you, Water, for the clarity you imparted. May we use what you've granted in the search for what is right."

Her mother blew out the southern candle. "Many thanks, Fire, for your strength and power. May we be able to use that energy when necessary."

"Gracious Air, thank you for bearing our magick and giving us discernment." Trisha extinguished the candle in the east.

All three women met in northern quadrant. "Thanks to Earth for keeping us stable and grounded as necessary, to receive what was given to us." Together they put out the flame of Earth.

Thus completing the ritual, the three ladies hugged and made their way into the kitchen. Trisha was the first to speak. "That was wonderful. I'm so glad you came over, Ti."

"Me, too. I've missed working with you and Mum. You did great leading, Mum."

"Well, considering I'm one of the leads for the coven I'm part of, it's a good thing." They all laughed. Jean continued, pouring a glass of lemonade for each of them. "You were very smooth on your transitions. I know you don't work with a group usually, so seeing you flow with the ceremony was wonderful, Ti."

Tiana blushed as she took a sip of her drink. "Personally, it was like I never left home. It's been a while since I felt that comfortable. I could definitely feel the working of the lunar energies."

Her aunt pulled out a covered dish from the oven. "Me, too. I brought over a stew that'll help restore us after using so much energy." Trisha paused and tilted her head. "You best call that man of yours so he doesn't get upset, Ti."

Ti looked at the clock. It was after eight and she remembered her words to Ian. Grinning at her aunt, she picked up the cordless phone and dialed Ian's cell number. When he answered, she spoke. "Hi, Ian." She listened for a moment. "I'm fine. We just finished doing our ritual and are eating supper. Once that's done and I make my goodbyes, I should be back at the hotel by ten or so."

"Don't rush on my account, Ti." Ian's voice sounded resigned. "Seems that someone figured it would be a good idea to attack a bunch of people with mace tonight, so I'm still doing the paperwork on that case."

"Ugh. You okay?" Tiana noticed that her mother and aunt were drawing closer, as if to listen to his words.

"Yeah." He paused. "Do me a favor tonight, Ti. Stay at your mother's."

"Why?"

She felt him hesitate, as if he didn't want to reveal why. The moment he decided to tell her, she felt his warmth wrapping around her. "Because, for some weird reason, I don't want you at the hotel room. I can't explain why, just that I think for tonight, it'd be safer."

"Hold on a moment." She covered the mouth of the phone. "Mum, can I stay the night?"

Jean nodded and lifted a brow at the phone. "Sure, what's wrong?"

"Ian's got a feeling and would prefer me to stay here."

Jean smiled and held out her hand. Reluctantly, Tiana handed her the phone. "Detective Spencer, this is Tiana's mother, Jean Merritt."

"Hello, Ms. Merritt."

"Please, call me Jean. When did you get this sensation about wanting Tiana to not come back?"

"About half an hour ago. I knew I was going to be running late, and the thought of her being alone in the hotel room made me nervous. I'm not sure why."

"You've got a good sense of intuition, Ian. I'm glad you're learning to trust in it and are open to what Tiana believes in." Jean pushed away Tiana's grabbing hands. "Listen well to those feelings, Ian. Sometimes they're the only things that help us to tap into our natural abilities that seem to be like magick. It might be that your subconscious picked up on something that your conscious hasn't put together yet. Tiana will stay here tonight, and if you'd like, you can come here for breakfast."

Tiana interrupted. "Mum, I've got a lecture to give in the morning."

"That would be great. We have to leave early, as Tiana's talking to the Metro force around eight-thirty."

"Not a problem. I'll have breakfast ready for you both. My sister, Trisha, will probably be here."

"Is this a 'meet the family' thing, Jean?" Ian asked.

Laughing, Jean handed Tiana the phone. "He wants to know if this is his way of meeting the family."

Tiana shook her head at her mother. "You're incorrigible at times, Mum." Speaking into the phone, Tiana answered Ian. "Yes. This is one of those things. Don't worry, Mum doesn't bite often; and lately, she's been quite mellow."

"What do I need to bring her, Tiana?"

"Anything you think she might like. Personally, I'd not bring her anything, but then again, I'm her daughter."

"I'll think of something. You sleep well tonight. I'll miss you, Ti." His voice dropped low. "I'd best get this done so I can get up early tomorrow."

"You dream sweet, Ian. See you in the morning."

"Night."

"Selene's blessings, Ian." Tiana hung up the phone. "Seems that since I'm here, it's time to party."

Both older women grinned. "Food and movies; this is gonna be great!" Trisha said as she handed a bowl of a thick stew to Tiana. "It's venison stew."

"Mmm, tastes great," Tiana commented as she took a small bite. "Then again, since you're the senior editor of a cooking magazine, I'd hope you could cook."

"Brat."

"What we watching?"

Jean swallowed a mouthful of the flavorful stew. "I've got some of the latest stuff from Hollywood, or we can watch a Pieter Aspe movie."

Tiana glared at her mother. "You mean to tell me that you were able to get one, when I've been waiting to get to Belgium to buy a copy?"

"I'm good like that. Pieter sent it himself. He knew that I wanted to see it, so he sent it as a birthday gift. He's such a good author, to keep track of his fans."

Tiana growled. "I could hate you, but considering I know you're going to let me borrow it after, I won't." Trisha's laugh joined in with Jean's.

"You're just jealous."

"Damn straight. I love his crime-fiction novels. It's not fair you've got the first one turned into a movie on DVD, though."

"Sure it is. Fair in that I'll share it with you."

"Yay!" Tiana grabbed her bowl and glass to head into the living room. "Let's clean up everything so we can watch it already."

"Yes, dear," Jean chuckled as she and Trisha followed Tiana to relax after their night of work.

* * * * *

He had noticed the increased patrols, but it wouldn't stop him. It hadn't done so ages ago, nor

265

would it stop his progress now. As he looked up at the full moon, he realized something had happened.

"I don't know what's pricking at my spirit, but I'm not going back," he muttered as he walked along the street. "There's no way that I'm going to go back to that hell."

Sensing someone was watching him, he slid deep into the shadows, his eyes darting around. Finally, he spotted her. *Oh, look, a female cop on patrol. How sweet. How utterly brill! This will cause an uproar like no other. That's it, my dear, come my way.*

The female officer spoke into her radio, then moved forward. Adjusting his positioning, the man smiled. "How lovely this will be --"

Then he stopped. Looking up at the moon, he decided that he'd wait. Something didn't seem quite right. He could wait until another time to kill this one. Observing her might be fun. Sliding off into darkness, the man waited and watched. Soon. Soon he'd make the entire city afraid.

Chapter Sixteen

Ian shook his head at Tiana as they sat in the car, heading back to the hotel. After an early-morning breakfast, Tiana had given a quick, in-depth talk about Jack the Ripper and his crimes.

Once the meeting was over, Ian took her back to the hotel to grab her materials for her talk at University College of London. After that, they wouldn't see each other until Wednesday. Ian was off on Tuesday, but he had a prior commitment to see his folks.

"I never got a chance to ask you, but what did you think of my mum?"

"She is as colorful behind the scenes as she is on screen. I really liked her," Ian responded with a smile. "I wasn't sure what to make of her at first, but she was grand, Ti."

She smiled at him, leaning over and kissing his cheek. "Thanks. I do love my mum. She isn't the usual garden variety of mother, but she was perfect for my needs," she said. "Well, most times she was." They both laughed.

Once at the hotel, they kissed and parted. "I'll call you tonight and tomorrow. What time will you be back from your London office, Ti?"

Blinking, Ti tilted her head and thought on that. "I'm not sure. You've got the address. If I'm not at the hotel, you can find me at my office. If I've got the skulls by then, I'll be working on them nonstop. My goal is simply getting it all done so the ladies can be reburied with dignity again."

"Sounds like a plan, darling," Ian whispered as he caressed her cheek. "Just be safe. I could feel your mum's concern and worry for you. So, trust me, I'm worried enough myself."

"I'll be fine. Either Kyle or Damian will bring the skulls. You won't have to worry on anyone else trying to come near me."

"Okay. Call me tonight?"

"About nine?"

"Great. I'll talk to you then, luv." Their kiss was one of emotions that neither seemed ready to state out loud to the other, but linked them together even more. When they pulled back, they were both gasping for air slightly.

Tiana watched Ian leave and then left for her talk. Such was her life.

* * * * *

Tuesday

It was an office day, so Tiana forced herself to get up, instead of sleeping in. Sleeping was for those who could afford the time, or for those who stayed up too late on the phone with men. The latter was her, she acknowledged ruefully, grumbling, as she got ready for work. She normally didn't open her office until ten in the morning, but today, she knew her time was a bit rushed. There were articles to work on and the last of the bog people to deal with.

Brushing her hair, Tiana grabbed her long coat. Luckily, her office wasn't too far away from the downtown area. She grabbed her briefcase, the corner of it catching on the fabric on the inner area of the Victorian trunk. As it ripped, Tiana heard the thud before she saw something glimmer past her eyes.

Putting down her briefcase, she examined the rip made by her briefcase. Her fingers traced the discolored wood area while picking up the small, bound journal that was wrapped with ribbons. Curious, she undid the ribbons and carefully opened up the first page of the book. "*This mirror book*

269

belongs to Patricia Grace Lester. Only those who wrote this book or are descendants may read the secrets inside."

Excitement reverberated deep inside Tiana. *This is it! I've found the mirror book!* Her fingers traced where the lining ripped away, where the small, long book had been easily hidden in the side panel of the lid. "Damn, you are good, Patricia. I promise I'll help solve your death and the deaths happening now. I'm not too sure what this all means, but I bow to the wisdom of the ancestors."

Placing the book in her briefcase, she then closed the trunk and locked it. Thrilled with her find, Tiana almost skipped past her car as she itched to read the book that had been lost. Mentally, she sent silent thanks to the elements and the deities for blessing her in this way. The ride to the office wouldn't take long, except she had to get breakfast. Damian had called the night before and told her that Kyle had business in London, so he would be bringing the skulls to her. Though Kyle had no idea what the packages were, they both speculated that he'd be tempted to look. Damian assured Tiana that he had done his usual trick of taping everything, to the point of needing scissors and a knife to get through to the boxes.

Tiana smiled at them laughing over Damian's idea of creating havoc, as she pulled into the small parking lot at Slice of Americana. Pain sliced at her heart as she walked toward the entrance. A new waitress greeted her. She asked to speak with Keith when he had a free moment. Sitting in a nearby booth, she watched as the woman approached Keith to tell him he was requested.

She lifted her hand in hello and the man was there instantly. "How are you doing?" she asked softly.

"Coping. I have a hard time that she's gone, you know."

"Yeah, me, too. You have no idea how hard it is for me. She and I talked almost nightly."

Keith nodded and squeezed her left hand. "Take off your coat and I'll make you something to eat."

"I wish I could, but I've got to open up my office today. Can you make me a take-out box?"

"Sure thing. I'm glad you came in, Ti. I don't blame you for what happened, and I was afraid you'd blame yourself over Hannah's death."

Tiana lowered her face and said nothing. Keith left her, murmuring he'd give her something that would perk her up. The new young waitress brought her a travel mug filled with coffee. "Thank you," Tiana said, her mind swirling with images of Hannah and Annie Chapman. Somehow, things were coming to a head and she planned to make sure that the killer didn't escape punishment as Jack the Ripper had so many years ago. It was as if he was recreating the

271

murders in order to prove he could do it again, just has he had so long ago.

"Here you go, Tiana. This should keep you full for a couple of hours." Keith handed her a bag with two containers and a special thermos. "The thermos has a new coffee blend for you to try. Let me know what you think. I'm considering adding it to the main list of coffees I offer."

Tiana shot a look at Keith. "I'm intrigued. I'll try it and let you know. How much do I owe you?"

"Nothing. Consider this my cheering up delivery for you."

"You don't need to do that," Tiana injected.

"Bah. I can do as I wish. Now, go, get to work." Keith shooed her out of the diner with a hug. "Call me and we'll talk a bit when you get time."

"This weekend, probably. I've got two projects going and a couple of other things to finish this week if possible."

"Sounds good. Take care of yourself, Tiana. We'll talk then."

Tiana got into her car, the aroma of food wafting inside. Digging into the bag, she opened up the smallest box and saw a Boston crème donut and other types of donuts inside. "I think I love you, Keith," she mumbled as she bit into the Boston crème. "Oh, yeah, this is heaven." Reasserting her normal routine, Tiana buckled up, carefully pulled out into traffic, and made her way to the office while polishing off the donut. As she waited at a stoplight, she listened to the BBC news on the radio, debating whether or not the British government was truly any different than the American one.

Deciding that governments were all a bit warped, Tiana licked her fingers as she went forward. Taking in some of the headline news from around the world, she made mental note to call her sister sometime this week to make sure she was doing fine in Egypt. Of course, that her sister almost looked Egyptian was one of those things that defied all explanation. Kit always said it was because she was meant to be there. Tiana always figured that Kit was reincarnated Egyptian royalty. Then again, Kit never denied that possibility. Grinning, Tiana pulled into her parking space on Dorset Street.

Though her office happened to be in a small building, Tiana loved it. She had bought a good portion of the first floor and had set it up as almost a twin to her office in Sheffield. The only difference was that the outer office had a place for a secretary, who was busy doing work as she entered.

"Morning, Marnie. I've got some donuts, if you're interested," Tiana stated as she hung up her coat.

"Thanks, Dr. Wells. What do you have?" The young woman had been one of Tiana's students and was doing the secretarial work on the side while she worked on her master's degree in anthropology.

"We have some glazed, a couple of creams, and three chocolates," Tiana teased, knowing which ones Marnie would love. Sure enough, the young woman took a glazed and two chocolates. Balancing her stuff, Tiana went into the small kitchen/break room down the side hall where she often ate while working this office.

Putting out the box with the donuts -- after snagging a chocolate-covered chocolate one -- Tiana opened up the bigger container and groaned hungrily. "Keith, I adore you beyond what anyone thinks. How can you be single when you cook like this?"

"Who is this Keith, and when can I marry him?" Marnie said as she went to the refrigerator and poured herself a glass of milk.

Tiana explained how to find the diner, as well as who Keith was. As she did that, she fixed Marnie a plate of the ultimate omelet, bacon, and sugar-dipped fruit. Marnie moaned as the smells reached her. "Yes, have some," Tiana quipped, handing her a plate. "There's too much for me to eat alone."

"You can't marry him. You've got someone named Ian, who's called twice so far this morning."

Tiana grinned. "He's something alright. How about I send you to Slice of Americana to get us lunch?

Then you can meet Keith for yourself and decide if he's your type."

"Great! I've put the messages on your desk. Also, there have been two calls from New Scotland Yard regarding your help on two separate cases."

Tiana poured the coffee into a mug. After adding some sugar and milk, she sipped on it. A contented sigh escaped and she sipped again to make sure it was really that good. "Oh, gods, my mum would kill for this blend. I'll have to buy her some for Yule." Turning to her assistant, she grinned. "I'll take care of those first, then. Kyle will be bringing by some packages for me. If I'm not here, which shouldn't be the case, have him put them in my office. Don't bother opening them. Damian made sure they were secured."

Marnie chuckled and took her plate of food back to the outer office. Tiana took her plate and her briefcase into her main office just down the small hall. A door in Tiana's office led to her work area. That room also had some windows, as well as a door to the parking lot. She liked it, as sometimes she'd lock up everything and could leave out of that door, setting the security system as she left at the end of a long day.

Taking in the stack of messages, Tiana sighed. Okay, doing this consulting was starting to cut into her time at the university. However, that was part of the agreement. She enjoyed helping others and wanted to be available for a variety of people, but the job was beginning to take on enormous proportions. Tiana didn't want to think on what she might have to do. She wasn't sure the time was right to expand. Though she knew of some forensic anthropologists, as well as forensic scientists, artists, and more, who'd love to be part of a consultancy, she wasn't the type who could manage an office of people. *Let's consider this topic later. Much later.*

* * * * *

Rubbing the back of her neck, Tiana wondered if there was a sign on her forehead that read, "Please make my life miserable." After talking with Inspector Saducci, she felt a bit better on things, but when she thought of all the messages she'd returned, the various cases she turned over to other people, the referrals to other qualified consultants, Tiana was seriously considering closing her consultancy.

A rumble in her stomach reminded her that Marnie had gone for lunch and it already was two o'clock. Putting her head in her hands, Tiana closed her eyes and tried to relax. It wasn't easy, but then again, she knew it wouldn't be. She admitted that it was time to hire another assistant and ask around to others in her fields, to see if they'd mind being part of a group that could be consulted on cases by various police departments in the United Kingdom and Ireland. Just considering the move, Tiana sighed again. She wasn't a businessperson, not in the strictest sense. It helped as she maintained part-time teaching, but it also meant that she had come far enough in the past couple of years to move forward.

"Tiana? Where are you?" The male voice sounded familiar.

"In my office, Kyle. Come on back!"

She got up and opened her door fully. Kyle carried in two decently large packages. Tiana grabbed one and placed it on the counter area in the back of the office. He placed the other beside it. Turning to her, he hugged her. "How goes it, Ti?"

Tiana waved her hands around. "It goes. How do you feel about being part of a part-time consultancy team, like what we have, but to more places?"

"What's the pay like?"

"Usual consultancy fee, and you can decline if you feel it's not suited to your skills."

"Count me in." Kyle's eyes raked over Tiana. "What's going on? You look a bit off your usual buoyancy."

Tiana motioned to one of the chairs as she sat in hers. When Kyle sat down, Tiana filled him in on the cases that had come her way, as well as the other offers, some of them bogus pleas for help and the others for which she wasn't suited. "So you see, it's growing, and I think having a group of us that can rotate would help the various police forces as well as prevent one person from being called upon all the time."

"Sounds reasonable. When you get the contracts and other things set into place, let me know. I take it that we'd hire someone to help Marnie with organizing things and more, right?"

"Definitely. There'd be a small fee off of what the consultant makes to pay for the office and people, but it'd be fair." Tiana smiled at her coworker. "I'm glad you're here. You interested in a case that requires you to do a confirmation of skeletal bones and a facial reconstruction?"

"Where at?"

"Oxford. They'll even ship the bones to the uni, if you wish."

"Really?"

"Yup. They're desperate for someone who can take the time to do a reconstruction." Tiana grinned at her friend. "Personally, I think you'd be a good consultant. They need someone who can take a hard-line with them and not let them run around with their flights of fancy."

"Now I'm interested." Kyle smiled. "Got any details regarding the case? Just the basics."

Tiana pulled out the file she'd created and handed it to him. "It's all yours. The contact numbers are on the top. Call them and let them know if you want the case. No major information beyond our usual basics, including evidence found at the recovery site."

"Thanks, Ti. Can I take this with me? I can swing down and see them before heading back to Sheffield."

"Really? You'd take the case?" Tiana felt her shoulders lighten slightly.

"Yes. It looks like it'd be great; plus, getting my name out there for consultant work will further my career beyond the research and publishing realm."

"Exactly. You explain things clearly and competently, plus you manage to make sure that people see things realistically, not just what they think is possible."

Kyle stood. "Thanks for this, Tiana. I'm going to grab lunch and then head out."

"You want to join me and Marnie for some food?"

"Nah. You two do what you need to. I'll let you know how the case shapes up." Kyle hugged Tiana, then left her office. "You take care of yourself and get some rest."

"Thanks again, Kyle. Let me know how it works out."

She watched her friend leave. Laughter welled up as Marnie whistled at Kyle and he returned the favor. Shaking her head, Marnie entered the office. "Explain to me why we put up with that man?"

"Because he's my friend and coworker?"

279

"That, too. I've got lunch and I think I'm in lust." Marnie led the way back into the kitchen. Tiana followed in the room and grinned knowingly. "Keith is hot, and more than that, he's sweet. He and I talked a bit, which is what took so long. He sent some special goodies."

As Marnie lifted out packages, Tiana peeked in each one, swooning over the various dishes to choose from. "Who does he think he's feeding, an army?"

"He said that you might want some for supper tonight."

"Heh. What a twerp. Got to love him."

"Oh, yeah. Told me to remind you to call him later." Marnie made up a plate of food and carried it to the table. Tiana did the same. The two women sat and chatted about the growth of the office, as well as what Tiana proposed for the future.

* * * * *

Ian sat behind his desk, finishing the paperwork for his latest case. Though he had grabbed something on the run, it hadn't been as satisfying as the breakfast he'd had with Tiana's mother. He wondered how her day was going and hoped she was having a better day than he was. He had planned to visit his folks, but John had called, telling him there was a break in the Nichols case. Now they were doing the clean up to make sure there was nothing that could be used to destroy the case.

His mind wandered a bit. Being with Tiana was definitely a heady experience. The way she had sucked on his cock had blown him away. She enjoyed pleasuring him just as much as he pleasured her. Smiling, he drifted off for a bit.

Ian smiled at Tiana. *"Lie back and trust me. When you want out, just tell me, okay? If you don't trust me, tell me."*

"Okay," Tiana said nervously as Ian used silk scarves to bind each hand and foot to the ends of the four-poster bed. She licked her lips. *"I do trust you, Ian. What do you plan on doing?"*

"Making you scream, my luv. I want to make you come so hard, so much, you will beg me to fuck you."

Tiana shot him a wicked look. *"I thought I did that already?"*

Ian brought the bowl on the nightstand closer. Taking a piece of ice, he let the cold water drip from his fingers over her naked breasts. As she gasped at the coldness, he smiled. *"No, not like this. I want it that you only need me. That the only thing worth having is my cock fucking you senseless."*

She said nothing as the ice cube touched a turgid nipple. Ian guided the piece of ice around the tip, letting the water dribble down her rounded breast.

Tiana gasped as he blew across the tops of her breasts. "You okay, Tiana?"

"Yes," she hissed as his mouth captured the taut nipple. "Oh, yes."

Ian slid the ice over the other nipple, causing it to contract just like the one in his mouth. Teasing it with his teeth, he felt Tiana's body tremble with passion. Releasing her nipple, he laved the other one with his tongue. She moved, trying to get out of her bonds, but was held fast. She was at his mercy and they both knew it. Licking her lips, she watched him, her eyes dark with desire and some other deep emotion.

Carefully, he stroked her skin with the ice cube until he reached her soft auburn curls. As he let the water drip onto them, she shimmied her hips as the cold contacted against her hot skin. "Does that feel good, Tiana? Do you like that?"

She said nothing as a moan erupted from her throat. He thought it was his name, but the teasing half crazed her. She knew what he was going to do next, and there was nothing she could do to stop him. His left hand parted her curls as the ice made its way slowly towards her hot pussy. Ian blew along the curls, urging the ice piece to slide over the edge. Once it touched her bare skin, Tiana shivered and moaned.

"Oh, gods, Ian, you're killing me!"

"No, I'm loving you, Tiana." He pressed the ice against her clitoris, then moved it toward her slit as

his mouth slid to take its place. Warmth upon the cold. The sensation was too much. Tiana screamed as she climaxed. Taking advantage, Ian pushed the ice piece inside her pussy, causing the inner muscles to contract tight against his fingers. Lapping at her entrance, Ian's mouth caught and swallowed her juices as she continued to tremble under his touch.

"I'm begging, please, Ian. Fuck me. Fuck me."

"How you doing, guv?"

Looking up at his partner, Ian grimaced. Shaking off his daydream, he tried to compose himself. *How am I doing? I want to not be here! I want to be having hot sex with a woman who makes my blood thrum with heat and passion!* "Honestly? I'd prefer a break. My parents were great about all this, but I hated that I had to do this."

"The price we pay to keep people safe, Ian."

"I know. How's the wife?"

"Much better." John hesitated and then spoke. "One of the police officers on patrol last night thought she spotted someone, but she couldn't make him out and wasn't sure it was possible, that the killer would be stalking the area. Gave her the creeps, it did."

"Where was she at?"

"Mitre Square area."

"Damn. So we've got nothing?"

John sat on the corner of Ian's roughened desk. "I wouldn't say that. I think we've got him scared and nervous with the increased patrols. That is a good thing, Ian. Maybe we'll scare him into making a mistake, and pick him up on something else."

Shutting down his computer, Ian leaned back. "We can hope. I don't know if it'll happen or not. Trace evidence has found some things that aren't related to the victims, but they're not sure if they match the other cases. If they do, then we've got a link between the cases that's physically oriented."

"Great. You look beat, Ian. Why don't you go and get something to eat? It's about six and you've been here since about ten. It's your day off. Go spend some time with your new lady love."

"What?" Ian looked at John.

"You think your partner can't see the change in you. My bet's on the lovely doctor."

"Bloody hell, John! I do like her, but business is business. You know that."

John shrugged. "Go do your thing. You need a break."

"Thanks, partner. I'll see you in the morning. Dr. Wells is at her office today. I'm going to head there."

"See you tomorrow."

Ian wondered how far Tiana had gotten in the facial reconstructions. Or if she'd be busy doing other aspects first. Perhaps he'd bring her some food and surprise her. He wanted to make sure she was doing okay. Though the killer hadn't attacked her, it didn't mean she couldn't be a target.

Getting to his car, Ian decided to shower and change first, then grab food and see Tiana. Liking the plan, he headed to make it a reality. He had to tell her his feelings, and soon. Time was closing in on them.

Chapter Seventeen

Tiana sat on her high-backed stool, fingers carefully smoothing the clay over the surface, creating the musculature. She had worked unswervingly since lunch. Now it was about eight o'clock, but she knew she had to do this quickly. The resonance and feelings from the skulls had almost unnerved her.

Never in her life had she ever thought she'd be sitting here with replicas of two skulls from Jack the Ripper's victims. Yet, these skulls belonged to Mary Kelly and Catherine Eddowes. She had decided on the left one, not sure why. Keeping the original skull next to the replica helped her to check and double-check her markers. Normally, a reproduction could take a week of sittings, but tonight she felt possessed; and though she skipped none of her steps, there was something in her fingers that made this come so quick, so pure, that Tiana feared and accepted that her special ability must be at work tonight.

As her fingers smoothed the clay over the eyes, creating eyelids, Tiana felt a tingling sensation run up her back, causing her to shiver. Blinking, she tried to get control of herself. Something began to emerge from the skull sitting next to the one she was working on. Wisps of a misty smoke seeped from it as though called by an ancient, powerful magic of which Tiana knew very little. Pulling back, Tiana watched in shock. Never had her ability to talk with the dead manifested like this.

"W-What the *hell!*" she gasped, as the smoke swirled and began to take on a vague form in front of her. "Who are you?"

"I'm Mary Kelly, Tiana. You knew this the moment you touched my skull."

The mist coalesced into the image of a young woman. Her blonde hair flowed around her shoulders; blue eyes glimmering with something mysterious, not quite definable. Mary looked almost touchable, not like the traditional ghost that was supposed to be transparent. The fact that the ghost was correct was another thing entirely. She hadn't even admitted to herself that she'd chosen Mary's skull, knowing it by touch.

"You know my name?"

"How could I not know the woman who'll put me to rest and put Jack back into the binding her ancestor had done so long ago?"

"What? I don't understand." Tiana stepped backwards, trying to comprehend how this ghost knew something she'd just figured out herself. *Didn't the journal say something like that? Miriam, maybe? Buck up, Ti. It's a spirit, just like you've dealt with before. You can deal with this. You can get answers.* Tiana noticed the woman looked like she did prior to Jack's brutal attack upon her body. "You know some say that you weren't killed, that it was another prostitute."

"Amazing what people will believe if it's repeated enough. Actually, I rented my room to another woman. She left shortly before my killer and I arrived." There was a pause. A small tear trickled down Mary's face, its trail ending as it splattered lightly on the floor. When Tiana looked down, it was gone. Her gaze went back to the ghostly figure in amazement. Sometimes she could speak to the dead, see their last memories, but this was beyond anything she'd ever done before.

"I knew there was a risk. Everyone knew what had happened to poor Catherine. However, I needed the money. I was about to lose my home, Tiana. There was nothing else I could do."

Tiana nodded and placed her right hand upon the ghost's arm. "I'm sorry about your death," she said gently. "Yours was the one that horrified me most when I first started reading about true crimes. Would you speak on what happened that night? I'd listen if you'd like to talk."

A soft sigh escaped the lips of the dead woman as she leaned against a low table. Sitting there, she looked at Tiana. *"It's been a long time since I've told anyone about this. Only to your ancestor, once she passed over."*

"My ancestor? Patricia?"

Mary smiled softly at Tiana's confusion. *"You are descended from witches, Tiana. Powerful witches. That pendant you wear is the legacy and the promise that they swore to uphold. She said one day that someone in her line would make sure my killer pays for the deaths he took. Until then, I'm not yet ready for the wheel of rebirth."*

"I'm glad she could help you." Tiana was intrigued as her fingers curled around the pewter pendant. Warmth greeted her fingers, and Tiana realized the source was from each person who'd owned the pendant, giving something of themselves to help the future generations. "Can you tell me more?"

"From what I was told, Patricia and others in her group tried to bind the evil to prevent more atrocities. Something didn't go right, though, because he didn't die or turn himself in. She said it wasn't until later, when she died while fighting him, that their blood commingled did the deed."

The frightening events of the unbinding spell crossed Tiana's mind. She cringed at the implications as she clasped the pendant in the palm of her hand. "Do you think—"

The sound of the door opening behind her cut her short.

"Tiana? You in here, luv?"

Ian stepped into the room and saw Tiana and a slender woman in Victorian clothing. Tiana held her breath for a moment, wondering if Ian saw Mary. "Who's that with you?"

The woman looked at Ian and shrieked, backing up into the corner.

"You. It's you! You shouldn't be here anymore!" With those words, Mary Kelly vanished into thin air.

Tiana turned to him, the terror from Mary filling her senses and her soul, certain questions making her leap to conclusions. Though she didn't want to ask, she knew she had to know. There was something in Mary's manner and emotions that was beyond understanding.

"Talk to me, Tiana," Ian said, "Who was that?"

"Go away," she said, staring at him in horror, "I can't believe... oh, gods, you're—"

Ian grabbed Tiana's arms. "I'm *what?*"

"You killed those women, didn't you?"

Ian released her arms abruptly, and the shocked look on his face made her think twice. Could she be mistaken in what Mary meant? She stepped away from Ian, her lover, the man she thought she was falling for. The coldness on his face scared her.

"Ian—"

"What do you want me to say, Tiana? That I did it and I'm Jack the Ripper?" His voice was hard as steel and colder than the frozen winters in northern England.

A shudder went through her as he stepped forward.

"Because this woman, or what have you, says 'You!'" he said icily. "Automatically, I'm the guilty party? I thought you knew me better than that. I thought you trusted me, Tiana."

Spinning on his heel, Ian stalked across the room for the door. On the threshold, he paused.

"My ancestor was Prince Albert," he said over his shoulder. "You figure it out."

The door slammed hard behind him.

Tiana sagged against the wall, her heart racing, mind spinning. She felt a splash of wetness and realized tears were streaking her cheeks.

What was it that Ian had said? His ancestor was the Prince Albert? Information raced through her head as she slid against the wall.

"Oh, my gods," she moaned. "What have I done?"

* * * * *

The man waited in the shadows of the buildings. Once again, he had managed to avoid being caught by the police that were out patrolling. They couldn't stop him. Though he had to do this murder a bit differently than he wanted, still, he accomplished his goal. It would break the cycle a bit, but the idea was what was important. To show that he was back and alive, ready to continue his killing spree! Moving the heavy bundle at his feet, he placed the young woman on the ground, making sure she was posed just so.

Looking down at the dead body, his grin grew. "Poor little lady, out all alone. You never thought the man you were helping was dangerous, did you? Now you've paid with your life. I so love how you whimpered as you felt the first stirrings of pain in your body."

The man looked up at the stars. "You will not win. I won't let you take me away like you did before. Dammit, I'm free and I'll remain so. All I need to do is find a way to get rid of that woman!"

Hearing footsteps, the man stepped back into the shadows. There wasn't much time, but the uproar would be major. Giving a deep, evil chuckle, the man walked toward the car he'd stolen earlier that day. *Get rid of it, then head for home.* "Then we can deal with the last hurrah. You, Dr. Tiana Wells, will be my grand finale before I begin anew!"

Chapter Eighteen

Two weeks later

Ian and John sat before the mounds of evidence. They had commandeered an empty office and begun placing various pieces of the cases together with the common factors. Though they realized the victims were totally random, there was a pattern that would help with the identification of the killer. Since Officer Tracey's death, the public was clamoring for answers. Unfortunately, there wasn't much to go on.

Both men looked at each other as they started putting up the pictures of the deceased. "Mate, this sucks. I hate that we've found nothing to help identify the killer."

"We don't know that for sure, John. We're still going over trace evidence from Lydia Tracey's body," Ian reminded his partner and friend. "Further, Dr. Wells and Al both spotted a couple of things that could help us identify the killer. They gave the samples over to the DNA lab. Give them some time to sort out the evidence they've found."

"Did they speculate on what they found?" John's voice was filled with repressed anger and a slight tinge of desperation. "I don't like the heat that's on us to find this guy. Hell, no one else has come up with anything."

"I know, John. But trust me, in time, there'll be something. It's been two weeks. Hopefully, the forensic department has some information for us."

"They bloody damn well better have something. This is giving me the fits, Ian." John slammed his hand down on the desk, causing pictures to scatter on the floor. "I'm to the point of not letting my wife out of the house without me."

Ian nodded and said nothing. He knew his partner needed to vent. It'd been two weeks since he and Tiana parted on bad terms. His body craved hers and his heart ached. But how could he trust her when she jumped to conclusions, instead of trusting in him? As it was, he'd shared his deepest secret with her, but in such a callous way, not in the way he had wanted to bring up the topic. How could he trust her to treat it seriously when she thought he was guilty of being the killer? *Did I jump away too soon without letting her explain herself? Maybe I'm an arse of the first order.*

A knock at the door grabbed his attention. "Come in, Officer."

The young man entered. "This arrived for you, sir. I was asked to bring it to you right away. It's from Dr. Wells." He handed Ian the package, then scampered out of the room.

Ian looked at the somewhat bulky envelope. He wasn't sure he wanted to open this packet from Tiana. He doubted it was about the cases, but you never knew.

"Well, you gonna open the package from the little lady?"

"I guess I could. It's probably some stuff on Jack the Ripper."

John looked at Ian, before shutting the door to the office. Ian looked up, staring at his friend. John grabbed a chair and sat across from him. "I don't know what happened between you and the lady doc; it's not my business. But whatever it is, it's made you crankier than normal. Ask yourself this—is what happened partially your fault, too?"

Ian growled. "You know nothing about it."

"Jack the Ripper, your family. Anything else beyond that?"

Ian shot a look of surprise at his partner. "How did you know?"

"I've known for years that you take one week a year to go over the evidence that is known. I know that once Dr. Wells showed you the connections between this case and Jack the Ripper, you've been excited and muted at the same time." John paused, looking as if he was trying to decide how to phrase things. "Look, mate, you and I know about your family's relation to Albert. I know you want to definitively clear his name. Don't blame you there; I'd want that, too, if he was mine."

"Then you realize how hard this is."

"Not like you, but I get an idea. I don't know what happened the night of the murder, but you hadn't told her about your personal connection to the case or that you look a lot like Albert did in his younger years, have you?"

Ian shook his head. Then something in John's words clicked. "Say that again."

"Say what? About your connection to the case?"

"No, the other part."

"That you look a lot like Albert?"

"Bingo!" Ian roared and started to open the package. "That's why that woman yelled. It has to be."

"Now you've lost me, Ian."

Ian started to open his mouth to explain, but stopped as a hand-drawn picture fell out first from the package. Looking at the face, he felt a shudder of revulsion course through him. Then he saw Tiana's handwritten letter.

Reading it, then going through the various pieces she'd included, Ian realized a few things that he'd already accepted, as well as some things of which he'd been unaware. Reading the journal entries by Tiana's ancestor, he looked again at the picture of the man she'd seen. "Do you know what this is, John?" Ian asked as he handed the picture of the man to his partner.

"Nope."

"A picture of Jack the Ripper, by someone who almost became his victim early on. Then later on, died at his hand."

"That's not possible, guv. The police would've had this picture if that were true. How do you know this?"

Ian passed over the notes that were copied from the journal, as well as the authentication that Tiana had done on the journals to prove they were from that time period. "Not me. Tiana. This was written by a relative of hers from that time."

"Bloody hell, man! Do you know that you're sitting on something that could break that case finally?"

Ian sat back and shook his head. "No. Not me. Tiana is ... This is hers, not mine." He looked at the other bundled papers and pictures, shaking his head. "She's even given me concrete evidence that Albert wasn't around during most of those murders."

"You're kidding."

"Nope. She's a bloody brilliant researcher and Ripperologist. Now I know why Al and the others look highly to her work. Tiana does all the necessary background research, so nothing is overlooked."

"True, but how is this going to help us find the killer?" John queried as he scanned the papers.

Ian held Tiana's letter in his hand, his mind working on the other pieces of information she'd pieced together regarding the killer, his motive, and her private opinion of who was actually doing the killing. Though he wanted to believe it was hogwash, there were things that were still in the files that others hadn't seen because papers had been confiscated and some stolen. He had seen some of them, and some of the markings that Tiana noticed were consistent with the hidden information that he had access to.

"She reminded me to call up the forensic department to see if they found a match for the fingerprint she lifted from the scarred area on Officer Tracey's arm."

John picked up the phone and called. "I'll ask. You're probably persona non grata with them."

Ian chuckled and nodded. "Al hasn't been nice at all since things happened." He continued to Tiana's thoughts about the things she'd seen during her full-moon ritual. The worry and the fact that she'd once again picked up her edged weapons had him fearful for her. There was something in him that still felt she was a probable target, though she dismissed the idea. Dammit, her emotions flowed over the paper and into his soul. *Perhaps there is something to magick, after all.*

"You're kidding, Al," John said, breaking into Ian's thoughts. He listened closer to his partner's side of the conversation. "No, we've not had contact with him. I know that he's a coworker of Dr. Wells, though. Hold on, explain this to Ian." His friend handed him the phone. "This isn't good, Ian."

Ian nodded and put the receiver up to his ear. "Ian Spencer here."

"Ian, this is Al. Listen to me, have you heard from Tiana today?"

"Just a package by courier. Why?"

"Bloody hell and damnation. We got the latent prints identified from the scar, as well as a couple of things where he left partial prints. The man is getting careless."

"Who?"

He heard his friend take a breath. This wasn't going to be something he liked. He knew he wouldn't already. Al never paused like that unless it was bad. Real bad.

"You need to find Tiana. She's in severe danger."

"What do you mean?"

Ian listened as Al explained exactly who those fingerprints belonged to and why Tiana was in danger.

Slamming the phone down, Ian growled. "Get back up and meet me at Tiana's London office. The damn bastard is going to kill her there. He's been playing with her!"

Ian rushed from the room, praying to his God and all the other gods, hoping he'd be there in time. He was afraid he'd lose her before he could tell her of his love. He had to make this all right, even if he wasn't completely at fault. She needed him, and he wouldn't be like others had been in her life and not be there.

Chapter Nineteen

Tiana pored over the autopsy results of the latest crimes and that of Jack the Ripper. The past two weeks without Ian had been harder than she thought possible, but until he read the evidence, there was no way of convincing him that she knew Prince Albert was innocent. There were various pieces of evidence, but the most important one was in the journal she held. Though she didn't know who the person was, she knew by various pictures that it wasn't Prince Albert. Other corroborating evidence, such as Albert being away for the various murders, helped to confirm that he wasn't Jack the Ripper. Rubbing her eyes, she refocused her concentration on the task at hand.

Dr. Campion had sent her copies of the trace evidence reports, comparing a couple of stray fibers that had been found consistently on the victims prior to her exams. She read over the reports again, comparing them to the ancient cases. Once again, she spotted something that made her consider something that couldn't be possible. Could it?

No doubt about it—they were the same, especially this last murder. Even the type of weapon used was so similar as to make no difference. Rolling her head forward to release the tension in her neck, she moaned softly as she felt the familiar pops telling her that she'd been sitting too long and hunching over her desk again. As her hand slipped on the papers, something captured her attention. Something she had known, but not realized. Rereading the piece of the trace evidence, including the one from the latest murder, the young female police officer, Tiana started putting together the chain of events.

The murder had been awful. Going in, facing Ian and Al, had been tough. More so, seeing the injuries that were replicas of Catherine Eddowes. There was nothing that could've prepared anyone for the damage Jack had inflicted upon the young woman. Her mind brought her back to the forensic autopsy room.

Tiana stood before the body of a woman torn almost to pieces by a madman. Though Ian said nothing, the coldness he showed her was nothing like the cold in her heart when she longed to be held by him.

Al broke the silence. "I've done my initial assessment, Tiana. Just need your expertise for the wounds again."

"Sure." Tiana felt like someone was choking her. Ever since last night, with how Ian left, she felt like something was missing in her soul. When she called Kit, her sister and mother had both yelled at her for not forcing Ian to listen, for not explaining what was going on with her. Though they understood, they reminded her of the responsibility that was hers as someone who was a Druid and walked that path. Now she stood here, the man she loved desperately not speaking to her. It hurt.

She began her assessment, calling out numbers, angles, and depths. Poking and prodding within the wounds, Tiana tried to keep her breakfast down as she continued the examination. The words from the long-ago autopsy on Catherine Eddowes entered her mind, as well as the words written by Patricia. She couldn't stop the tears from flowing as she slowly went down the body, cataloging the various injuries.

At the end, Tiana spoke, her voice soft from the pain she felt for this dead woman who represented Catherine Eddowes's death. "The man has once again presented us with a death that is similar to the Jack the Ripper killing of Catherine Eddowes. Though this is circumstantial, based upon the various testimonies found by the autopsy reports, I can safely say that this

killer is trying his utmost to copy the actions done
before. If the slit was done from behind, which I think
might be the case, then he's more than likely right-
handed, though he seems to have some talent to work
with his left hand. Dr. Tiana Wells."

When Ian walked past her in the changing room,
she had grabbed his arm. "Ian, we need to talk. I know
that your ancestor—"

"I don't want to speak on this, Tiana. You
obviously think I'm guilty."

"That's not true. I was reacting to Mary's
emotions. Please!"

Ian walked off, leaving Tiana alone once more.

She had sent him a long, rambling letter
explaining why she'd reacted the way she had that
night. In the packet, she also included all of the
information she had on Prince Albert -- his
movements, letters that helped clear him, and other
tidbits collected by her and other Ripperologists.
Because she figured he might need it, Tiana included
all the evidence regarding her great-great-
grandmother and the various pieces of confirmed
information regarding Albert's whereabouts during
those vital times. Tiana hoped that, somehow, he'd
realize she had been drawn into the emotions but
realized her mistake. She missed him; she was in love
with him and hated that they were apart like this.

Reading the information that she'd just gotten at her London office, her disbelief turned slowly into certainty. How could she have not seen the evidence? There was too much there to dismiss casually, especially considering the timings. Part of her railed against the truth, but the logical part of her brain insisted that she accept the facts of the case, and her intuition. She recalled who had been in the office the day she handed over the reconstructions and the original skulls to Inspector Frederick Saducci. She remembered the conversation regarding how vicious Jack had been, and once again, the defense of the killer's actions by the only man who knew as much as she did about the crimes.

"Oh, shit! That's the link. I know who Jack's possessed," Tiana whispered, her fear cloaking her body. It couldn't be true. There was no way that it could be him, could it?

A scratching sound caused her to jump in her chair and whirl around.

A distorted face in the door window grinned its menace.

"Jack's back, Tiana," growled the man as he kicked open her door, the knife glinting in his hand. "There's not a damn thing you or anyone else can do to stop me."

Tiana's hand felt in her desk and palmed the knife she'd put in her drawer after everything happened.

Silently, she thanked her aunt for the warning. She scrambled, putting distance between herself and Kyle, her friend who was now the living essence of Jack the Ripper. Her heart beat rapidly as she tried to take in the truth that she'd denied for so long. Pieces of the puzzle began falling into place, causing Tiana to panic even more.

"Kyle, listen to me. You need help," she said quickly, as reasonably as she could manage, shoving another chair between them. "We've got to get Jack captured and out of you."

"Don't you recognize this place, Tiana? Or the address? This lovely London office you have was once the residence of my last known victim, or in this case, the last reenactment before I begin anew!"

Tiana thought for a moment. *Was this building on the original spot where Mary Kelly had died?* There was no time to dwell on it. Her only hope was to get to the door that connected to her studio, so she could get out of the building, away from Kyle. Part of her still couldn't believe her friend could be guilty of those murders, even if he was under the influence of Jack's spirit.

"Kyle, how did this happen? You're not a murderer." She pushed her desk at Kyle-Jack to stop his forward motion, while she made her way to the side door in the room.

"How little you know me after all this time, Ti," the man whispered, the knife brandished before him. "I've been arrested before on assault charges, but they were dropped for lack of evidence."

"Kyle! Listen to me; I know why you're acting like this. You can break free of him. I promise."

The man laughed, a sound so ugly and evil, she cringed as she felt the door handle caress her skin. "What if I don't want to be free of him? I'm enjoying the killing. The way he works is indescribable, but he has plans for you. I have plans for you. Your family will pay for what was done before!"

Tiana turned the knob slowly, grateful she hadn't locked it. "You mean Patricia?"

"The woman who you're the spitting image of. She found me, you know. I couldn't believe she recognized me from that one look at the church. How *dare* she tell me that I'd be stopped? I showed her, though. When it was all said and done, she was the one who died." Kyle-Jack growled. "Then I died shortly after, her curse binding me until you freed me."

"The spell," Tiana whispered. "I thought I felt something."

"I was freed by you. I won't be put back in there, Tiana. I won't."

"Kyle, it's not you; it's that dangerous spirit inside you. Please, Kyle, fight it. Fight it, for our friendship."

Her voice cracked in desperation, sweat dripping down her back as fear fought to overtake her.

The knife came down on the desk in front of her. "No! You're going to be a testament to the brilliance of Jack the Ripper."

Tiana grabbed a book from the bookshelf in front of her and threw it at Kyle-Jack, then opened the door, bolting through. Locking it as she pulled it shut, she heard him cursing as he tried to unlock it. She knew that there was only a minute or two before he managed to unlock it. Damn her stupid need for easy access; that lock could be undone from either side.

Running, she tripped a bit as she ran into her stool. The art room was bright with light-colored walls and track illumination overhead. The pounding of her heart filled her ears as she tried to regain her balance and head for the exit. Suddenly a hand grabbed her. As she tried to scream, a hand clamped over her mouth.

"I don't think so, dear heart," Kyle-Jack said, the glint of the knife catching her eye before it slid gently against her neck.

Panic welled up in her. This was just like before. Feeling sick, she tried to take slow, open-mouthed breaths. "Please, Kyle, don't do this. Please," she begged, her body trembling.

"Are you frightened, Ti?" Seeing her nod, he smiled. "Good. Doesn't this bring back the most enjoyable memories for you?"

"No. Please, Kyle, you're scaring me," she pleaded, sliding the sheath off her knife as she prayed for the strength necessary.

"Good. You need to be scared, Tiana." The voice got a bit more cultured, but still was menacing. "You and yours have been a pain in my side for too long. I'm tired of being caged. With your death, there will be no way to bind me anymore."

"Why did they bind you?" Tiana's thoughts were to keep him talking. Perhaps she'd be able to get him where she needed, in order to do the spell that she'd been memorizing from the mirror book. Supposedly, the binding spell had been passed down,. It had looked powerful and something not done on a whim. "Please, I don't understand all of this."

The laugh was low and completely unnerving. Tiana almost dropped her knife, but gripped it tighter as she knelt before the tall man. She looked up; his eyes were more menacing and dead than at any time she'd known him. The man grabbed her pendant and pulled it away. "Goddamned pendant!"

"What?"

"She said the pendant helped her to formulate the binding. I won't let you use it against me." He slipped it in a pocket. "You want to know why you're going to die?"

"Yes."

"I do enjoy toying with my victims. The police officer broke too early, you know." He sighed as if her early death had created problems for him.

Tiana knew he had literally gotten off over the officer's death. It was a piece of evidence that had almost been missed. Hopefully, someone would put the pieces together, if she didn't live through this. *Ian, if you can hear me, please know I love you.*

"Your family has issues with interfering in things that don't include them. She'd have lived, had she and her friends stayed out of it." The man slid the blade against Tiana's neck, causing a pricking sensation that she remembered all too well. "I love how the blood beads against your neck. Then again, you've already done this once before, haven't you, Tiana?"

"Yes. Please tell me more." Tiana felt tears roll down her face. The horror of facing death by knife again had haunted her, and now it was coming true. There was nothing she could do, even if she was able to use the knife in her hand against him. He'd kill her as soon as she stabbed him.

"I knew Patricia from before, you know. She and I were in similar circles. That night, when I saw her in the church, I thought she'd make an excellent victim because, honestly, if she wasn't a whore, would she have come down to the East End to really help others?" The man considered his own question. "No, but she would interfere. After I killed Mary Kelly, I felt lost and a bit out of control. I headed away from London. No one ever considered it unusual. I did come back at times, you know."

"Yes, I do know. The torso."

"You are good, my dear. When Patricia came to Cornwall, I heard about it and met up with her. At the time, there were a couple of people around. She told me that she and her friends had bound my spirit and that if I tried to kill again, I'd die and would never be free, unless someone of hers released me."

"Fuck!"

"Yes, you freed me. How ironic, isn't it? The woman I killed caused my death, but her descendant allowed me to find an avatar for my spirit. Now, you'll die, and once again, I'll be free from the bindings."

Suddenly, Tiana felt a chill, signaling that someone had opened the door between her office and the studio. Then there came Patricia's voice. *Hold on, my precious granddaughter. Know that you're not alone. Your love and I are here to help. You need to cut him. Make him bleed and rage.*

No, I can't. He'll hurt and kill me. He's going to make me into Mary Kelly!

Patricia seemed to squeeze her hand. *Listen to me, Tiana. You're fine. He won't expect you to try something. Remember that the man who knows you doesn't realize how far you've come in conquering your fear of weapons. Use it now and get him off guard. Then duck.*

Tiana wanted to shake her head. Could she really pull this off? Do I have a choice? Raising her head to her captor, Tiana spoke softly, but confidently. "So you mean, if I do a binding spell, I could put you back in your place."

"Yes, but you'd need blood. Something you're not willing to deal with, remember? You're so damn afraid of knives, it makes this even more fun," Kyle-Jack snarled triumphantly.

"You'd think that, wouldn't you?"

He glared at her. "What do you mean?"

She moved one arm up, pushing away his knife hand as she brought up her other hand and stabbed him hard in the belly. Then she rolled backwards, trying to get out of the way. A gunshot rang out as he fell to his knees. "You bitch, you tricked me!"

"I'm no one's victim anymore, Kyle. You of all people should've known that." Tiana glanced at Ian, who knelt next to the counter.

"You okay, Ti?"

She rubbed her neck and coughed. "Yes. But I need to do the spell."

Kyle tried to stand up, and Ian rushed him and knocked him down, causing the knife to slide against the tiled floor, away from them both. Tiana rushed over and grabbed the pendant from Kyle's pocket as Ian tried to cuff him. He struggled as Tiana rubbed blood from her neck as well as blood from Kyle upon the pendant.

Standing back, she called upon the elements. "Hear me, O Earth, Air, Water, and Fire. Guide me and protect me as I work this magick."

Looking at Kyle, she stepped forward as Ian finished getting the man's hands cuffed behind his back. He nodded at Tiana as he moved back.

"Your work of evil is over; your time here on earth is done. By those whose blood you've spilt time and again, they claim vengeance. I bind you to the world beyond; never again shall you be free. I bind you to the spirit realm, far away from me."

Tiana coughed as she tried to finish the binding spell. Warmth flooded her hands as the pendant glowed, the filigree workings shining with an unearthly flame. Tiana stepped closer and placed the pendant against Kyle's chest. "Your life is done, spirit bound. Your blood is spilt upon hallow ground. Just as you killed in this area so long ago, I now claim justice for the women slain by your hand. Balance demands your death, and forever bound from coming back, you're condemned to the spirit plane, never to come back or interfere with human life once more."

Suddenly, a sound of singing filled her ears as she heard the binding spell from ancient times spill from her lips. Though she didn't understand the Old English words fully, she allowed the power to flow through her, capturing the spirit and binding it with something other than metal handcuffs. An unholy scream filled the air and then quiet settled through the office.

Tiana collapsed on her knees as tears flooded down her cheeks. Ian rushed to her side and held her.

"Shh, it's okay, Ti. You did it. You did it."

She looked up at him, her eyes wet, her heart petrified. "You came. How did you know?"

"Al gave me the results and said that he tried calling here to warn you but you didn't answer."

"He cut my phone lines, didn't he?"

Ian nodded and held her close, her heart pounding out the same rhythm as his. She allowed his warmth to fill her as she felt her body shiver, as the adrenaline rush ended. "Ian, I need to tell you—"

"I got your package." He daubed at the small pearls of blood on her neck with his handkerchief. "I was wrong, you know. I should've told you about my family history and I didn't. It's just hard knowing he's a suspect."

"But he's not, not by those who know the evidence, Ian."

"I know that now, but in my foolishness, I almost lost the woman I love." He stopped and looked at her, his eyes holding her green ones. "I don't know if you can forgive me for being an ass, but I do love you, Tiana."

"I love you, too, Ian. More than I thought ever possible." Tiana coughed. Her eyes glanced at the dead man in her studio. "What will happen?"

"Everyone put your hands up!" John entered the room with two other officers.

"You're a bit late, John. The man is dead." Ian handed over his weapon. "He sliced at Tiana's throat. She managed to stab him, and when she moved, I shot him."

John nodded. "I heard it from the corridor." His voice lowered. "I wanted to give you both some time, but this mess has to be dealt with."

"Thanks, John. What now?"

His voice rose. "Well, technically, you're suspended until this gets cleared up, but with Tiana and me as witnesses, it shouldn't take long."

Ian nodded. "The usual procedure, then."

"Well, considering that we don't normally allow officers to carry firearms ..."

Ian shrugged. "I've got a permit to carry one."

"Good."

Tiana looked from one man to another. "Can I get some water and some bandages?"

Both men scurried to fill her request as emergency service personnel showed up. Once she was taken care of and the body was removed, Tiana sighed. She wasn't sure how long this mess would take to be resolved, but knowing that Ian loved her made it much easier.

* * * * *

Later on, she sat wrapped in her robe on the hotel bed, with Ian cradling her. Tiana grinned up at him. He shook his head at her. "What?" she demanded.

"You're adorable, Tiana Wells."

She lifted an eyebrow at him. "Adorable?"

"Loveable, huggable, and wonderful. How's that?"

She kissed his cheek and leaned against him. "I love you, Ian Spencer. Thank you for today."

"For almost letting you get killed?"

"No, for coming to my rescue and being there when I needed you most. I trust you like none other, and without you there, I might've died." Her fingers caressed his cheek. His hand wrapped around hers.

"Marry me."

"What?" She looked at him, her head tilting to the left. "Did you just ask what I thought I heard?"

Ian chuckled. "I'm not letting you go. The only way to ensure that is by having you married to me."

"What about my job?"

"You can do the consulting. If you mean the uni, aren't there others that might like you as well?"

Tiana sighed. "This is true. Can we discuss the job thing after we talk about the marriage thing?"

"You are going to marry me, right?"

Tiana grinned. "Well, considering that I think my mother has given up hope of ever having grandchildren, it might be a good idea if we get married and give her one or two to spoil."

Ian kissed her passionately. When they separated, he smiled lovingly at her. "I even promise to let the kids be raised in both traditions."

"Good, you don't want to fight with Mum."

"Um, no."

Tiana laughed as Ian joined in. Finally, she'd put the past behind her and found a man who loved and accepted her. It was simply amazing that through a historical murderer and his current-day incarnation, Tiana had managed to find love and completion. She silently thanked Patricia as she leaned against the man she loved.

Author Notes

You'll notice a few things in this book that might not match up to your memories regarding Jack the Ripper. <grins> There are some reasons for this. One, I went back to review all the evidence and spent a long time gathering articles, information, and reading a lot of books regarding who Jack the Ripper was. You won't find that answer here in this book. What you will find is who he wasn't; well, at least according to the research I've done. Right now, I need to give a huge thank you to a wonderful site, www.casebook.org. It's one of the best sites online regarding Jack the Ripper. Without this fantastic site, I couldn't have done half the research I was able to accomplish. Go to this site if you really want to learn more about Jack the Ripper and the Whitechapel murders. I referenced many of the articles within that site, as well as various books, and people I know who have a thing for Jack the Ripper, in order to write this story. All hail the wonderful contributors for the site and the message forum for their tremendous knowledge. Hoorah!

One thing I've noticed in all of my research is that no one is quite sure if Jack started killing prior to Polly Nichols's death or if he ended with Mary Kelly's. For me, in reviewing evidence, making comparative notes of wounds, etc., I've made some changes in the canonical list of the murders. This might create some ire in Ripperologists, but in my defense, I've taken the time to look at many things and ask many people who know more than I do, and I fully take the blame in creating this list. Do I believe that Martha Tabram, once considered a Ripper victim, then decanonized, is a Ripper victim? Yes, I really do. By the same token, I have sincere doubt that Elizabeth Stride was one of Jack's victims, based upon evidence available to me. I know that some people will point out that he was interrupted, but when you look at the timetables, the type of knife used, the types of wounds, the distance that had to be traveled, and how he'd have needed to coerce Catherine Eddowes to go with him, I doubt that Elizabeth was his victim. Again, this is just my take on one of the most fascinating unsolved serial murder cases in history. Could I be wrong? Yes, I could be extremely wrong in how I'm viewing this. I'll leave it up to the Ripperologists to crucify me. And, note, I do so willingly. These people know more about this than I can ever comprehend in a lifetime. My goal is to give them something enjoyable to read regarding this fascinating mystery and perhaps, in my own way, give some of my own theories to what happened.

As for not saying whom I think Jack was, there are reasons for that. I don't think there's enough evidence to finger a suspect after all this time. Further, for me, it wasn't a matter of who he was, just who he wasn't. Sometimes, we have to start with a list and get rid of those who are suspects in order to narrow the field down. I hope that my reasoning for who Jack isn't is logical and rational. Jack the Ripper isn't the first serial killer in history, but he's one of the best-known, due to his crimes remaining unsolved, the time period in history when he was active, and the murders seeming to stop so suddenly -- though if you read contemporary newspaper accounts, there were more murders after Mary Kelly that some people do attribute to Jack. Is it possible that Jack continued to kill after the last found murder? No one really knows for sure, but somehow, unless he himself died, I think he never stopped, though he might've changed venues. Again, that's rampant speculation on my part.

One thing that always amazed me about these murders is that MO, modus operandi, stayed consistent, though the killing blows were not always the same. When I went through the victims' wounds and made a chart on them, I noticed that there were some great similarities as well as differences. This could be attributed to many things, including the escalation of his temper, what amount of time he had in order to accomplish his deed, and location. One thing I noted was the increase of brutality with each murder, except for Elizabeth Stride. In the book, I deal with that issue as something Tiana, the heroine, also saw as too many anomalies, which made her think Elizabeth wasn't a Ripper victim. Why did Jack center on low-end prostitutes? Was he thinking of his mother a prostitute and killing her through those unfortunate victims? Was he trying to clean up London from the diseases that could be spread by these ladies? We might never know why Jack chose the victims he did, but the theories put out by many psychologists and others help us to glimpse into that time and perhaps into the heart of a killer.

Forensic facial reconstruction is science and an art form, in my eyes. Many people have seen documentaries or crime stories on television that show those reconstructionists at work. Theirs is a skill I would love to have, but know I've not the patience to acquire, much less the ability to work like they do. Last year, I was introduced to the computer graphics world, where forensic reconstruction is going. Amazing. Given a glimpse into how much work goes into the computer program to help with variabilities, tissue depths, mapping the skull, had me bowled over. I must thank Dr. Damian Schoffield for sharing his knowledge of this field. He was the inspiration for Tiana's occupation and coworkers. These men at Sheffield University are truly gifted, not just in creating reconstructions that are so lifelike, but also in the ability to explain the procedures they use in such a way that someone like me, a neophyte, can understand.

Normally, I include many of the references I used in the research of my books that have historical backgrounds. For this book, it'd take a good portion of space, so I'm going to give you some of my main references. If you'd like a complete listing, please feel free to email me at cynnara@gmail.com and I'll send you the list of books, websites, and more that I used.

http://www.casebook.org -- Casebook (The best Jack the Ripper site, by far.)

http://www.bbc.co.uk/arts/ripper/ -- Stalking the Ripper

http://www.bbc.co.uk/history/historic_figures/ripper_jack_the.shtml -- Jack the Ripper

http://news.bbc.co.uk/1/hi/uk/1286183.stm -- Jack the Ripper letter made public

http://news.bbc.co.uk/1/hi/uk/3544233.stm -- More than one "Jack the Ripper"

http://news.bbc.co.uk/1/hi/uk/172290.stm -- Ripper diary has historians stumped

http://www.crimelibrary.com/jack/jackmain.htm -- Crime Library's Jack the Ripper

http://www.met.police.uk/history/ripper.htm -- Metropolitan Police Service History -- Jack

http://www.pro.gov.uk/virtualmuseum/maingalleries/crime/jack/default.htm --

Public Record Office Virtual Museum -- Jack the Ripper

http://hosted.ray.easynet.co.uk/serial_killers/whitecha.html -- Serial Killers Casefiles -- Jack the Ripper

Cynnara Tregarth

Born in Chicago, currently living in the Peninsula state, aka Florida, Cynnara loves to write, has always been writing or telling stories. Unfortunately for her, it means that her sense of direction sucks on occasion, but she can tell you all about ancient history. She always writes hot, but on occasion, delves into various other genres. Her first love is paranormal with various other genres tossed in for good measure.

You can visit Cynnara on the Web at www.cynnara.com, or email her at cynnara@gmail.com.

Other Books by Cynnara Tregarth

Loose Id Publishing
- Treaty of Desire
- Cupid Shoots, She Scores
- Games Empaths Play
- Match Game: Ghost Style
- Pirate Queen's Rebellion

Changeling Press
- Dragon Chef: Pixified

Etopia Press
- Love Games

Self Published Books
- Mark of the Blood (Book 1 of the Marauders)
- Call of the Wylde (Book 2 of the Marauders)
- Bardic Tales (Book 3 of the Marauders) (Coming Soon!)
- Ride Me, Baby
- Shades of Fyre (Book 1 of the Elemental Guardians) (Coming Soon!)
- Jack's Back

www.ingramcontent.com/pod-product-compliance
Lightning Source LLC
Chambersburg PA
CBHW051407170626
46809CB00006B/2053